A CHARGE of VALOR

(BOOK #6 IN THE SORCERER'S RING)

MORGAN RICE

Books by Morgan Rice

THE SORCERER'S RING
A QUEST OF HEROES (BOOK #1)
A MARCH OF KINGS (BOOK #2)
A FEAST OF DRAGONS (BOOK #3)
A CLASH OF HONOR (BOOK #4)
A VOW OF GLORY (BOOK #5)
A CHARGE OF VALOR (BOOK #6)
A RITE OF SWORDS (BOOK #7)
A GRANT OF ARMS (BOOK #8)
A SKY OF SPELLS (BOOK #9)
A SEA OF SHIELDS (BOOK #10)
A REIGN OF STEEL (BOOK #11)

THE SURVIVAL TRILOGY
ARENA ONE (Book #1)
ARENA TWO (Book #2)

the Vampire Journals
turned (book #1)
loved (book #2)
betrayed (book #3)
destined (book #4)
desired (book #5)
betrothed (book #6)
vowed (book #7)
found (book #8)
resurrected (book #9)
craved (book #10)

"Cowards die many times before their deaths;
The valiant never taste of death but once."

--William Shakespeare
Julius Caesar

CHAPTER ONE

Gwendolyn lay face down in the grass, feeling the cold winter breeze rush over her bare skin, and as her eyes fluttered open, slowly, distantly, the world came back into focus. She had been in some faraway place, in a field radiant with sunlight, flowers, Thor and her father by her side, all of them laughing and happy. Everything had been perfect in the world.

But now, as she peeled open her eyes, the world before her could not have been more different. The ground was hard, cold, and standing over her, slowly gaining his feet, was not her father, not Thor—but a monster: McCloud. Done with her, he slowly rose, buckled his pants, and gazed down with a satisfied look.

In a rush, it all came back to her. Her surrender to Andronicus. His betrayal. Her being attacked by McCloud. Her cheeks flushed red as she realized how naive she had been.

She lay there, her whole body hurting, her heart breaking, and more than any time in her life, she wanted to die.

Gwendolyn opened her eyes further and saw Andronicus' army, scores of soldiers, all watching the scene, and her shame deepened. She should have never surrendered to this creature; she wished, instead, she had gone down fighting. She should have listened to Kendrick and the others. Andronicus had played to her sacrificial instincts, and she had fallen for it. She wished she would have met him in battle: even if she had died, at least then she could have gone down with her dignity, her honor, intact.

Gwendolyn knew with certainty, for the first time in her life, that she was about to die. But somehow, that no longer bothered her. She no longer cared about dying—she just cared about dying *her* way—and she wasn't ready to go down yet.

As she lay there, face down, Gwendolyn furtively reached out and grasped a clump of dirt in one hand.

"You can get up now, woman," McCloud ordered gruffly. "I'm through with you. It's time for others to have a turn."

Gwen clutched the dirt so hard her knuckles turned white, and she prayed that this worked.

In one quick motion she spun around and threw the clump of dirt into McCloud's eyes.

He had not expected it, and he screamed and stumbled back, raising his hands to try to pull the dirt out of his eyes.

Gwen took advantage of the moment. Raised in King's Castle, she had been reared by the King's warriors, and they had always taught her to attack a second time, before your enemy had a chance to recover. They had also taught her a lesson she had never forgotten: whether she carried a weapon or not, she was always armed. She could always use the enemy's weapon.

Gwen reached over, extracted the dagger from McCloud's belt, raised it high, and plunged it between his legs.

McCloud shrieked even louder, removing his hands from his eyes and grabbing his groin. Blood flowed between his legs, as he reached down and pulled out the dagger, gasping.

She was thrilled with herself for landing the blow, for getting at least this small revenge. But to her surprise, the blow, which would have downed anyone else, did not stop him. This monster was unstoppable. She had wounded him badly, right where he deserved it, but had not killed him. It had not even made him sink to his knees.

Instead, McCloud extracted the dagger, dripping with blood, and sneered down at her with a look of death. He began to descend for her, clutching the dagger with shaking hands, and Gwendolyn knew her time had come. At least she would die with some small satisfaction.

"Now I'm going to carve out your heart and feed it to you," he said. "Prepare to learn what real pain means."

Gwendolyn braced herself for the dagger plunge, prepared to meet a painful death.

A scream rang out, and after a shocked moment, Gwendolyn was surprised to realize that the scream was not her own. It was McCloud; he was shrieking in agony.

Gwen lowered her hands and looked up, confused. McCloud had dropped the dagger. She blinked several times, trying to understand the sight before her.

McCloud stood there with an arrow lodged in his eye. He shrieked, blood pouring from his eye, as he raised a hand and grabbed at the arrow. She could not understand. He had been shot. But how? By whom?

Gwen turned in the direction from which the arrow had sailed, and her heart soared to see Steffen, standing there, holding a bow, hiding amidst a huge group of soldiers. Before anyone else could figure out what was going on, Steffen fired off six more arrows, and

3

one by one, the six soldiers standing beside McCloud fell, arrows piercing through all of their throats.

Steffen reached back to fire more, but he was finally spotted and pounced on by a large group of soldiers, who subdued him and pummeled him down to the ground.

McCloud, still shrieking, turned and ran off into the crowd. Amazingly, he was still not dead. She hoped that he would bleed to death.

Gwen's heart soared with gratitude for Steffen, more than he would ever know. She knew she would die here today by someone else's hand, but at least now it would not be by McCloud's.

The camp of soldiers quieted as Andronicus arose and marched slowly towards Gwendolyn. She lay there and watched him approach, impossibly tall, like a mountain moving her way. Soldiers fell in behind him as he came closer, the battlefield deathly silent, the only sound that of the whipping wind.

Andronicus stopped a few feet away, looming over her, looking down, expressionless. He reached up and slowly fingered the shrunken heads on his necklace, and an odd sound came from the bowels of his chest and throat, like a purring noise. He seemed to be both angry and intrigued at the same time.

"You have defied the great Andronicus," he said slowly, the entire camp listening to his every word, ancient and deep. His voice boomed with authority and resonated across the plains. "It would have been easier if you had submitted to your punishment. Now you will have to learn what real pain means."

Andronicus reached down and drew a sword longer than Gwen had ever seen. It must have been eight feet long, and its distinctive ring echoed across the battlefield. He held it high, turning it in the light, the reflection so strong that it blinded her. He examined it himself as he twisted it in his hands, as if seeing it for the first time.

"You are a woman of noble birth," he said. "It suits you that you should die by a noble sword."

Andronicus took two steps forward, grabbed the hilt with both hands, and raised the sword higher.

Gwendolyn closed her eyes. She heard the whistling of the wind, the movement of every blade of grass, and there came flashing through her mind random memories from her life. She felt the completion of her life, felt everything she had done, everyone she had loved. In her final thoughts, Gwen thought of Thor. She reached down to her neck and clasped the amulet he had given her, held it tight in her fist. She could feel the warm power radiating through it, this ancient red stone, and she remembered Thor's words as he had given it to her: this amulet can save your life. Once.

She clutched the amulet tighter, throbbing in her palm, and she prayed to God with every fiber of her being.

Please God, let this amulet work. Please, save me, just this one time. Let me see Thor again.

Gwendolyn opened her eyes, expecting to see Andronicus's sword flashing down at her—yet what she saw surprised her. Andronicus stood there, frozen, looking over her shoulder, as if watching someone approach. He appeared to be surprised; even confused, and it was not an expression which she had ever expected to see him wear.

"You will lower your weapon now," a voice rang out behind Gwendolyn.

Gwendolyn was electrified at the sound of that voice. It was a voice she knew. She spun, and she was shocked to see standing there a person who she knew as well as her own father.

Argon.

There he stood, dressed in his white robes and hood, his eyes shining with an intensity greater than she had ever seen, staring right at Andronicus. She and Steffen lay on the ground between these two titans. They were two creatures of incredible force, one of the darkness, and one of the light, standing off against each other. She could almost feel the spiritual war raging above her head.

"Will I?" Andronicus mocked, smiling back.

But in Andronicus' smile, Gwen could see his lips tremble, could see, for the first time, something like fear in Andronicus' eyes. She had never thought she would see that. Andronicus must have known of Argon. And whatever it was he knew, it was enough to make the most powerful man in the world afraid.

"You will harm the girl no further," Argon said calmly. "You will accept her surrender," he said, taking a step closer, his eyes shining, hypnotizing. "You will allow her to retreat to her people. And you will allow her people to surrender, if they choose. I will only tell you this one time. You would be wise to accept it."

Andronicus stared back at Argon and blinked several times, as if undecided.

Then finally, he leaned back his head and roared with laughter. It was the loudest and darkest laughter Gwen had ever heard, filling the entire camp, seeming to reach up to the very sky.

"Your sorcerer's tricks won't work on me, old man," Andronicus said. "I know of the Great Argon. There was a time when you were powerful. More powerful than man, than dragons, than the sky itself, or so they say. But your time has passed. Now it is a new time. Now it is a time for the great Andronicus. Now, you are but a relic, a remnant of some other time, when the MacGils ruled, when magic was strong. When the Ring was indefensible. But your fate is tied to the Ring. And now the Ring is weak. Like you.

"You are a fool to confront me, old man. Now you will suffer. Now you will learn the strength of the Great Andronicus."

Andronicus sneered and raised his sword again, towards Gwendolyn, this time looking right at Argon.

"I'm going to kill the girl slowly, before your eyes," Andronicus said. "Then I will kill the hunchback. Next, I will maim you, but leave you alive as a walking symbol of the power of my greatness."

Gwendolyn braced herself and flinched as Andronicus brought the sword down for her head.

Suddenly, something happened. She heard a sound cut through the air, like that of a thousand fires, followed by Andronicus' scream.

She opened her eyes in utter disbelief to see Andronicus' face contorted in pain, dropping his sword and kneeling to the ground. She watched Argon take a step forward, then another, holding out a single palm, which was radiating a ball of violet light. The ball grew larger and larger, enveloping Andronicus as Argon continued walking forward, expressionless, getting closer and closer to Andronicus as he held out his palm.

Andronicus curled up into a ball on the ground, as the light enveloped him.

A gasp erupted from his men, but none dared approach. Either they were afraid, or Argon had cast some sort of spell to make them powerless.

"MAKE IT STOP!" Andronicus screamed, reaching up and grabbing his ears. "I BEG YOU!"

"You will do no further harm to the girl," Argon said slowly.

"I will do no further harm to the girl!" Andronicus repeated, as if in a trance.

"You will release her now and allow her to return to her people."

"I will release her now and allow her to return to her people!"

"You will give her people a chance to surrender."

"I will give her people a chance to surrender!" Andronicus shrieked. "Please! I will do anything!"

Argon breathed deep, then finally stopped. The light disappeared from his hand, as he slowly lowered his arm.

Gwen looked up at him in shock; she had never seen Argon in action, and she could hardly comprehend his power. It was like watching the heavens open up.

"If we meet again, great Andronicus," Argon said slowly, looking down as Andronicus lay there whimpering, "it will be on your way to the darkest realms of death."

CHAPTER TWO

Thor struggled, held firmly in place by the Empire soldiers, and watched helplessly as Durs, a man he once thought of as a brother, raised a sword to kill him.

Thor shut his eyes and braced himself, knowing his time had come. He kicked himself for being so stupid, so trusting. They had set him up all along, a lamb led to slaughter. Even worse, as the leader, the other boys had looked to Thor for guidance. He had not only let himself down, he had let all the others down with him. His naiveté, his trusting nature, had endangered them all.

As Thorgrin struggled, he tried with all he had to summon his power, to call it up from somewhere deep inside himself, just enough power to break free of his bonds, to fight back.

Yet, try as he did, it would not come. His own strength was just not enough to break free of all the soldiers holding him down.

Thor felt the wind caress his face as Durs lowered the sword, and braced himself for the imminent impact of steel. He was not ready to die. In his mind he saw Gwendolyn, in the Ring, waiting for him. He felt he had let her down, too.

Thor heard a sudden noise of flesh meeting flesh, and opened his eyes and was surprised to see that he was still alive. Durs' arm froze there, in mid-air, his wrist caught by the hand of a huge Empire soldier who towered over Durs—no easy feat, considering Durs' size. He held Durs' wrist just inches away from impaling Thor.

Durs turned to the Empire soldier, surprise in his face.

"Our leader does not want them dead," the soldier muttered darkly to Durs. "He wants them alive. As prisoners."

"No one told us that," Durs protested.

"The deal was that we would get to kill them!" Dross added.

"The terms of the deal have changed," the soldier answered.

"You can't do that!" Drake called out.

"Can't we?" he answered darkly, turning to him. "We can do anything we want. In fact, you are now our prisoners, too." The soldier smiled. "The more Legion we have for ransom, the better."

Durs looked back at the soldier, his face falling in outrage, and a moment later, chaos erupted as the three brothers were pounced upon by dozens of Empire soldiers, who tackled them down to the ground and bound their wrists.

Thor took advantage of the chaos and turned and searched for Krohn, who he spotted just a few feet away, lurking in the shadows, loyally close to his side.

"Krohn, help me!" Thor screamed. "NOW!"

Krohn leapt into action with a snarl, flying through the air, landing his fangs on the throat of the Empire soldier holding Thor's wrist. Thor wriggled free and Krohn leapt from one soldier to the next, biting and clawing them until Thor could break free and grab his sword. Thor then spun around and in a single blow, chopped off three of their heads.

Thor darted over to Reece, closest to him, and stabbed his captor in the heart, freeing him and allowing him to draw his sword and join the fight. The two of them fanned out and hurried to their Legion brothers, attacking their captors and freeing Elden, O'Connor, Conval and Conven.

The other soldiers were distracted by detaining Drake, Durs and Dross, and by the time they turned around and figured out what was going on, it was too late. Thor, Reece, O'Connor, Elden, Conval and Conven were free, all with weapons in hand. They were still badly outnumbered, and Thor knew the fight would not be easy. But at least know they had a fighting chance. Undaunted, they all charged the enemy with abandon.

The hundred Empire soldiers attacked and Thor heard a screech high overhead and looked up to see Estopheles. His falcon swooped down and scratched the eyes of the lead Empire soldier, who fell to the ground flailing. Estopheles then scratched several others, taking them down one at a time.

As they charged, Thor placed a rock in his sling and hurled it, striking one soldier in the temple and knocking him down before he could reach them; O'Connor managed to fire off two arrows, both landing with deadly precision, and Elden hurled a spear, impaling two soldiers, dropping at their feet. It was a good start—but there remained a hundred soldiers left to kill.

They met in the middle with a great battle cry. As he had been taught, Thor focused on one soldier in particular, choosing the biggest and meanest one he could find, and raising his sword high. There was a great clang of metal as Thor's sword was blocked by the man's shield, and the man immediately brought a hammer down for Thor's head.

Thor sidestepped, and as the hammer plunged down into the earth, Thor pulled the dagger from his belt and stabbed him; he collapsed, dead.

Thor raised his shield in time to block the sword blows of two attackers, then parried with his own, killing one of them. He was about to swing at the other, when he caught a glimpse of a sword slashing down at him from behind; he had to spin around and block that with his shield.

Thor was getting attacked from all sides now, badly outnumbered, and it was all he could do just to keep the blows from raining down on him. He had no time or energy to attack—only to defend. And more and more soldiers kept coming at him.

Thor looked over and saw his Legion brothers were in the same predicament: they each managed to kill one or two soldiers—but badly outnumbered, they paid a price, receiving minor wounds from all sides. Thor could tell that they were losing ground—even with Krohn jumping in and attacking, and even with Indra helping, picking up rocks and hurling them at the group of soldiers. It would only be a matter of time until they were surrounded and finished off.

"Free us!" came a voice.

Thor turned to see Drake, bound by ropes with his brothers, just a few feet away.

"Free us!" Drake repeated, "and we will help you fight them! We fight for the same cause!"

As Thor raised a shield to block yet another great blow, this from a battle axe, he realized that having three more hands would help greatly. Without them, they clearly had no chance of defeating all of these soldiers. Thor didn't feel he could trust the three brothers anymore, but at this point he felt he had nothing to lose by trying. After all, the three brothers had motivation to fight, too.

Thor blocked yet another sword blow, then dropped to his knees and rolled over, through the crowd, several feet, until he reached the three brothers. He jumped up and slashed their ropes one at a time, protecting them from blows, as they each drew their swords and jumped into the mix.

Drake, Dross and Durs charged the thick crowd of Empire soldiers and attacked, slashing, thrusting, jabbing. They were each large and skilled, and they caught the Empire soldiers off guard, immediately killing several of them, and helping the odds. Thor felt mixed feelings about freeing them, after what they had done—but given the circumstances, it seemed to be the wisest choice. Better that than death.

Now there were nine of them against the remaining eighty or so soldiers. The odds were still terrible, but at least better than they were.

The Legion brothers fell back on their training skills, on the drills ingrained in them during the Hundred, the countless times they had been trained to fight while encircled and outnumbered; they did as Kolk and Brom trained them to do: they fell back and formed a tight circle, backs to each other, and fought off the encroaching Empire soldiers as one unit. They were emboldened by the arrival of the three extra fighters, and they each caught a second wind, and fought back more vigorously than before.

Conval extracted his flail and swung it wide and struck the enemy again and again, managing to take out three Empire soldiers before the chain was snatched away from him. His brother Conven used a regular mace, aiming low and taking out soldiers' legs with the studded metal ball. O'Connor couldn't use his bow in such short range, but he managed to extract two throwing daggers from his waist and threw them into the crowd, killing two soldiers. Elden wielded his two-handed war hammer ferociously, raining great blows all around him. And Thor and Reece blocked and parried with their swords expertly. For a moment, Thor was feeling optimistic.

Then, out of the corner of Thor's eye, he detected something that disturbed him. He spotted one of the three brothers turning and charging across the circle of Legion; Thor turned and saw Durs. He was charging, not for an Empire soldier, but for him. For Thor. Right for his back.

It happened too quickly, and Thor, fighting off two Empire soldiers before him, could not turn in time.

Thor knew he was about to die. About to be stabbed in the back by a boy he had once thought of as a brother, by a boy whom he had, naively, trusted twice.

Suddenly Conval appeared in front of Thor, to protect him.

And as Durs lowered his sword for Thor's back, it found a target in Conval's chest instead.

Thor turned and screamed: "CONVAL!"

Conval stood there, frozen, eyes wide in a death stare, as he looked down at the sword plunged through his heart, the blood gushing down his torso.

Durs stood there, staring back, equally surprised.

Conval collapsed to his knees, blood gushing from his chest. Thor watched, in slow motion, as Conval, a close Legion brother, a boy he had loved like a brother, fell face-first to the ground, dead. All to save Thor's life.

Durs stood over him, looking down, appearing shocked by what he had just done.

Thor lunged forward to kill Durs—but Conven beat him to it. Conval's twin rushed forward and swung his sword wide, decapitating Durs, whose limp body fell to the earth.

Thor stood there and felt hollowed out, crushed by guilt. He had made one too many mistakes in judgment. If he had not freed Durs, Conval might be alive right now.

With their backs exposed to the Empire, it gave the Empire soldiers an opportunity. They all rushed in through the open circle, and Thor felt a war hammer smash him on the back of the shoulder blade; the strength of the blow sent him down to the ground, face-first.

Before he could rise, several soldiers pounced on him; he felt their feet on his back, then felt one soldier reach down, grab his hair, and lean over him with a dagger.

"Say goodbye, young one," the soldier said.

Thor closed his eyes, and as he did, he felt himself transported to another world.

Please God, Thor said to himself. *Allow me to live this day. Just give me the strength to kill these soldiers. To die some other day, in some other place, with honor. To live long enough to avenge these deaths. To see Gwendolyn one last time.*

As Thor lay there, watching the dagger come down, he felt time slow to a near stop. He felt a sudden rush of heat, up his legs and torso and arms, all the way through his palms, to the tips of his fingers, a tingling so intense he could not even close his fingers. The incredible rush of heat and energy was ready to burst right through him.

Thor spun around, feeling charged with a new strength, and aimed his palm at his attacker. A white orb of light emanated from his palm and sent his attacker flying across the battlefield, knocking back several other soldiers with him.

Thor stood, overflowing with energy, and aimed his palms throughout the battlefield. As he did, white orbs of light went everywhere, creating waves of destruction, so fast and intense, that within minutes, all of the Empire soldiers lay in a great heap, dead.

As the heat of the moment calmed, Thor took stock. He, Reece, O'Connor, Elden, and Conven were alive. Nearby were Krohn and Indra, also alive, Krohn breathing hard. All the Empire soldiers were dead. And at their feet lay Conval, dead.

Dross was dead, too, an Empire sword thrust through his heart.

The only one left alive was Drake. He lay there, moaning on the ground with a stomach wound from an Empire dagger. Thor marched over to him as Reece, O'Connor and Elden dragged him roughly to his feet, groaning in pain.

Drake, wincing in pain, sneered back insolently, semi-conscious.

"You should have killed us from the start," Drake said, blood dripping from his mouth, breaking into a long cough. "You were always too naïve. Too stupid."

Thor felt his cheeks redden, even more furious at himself for believing them. He was furious, most of all, that his naiveté resulted in Conval's death.

"I'm only going to ask you this once," Thor growled. "Answer me truthfully, and we will let you live. Lie to us, and you will follow the way of your two brothers. The choice is yours."

Drake coughed several times.

"Where is the Sword?" Thor demanded. "The truth this time."

Drake coughed again and again, then finally lifted his head. He looked up and met Thor's eyes, and his stare was filled with hate.

"Neversink," Drake finally answered.

Thor looked at the others, who all looked back at him, confused.

"Neversink?" Thor asked.

"It is a bottomless lake," Indra chimed in, stepping forward. "On the far side of the Great Desert. It is a Lake of the deepest depths."

Thor scowled back at Drake.

"Why?" he asked.

Drake coughed, getting weaker.

"Gareth's orders," Drake said. "He wanted it cast into a place from which it would never return."

"But why?" Thor pressed, confused. "Why destroy the Sword?"

Drake looked up and met his eyes.

"If he could not wield it," Drake said. "Then no one could."

Thor looked at him long and hard, and finally, he felt satisfied that he was telling the truth.

"Then our time is short," Thor said, preparing to go.

Drake shook his head.

"You will never get there in time," Drake said. "They are days ahead of you. The Sword is already lost forever. Give up and return to the Ring and spare yourselves."

Thor shook his head.

"We don't think as you," he replied. "We don't live to save our lives. We live for valor, for our code. And we will go wherever that takes us."

"You see where your valor has taken you now," Drake said. "Even with your valor, you're a fool, just like the rest of them. Valor is worthless."

Thor sneered back at him. He could hardly believe that he'd been raised in a house, had spent his whole childhood, with this creature.

Thor's knuckles whitened as he squeezed his sword hilt, wanting more than ever to kill this boy. Drake's eyes followed his hands.

"Do it," Drake said. "Kill me. Do it once and for all."

Thor stared back long and hard, itching to do it. But he had given Drake his word that if he told the truth, he would not kill him. And Thor was always good to his word.

"I will not," Thor said finally. "As much as you may deserve it. You will not die by my hand, for then I would be as low as you."

As Thor began to turn away, Conven rushed forward and shrieked:

"For my brother!"

Before any of them could react, Conven raised his sword and thrust it through Drake's heart. Conven's eyes were alight with madness, with grief, as he held Drake in a death embrace and watched Drake's limp body fall to the ground, dead.

Thor looked down and knew the death would mean little consolation for Conven's loss. For all of their loss. But, at least, it was something.

Thor looked out at the vast stretch of desert before them and knew the Sword was somewhere beyond its borders. It seemed like a planet away. Just as he thought their journey was complete, he realized it had not yet even begun.

CHAPTER THREE

Erec sat amongst the scores of knights in the Duke's hall of arms inside his castle, secure behind the gates of Savaria, all of them bruised and battered from their encounter with those monsters. Beside him sat his friend Brandt, who held his head in his hands, as did many of the others. The mood in the chamber was glum.

Erec felt it, too. Every muscle in his body ached from the day's battle with that lord's men and with the monsters. It had been one of the toughest days of battle he could remember, and the Duke had lost too many men. As Erec reflected, he realized that if it had not been for Alistair, he and Brandt and the others would be dead right now.

Erec was overwhelmed with gratitude for her—and even more, with a renewed love. He was also intrigued by her, more so than he had ever been. He had always sensed that she was special, even powerful. But this day's events had proved it to him. He had a burning desire to know more about who she was, about the secret of her lineage. But he had vowed not to pry—and he always kept his word.

Erec couldn't wait until this meeting was over, so he could see her again.

The Duke's knights had all been sitting here for hours, recovering, trying to figure out what had happened, arguing about what to do next. The Shield was down, and Erec was still trying to wrap his mind around the ramifications. It meant that Savaria was now prone to attack; even worse, messengers had streamed in with news of Andronicus' invasion, of what had happened at King's Court, at Silesia. Erec's heart sank. His heart tugged at him to be with his brothers in the Silver, to defend his home cities. But here he was, in Savaria, and this was where fate had put him. He was needed here, too: the Duke's city and people were, after all, a strategic part of the MacGil empire, and they also needed defending.

But with the new reports flooding in of Andronicus sending one of his battalions here, to attack Savaria, Erec knew that his million-man army would soon spread to every corner of the Ring. When he was done, Andronicus would leave nothing. Erec had heard stories of Andronicus' conquests his entire life, and he knew that he was a cruel man without equal. By the simple law of numbers, the Duke's few hundred men would be helpless to stand up against them. Savaria was a doomed city.

"I say we surrender," said the Duke's advisor, a grizzled old warrior who sat slumped over a long, rectangular wooden table, lost in a mug of ale, slamming his metal gauntlet on the wood. All the other soldiers quieted and looked to him.

"What choice do we have?" he added. "It is but a few hundred of us against a million of them."

"Perhaps we can defend, at least hold the city," said another soldier.

"But for how long?" asked another.

"Long enough for MacGil to send reinforcements, if we can hold out long enough."

"MacGil is dead," another warrior answered. "No one is coming to help us."

"But his daughter lives," another countered. "As do his men. They would not abandon us here!"

"They can barely defend themselves!" another protested.

The men broke out into agitated mumbling, all arguing with each other, speaking over each other, going around and around in circles.

Erec sat there, watching it all, and feeling hollowed out. A messenger had arrived but hours ago and had delivered the dreadful news of Andronicus' invasion—and also, for Erec, the even worse news, just reaching him now, that MacGil had been assassinated. Erec had been so far away from King's Court for so long, it was the first time he had received the news—and when he had, he felt as if a dagger had been plunged into his heart. He had loved MacGil as a father, and his loss left him feeling more empty than he could say.

The room grew quiet as the Duke cleared his throat and all eyes turned to him.

"We can defend our city against an attack," the Duke said slowly. "With our skills and the strength of these walls, we can hold it against an army even five times our numbers—perhaps an army even ten times our numbers. And we have enough provisions to withhold a siege for weeks. Against any regular army, we would win."

He sighed.

"But the Empire boasts no regular army," he added. "We cannot defend against one million men. It would be futile."

He paused.

"But so would surrender. We all know what Andronicus does to his captors. It appears to me that we will all die either away. The question is whether we die on our feet, or die on our backs. I say, we die on our feet!"

The room erupted into a cheer of approval. Erec couldn't agree more.

"Then we have no other course of action left," the Duke continued. "We will defend Savaria. We will never surrender. We may die, but we will all die together."

The room fell into a heavy silence, as the others gravely nodded to each other. It seemed as if they were all searching for another answer.

"There is one other way," Erec said finally, speaking up.

He could feel all eyes turn and stare at him.

The Duke nodded his way, for him to speak.

"We can attack," Erec said.

"Attack?" the soldiers called out in surprise. "The few hundred of us, attacking one million men? Erec, I know you are fearless. But are you mad?"

Erec shook his head, deadly serious.

"What you fail to consider is that Andronicus' men would never expect an attack. We would gain the element of surprise. As you say, sitting here, defending, we will die. If we attack, we can take out a lot more of them; more importantly, if we attack in the right way, and at the right place, we might do more than just hold them back—we might actually win."

"Win!?" they all called out, looking at Erec, completely bewildered.

"What do you mean?" asked the Duke.

"Andronicus will expect us to be here, to sit back and defend our city," Erec explained. "His men will never expect us to be holding a random chokepoint outside our city's gates. Here in the city, we have an advantage of strong walls—but out there, in the field, we have the advantage of surprise. And surprise is always greater than strength. If we can hold a natural chokepoint, we can funnel them all to one spot, and from there we can attack. I speak of the Eastern Gulch."

"The Eastern Gulch?" a soldier asked.

Erec nodded.

"It is a steep crevice between two cliffs, the only pass-through in the Kavonia Mountains, a good day's ride from here. If Andronicus' men come to us, the most direct way will be through the Gulch. Otherwise, they will have to scale the mountains. The road from the north is too narrow and too muddy this time of year—he would lose weeks. And from the south he would have to breach the Fjord River."

The Duke look admiringly at Erec, rubbing his beard, thinking.

"You may be right. Andronicus may just lead his men through the gulch. For any other army it would be an act of supreme hubris. But for him, with his million men, he might just do it."

Erec nodded.

"If we can get there, if we can beat them to it, we can surprise them, ambush them. With a position like that, a few can hold back thousands."

All the other soldiers looked at Erec with something like hope and awe, as the room was blanketed with a thick silence.

"A bold plan, my friend," the Duke said. "But then again, you are a bold warrior. You always have been" The Duke gestured to an attendant. "Bring me a map!"

A boy ran from the room and came back through another door holding a large scroll of parchment. He rolled it out on the table, and the soldiers gathered around, studying it.

Erec reached out and found Savaria on the map and traced a line with his finger, east, stopping at the Eastern Gulch. A narrow crevice, it sat surrounded by mountains as far as the eye could see.

"It is perfect," a soldier said.

The others nodded, rubbing their beards.

"I have heard stories off a few dozen men holding off thousands at the gulch," one soldier said.

"That is an old wives' tale," another soldier said, cynically. "Yes, we will have the element of surprise. But what else? We will not have the protection of our walls."

"We will have the protection of nature's walls," another soldier countered. "Those mountains, hundreds of feet of solid cliff."

"Nothing is safe," Erec added. "As the Duke said, we die here, or we die out there. I say we die out there. Victory favors the bold."

The Duke, after a long time rubbing his beard, finally nodded, leaned back and rolled up the map.

"Prepare your arms!" he called out. "We ride tonight!"

*

Erec, dressed again in full armor, his sword swinging at his waist, marched down the hall of the Duke's castle, going the opposite way of all the men. He had one important task left before he departed for what could be his final battle.

He had to see Alistair.

Since they had returned from the day's battle, Alistair had waited in the castle, down the hall in her own chamber, waiting for Erec to come to her. She was waiting for a happy reunion, and his heart sank as he realized he would have to share with her the bad news that he would be leaving again. He felt some sense of peace knowing that she would at least be here, safe within these castle walls, and he felt more determined than ever to keep her safe, to keep back the Empire. His heart ached at the idea of leaving her—he had wanted nothing but to spend time with her since their vow to marry. But it just did not seem meant to be.

As Erec turned the corner, his spurs jingling, his boots echoing in the emptying castle halls, he braced himself for the goodbye, which he knew would be painful. He finally reached an ancient, arched wooden door, and knocked gently with his gauntlet.

There came the sound of footsteps crossing the room, and a moment later, the door opened. Erec's heart soared, as it did every time he saw Alistair. There she stood, in the doorway, with her long, flowing blonde hair and large crystal eyes, staring back at him like an apparition. She seemed more beautiful every time he saw her.

Erec stepped inside and embraced her, and she hugged him back. She held him tightly, for a long time, not wanting to let go. He did not either. He wished more than anything that he could just shut the door behind him and stay here with her, for as long as he could. But it was not meant to be.

The warmth and feel of her made everything right in the world, and he was reluctant to let go. Finally, he pulled back and looked into her eyes, which were glistening. She glanced down at his armor, his weapons, and her face fell as she realized he was not staying.

"Are you leaving again, my Lord?" she asked.

Erec lowered his head.

"It is not my wish, my lady," he replied. "The Empire approaches. If I stay here, we will all die."

"And if you leave?" she asked.

"I will likely die either way," he admitted. "But this will at least give us all a chance. A tiny chance, but a chance."

Alistair turned and walked to the window, looking out over the Duke's courtyard in the setting sun, her face lit by the soft light. Erec could see the sadness etched across it, and he came to her and brushed the hair off her neck, caressing her.

"Do not be sad, my lady," he said. "If I survive this, I will return to you. And then we shall be together, forever, free from all dangers and threats. Free to finally live our lives together."

Sadly, she shook her head.

"I'm afraid," she said.

"Of the approaching armies?" he asked.

"No," she said turning to him. "Of you."

Erec looked back, puzzled.

"I'm afraid that you will think of me differently now," she said, "since you saw what happened on the battlefield."

Erec shook his head.

"I do not think of you differently at all," he said. "You saved my life, and for that I'm grateful."

She shook her head.

"But you also saw a different side of me," she said. "You saw that I'm not normal. I'm not like everybody else. I have a power within me which I do not understand. And now I fear you will think of me as some sort of freak. As a woman you no longer want for your wife."

Erec's heart broke at her words, and he stepped forward, took her hands earnestly in his, and looked into her eyes with all the seriousness he could muster.

"Alistair," he said. "I love you with everything that I am. There has never been a woman that I have loved more. And there never will be. I love all that you are. I see you no differently as anyone else. Whatever powers you have, whoever it is that you are—even if I do not understand it, I accept all of it. I'm grateful for all of it. I vowed not to pry, and I shall keep that vow. I will never ask you. Whatever it is that you are, I accept it."

She stared back at him for a long time, then slowly, she broke into a smile, and her eyes fluttered with tears of relief and joy. She turned and embraced him, hugging him tightly, with everything she had.

She whispered in his ear: "Come back to me."

CHAPTER FOUR

Gareth stood at the cave's edge, watching the sun fall, and waited. He licked his dry lips and tried to focus, the effects of the opium finally wearing off. He was lightheaded, and hadn't drank or eaten in days. Gareth thought back to his daring escape from the castle, slinking out through the secret passageway behind the fireplace, right before Lord Kultin had tried to ambush him, and he smiled. Kultin had been smart in his coup—but Gareth had been smarter. Like everyone else, he had underestimated Gareth; he hadn't realized that Gareth's spies were everywhere, and that he'd known about his plot almost instantly.

Gareth had escaped just in time, right before Kultin had ambushed him and before Andronicus had invaded King's Court and razed it to the ground. Lord Kultin had done him a favor.

Gareth had taken the ancient, secret passageways out of the castle, twisting and turning beneath the ground, finally letting him out in the countryside, surfacing in a remote village miles from King's Court. He had surfaced near this cave, and he had collapsed upon reaching it, sleeping throughout the day, huddled up and shivering in the relentless winter air. He wished that he had brought more layers of clothing.

Awake, Gareth crouched and eyed, in the distance, the small farming village; there were a handful of cottages, smoke rising from their chimneys, and throughout were Andronicus' soldiers marching through the village and the countryside. Gareth had waited patiently until they dispersed. His stomach ached with hunger, and he knew he needed to make it to one of those houses. He could smell the food cooking from here.

Gareth sprinted from the cave, looking every which way, breathing hard, frantic with fear. He hadn't ran in years, and he gasped from the effort; it made him realize how thin and sickly he had become. The wound in his head, where his mother had hit him with the bust, throbbed. If he survived all this, he vowed to kill her himself.

Gareth ran into the town, luckily escaping detection from the few Empire soldiers who had their backs turned to him. He sprinted to the first cottage he saw, a simple one-room dwelling like the others, a warm glow coming from inside. He saw a teenage girl, perhaps his age, walking through the open door with a stack of meat, smiling, accompanied by a younger girl, perhaps her sister, maybe ten—and decided this was the place.

Gareth burst through the door with them, following them in, slamming the door behind them and grabbing hold of the younger girl from behind, his arm around her throat. The girl screamed out, and the older girl dropped her platter of food, as Gareth pulled a knife from his waist and held it to the young girl's throat.

She screamed and cried.

"PAPA!"

Gareth turned and looked around the cozy cottage, filled with candlelight and the smell of cooking, and he saw, besides the teenage girl, a mother and a father, standing over a table, looking back at him, wide-eyed with fear and anger.

"Stay back and I won't kill her!" Gareth screamed out, desperate, backing away from them, holding the young girl tight.

"Who are you?" the teenage girl asked. "My name is Sarka. My sister's name is Larka. We are a peaceful family. What do you want with my sister? Leave her alone!"

"I know who you are," the father squinted down at him in disapproval. "You were the former King. MacGil's son."

"I am *still* King," Gareth screamed. "And you are my subjects. You will do as I say!"

The father scowled down at him.

"If you are King, where is your army?" he asked. "And if you are King, what business have you taking hostage a young, innocent girl with a royal dagger? Perhaps the same royal dagger you used to kill your own father?" The man sneered. "I have heard the rumors."

"You have a fresh tongue," Gareth said. "Keep talking, and I will kill your little girl."

The father swallowed, his eyes widening with fear, and he fell silent.

"What do you want from us?" the mother cried out.

"Food," Gareth said. "And shelter. Alert the soldiers to my presence, and I promise I will kill her. No tricks, you understand? You let me be, and she will live. I want to spend the night here. You, Sarka, bring me that platter of meat. And you, woman, stoke the fire and bring me a mantle to drape over my shoulders. Move slowly!" he warned.

Gareth watched as the father nodded to the mother. Sarka gathered the meat back onto her platter, while the mother approached with a thick mantle and draped it over his shoulders. Gareth, still trembling, backed up slowly towards the fireplace, the roaring fire warming his back as he sat down on the floor beside it, holding Larka securely, who was still crying. Sarka approached with the platter.

"Set it down on the floor beside me!" Gareth ordered. "Slowly!"

Scowling, Sarka did so, looking down at her sister in concern and slamming it down on the floor beside him.

Gareth was overwhelmed by the smell. He reached down and grabbed a hunk of meat with his free hand, holding the dagger to Larka's throat with the other; he chewed and chewed, closing his eyes, relishing each bite. He chewed faster than he could swallow, food hanging from his mouth.

"Wine!" he called out.

The mother brought him a sack of wine, and Gareth squeezed it into his full mouth, chasing it down. He breathed deeply, chewing and drinking, starting to feel himself again.

"Now let her go!" the father said.

"No chance," Gareth answered. "I will sleep the night here, like this, with her in my arms. She will be safe, as long as I am. Do you want to be a hero? Or do you want your girl to live?"

The family looked at each other, speechless, hesitant.

"Can I ask you one question?" Sarka asked him. "If you are such a good king, why would you treat your subjects this way?"

Gareth stared back, puzzled, then finally leaned back and broke out into laughter.

"Whoever said I was a good king?"

CHAPTER FIVE

Gwendolyn opened her eyes, feeling the world moving around her, and struggled to figure out where she was. She saw, passing by her, the huge, arched red stone gates of Silesia, saw thousands of Empire soldiers watching her in wonder. She saw Steffen, walking beside her, and she watched as the sky, bounced up and down. She realized she was being carried. That she was in somebody's arms.

She craned her neck and saw the shining, intense eyes of Argon. She was being carried, she realized, by Argon, Steffen by their side, the three of them walking openly through the gates of Silesia, past thousands of Empire soldiers, who parted ways for them and stood there, staring. They were surrounded by a white glow, and Gwendolyn could feel herself immersed in some sort of protective energy shield in Argon's arms. She realized he was casting some sort of spell to keep all the soldiers at bay.

Gwen felt comforted, protected in Argon's arms. Every muscle in her body ached, she was exhausted, and she didn't know if she could walk if she tried. Her eyes fluttered as they went, and she watched the world pass by her in snippets. She saw a piece of a crumbling wall; a collapsed parapet; a burnt-out dwelling; a pile of rubble; she saw them cross through the courtyard, reach the farthest gates, at the edge of the Canyon; she saw them pass through these, too, the soldiers stepping aside.

They reached the Canyon's edge, the platform covered in metal spikes, and as Argon stood there, it lowered, taking them back into the depths of lower Silesia.

As they entered the lower city, Gwendolyn saw dozens of faces, the concerned, kind faces of Silesian citizens, watching her pass as if she were a spectacle. They all stared back with looks of wonder and concern as she kept descending to the main square of the city.

As they reached it, hundreds of people crowded around them. She looked out and saw familiar faces—Kendrick, Srog, Godfrey, Brom, Kolk, Atme, dozens of Silver and Legion she recognized.... They gathered around her, distress in their faces in the early morning sun, as the mist swirled in off the Canyon, and a cold breeze stung

24

her. She closed her eyes, trying to make all this go away. She felt as if she were a thing on display, and felt crushed to the depths. She felt humiliated. And she felt she had let them all down.

They continued, past all the people, through the narrow alleyways of the lower city, through another arched entranceway, and finally into the small palace of lower Silesia. Gwen faded in and out of consciousness as they entered a magnificent small, red castle, up a set of stairs, down a long corridor, and through another high arched doorway. Finally, a small door opened and they entered a room.

The room was dim. It appeared to be a large bedroom, with an ancient four-poster bed in its center, a roaring fire in an ancient marble fireplace not far from it. Several attendants stood about the room, and Gwendolyn felt Argon bring her to the bed, laying her down gently on it. As he did, scores of people gathered, looking down at her with concern.

Argon withdrew, took several steps back and disappeared amidst the crowd. She looked for him, blinking several times, but she could no longer find him. He was gone. She felt the absence of his protective energy, which had been enveloping her like a shield. She felt colder, less protected, without him around.

Gwen licked her chapped lips, and a moment later felt her head being propped up from behind, set under a pillow, and a jug of water being put to her lips. She drank and drank, and realized how thirsty she was. She looked up and saw a woman she recognized.

Illepra, the royal healer. Illepra looked down, her soft hazel eyes filled with concern, giving her water, running a warm cloth over her forehead, wiping the hair from her face. She lay a palm on her forehead, and Gwen felt a healing energy pass through her. She felt her eyes getting heavy, and soon she found them closing against her will.

*

Gwendolyn did not know how much time had passed when she opened her eyes again. She still felt exhausted, disoriented. In her dreams she had heard a voice, and now she heard it again.

"Gwendolyn," came the voice. She heard it echo in her mind, and wondered how many times he had called her name.

She looked up and recognized Kendrick, looking down at her. Standing beside him was her brother Godfrey, along with Srog, Brom,

Kolk and several others. On her other side stood Steffen. She hated the expressions in their faces. They looked at her as if she were a thing to pity, as if she had returned from the dead.

"My sister," Kendrick said, smiling. She could hear the concern in his voice. "Tell us what happened."

Gwen shook her head, too tired to recount everything.

"Andronicus," she said, her voice hoarse, coming out more like a whisper. She cleared her throat. "I tried…to surrender myself…in return for the city…I trusted him. Stupid…."

She shook her head again and again, a tear rolling down her cheek.

"No, you are *noble*," Kendrick corrected, clasping her hand. "You are the most courageous of us all."

"You did what any great leader would have done," Godfrey said, stepping forward.

Gwen shook her head.

"He tricked us…" Gwendolyn said, "…and he attacked me. He had McCloud attack me."

Gwen couldn't help it: she began to cry as she spoke the words, unable to hold it back. She knew it was not leader-like to do so, but she could not help herself.

Kendrick clasped her hand tighter.

"They were going to kill me…" she said. "…but Steffen saved me…"

The men all looked to Steffen with a new respect, who stood loyally by her side, bowing his head.

"What I did was too little and too late," he replied humbly. "I was one man against many."

"Even so, you saved our sister, and for that we shall always be in your debt," Kendrick said.

Steffen shook his head.

"I owe her a far greater debt," he responded.

Gwen teared up.

"Argon saved us both," she concluded.

Kendrick's face darkened.

"We will avenge you," he said.

"It is not myself I'm worried about," she said. "It is the city … our people … Silesia … Andronicus … he will attack…."

Godfrey patted her hand.

"Don't you worry about that now," he said, stepping forward. "Rest. Let us discuss these things. You are safe now, here."

Gwen felt her eyes closing on her. She didn't know if she was awake or dreaming.

"She needs to sleep," Illepra said, stepping forward, protective.

Gwendolyn dimly heard all of this as she felt herself growing heavier and heavier, drifting in and out of consciousness. In her mind flashed images of Thor, and then, of her father. She was having a hard time discerning what was real and what was a dream, and she heard only snippets of the conversation above her head.

"How serious are her wounds?" came a voice, maybe Kendrick's.

She felt Illepra run her palm across her forehead. And then the last words she heard, before her eyes closed on her, were Illepra's:

"The wounds to the body are light, my Lord. It is the wounds to her spirit that run deep."

*

When Gwen woke again, it was to the sound of a crackling fire. She could not tell how much time had passed. She blinked several times as she looked around the dim room, and saw the crowd had dispersed. The only people who remained were Steffen, sitting in a chair by her bedside, Illepra, who stood over her, applying a salve to her wrist, and just one other person. He was a kind, old man who looked down at her with worry. She almost recognized him, but had a hard time placing it. She felt so tired, too tired, as if she hadn't slept in years.

"My lady?" the old man said, leaning over. He held something large in both hands, and she looked down and realized it was a leather-bound book.

"It is Aberthol," he said. "Your old teacher. Can you hear me?"

Gwen swallowed and slowly nodded, opening her eyes just a bit.

"I have been waiting hours to see you," he said. "I saw you stirring."

Gwen nodded slowly, remembering, grateful for his presence.

Aberthol leaned over and opened his large book, and she could feel the weight of it on her lap. She heard the crackling of its heavy pages as he flipped them back.

"It is one of the few books that I salvaged," he said, "before the burning of the House of Scholars. It is the fourth annal of the

MacGils. You have read it. Hidden inside are stories of conquest and triumphs and defeats, of course—yet there are also other stories. Stories of great leaders wounded. Of wounds to the body, and wounds of the spirit. There all sorts of injuries imaginable, my lady. And this is what I came to tell you: even the best of men and women have suffered the most unimaginable treatment, injuries and torture. You are not alone. You are but a speck in the wheel of time. There are countless others who suffered far worse than you—and many who survived and who went on to become great leaders.

"Do not feel ashamed," he said, grasping her wrist. "That is what I want to tell you. *Never* be ashamed. There should be no shame in you—only honor and courage for what you have done. You are as great a leader as the Ring has ever seen. And this does not diminish it in any way."

Gwen, touched by his words, felt a tear fell roll down her cheek. His words were just what she needed to hear, and she felt so grateful for them. Logically, she knew and understood he was correct.

Yet emotionally, she was still having a hard time feeling it. A part of her could not help but feel as if somehow she had been damaged forever. She knew it was not true, but that was how she felt.

Aberthol smiled, as he held out a smaller book.

"Remember this one?" he asked, turning back its red leather-bound cover. "It was your favorite, all through childhood. The legends of our fathers. There's a particular story in here I thought I would read to you, to help you idle away the time."

Gwen was touched by the gesture, but she could take no more. Sadly, she shook her head.

"Thank you," she said, her voice hoarse, another tear rolling down her cheek. "But I can't hear it right now."

His face fell in disappointment, then he nodded, understanding.

"Another time," she said, feeling despondent. "I need to be alone. If you would, please, leave me. All of you," she said, turning and looking at Steffen and Gwen.

They all rose to their feet and bowed their heads, then turned and hurried from the room.

Gwen felt guilty, but she couldn't stop it; she wanted to crumple into a ball and die. She listened to their steps cross the room, heard the door close behind them, and looked up to make sure the room was empty.

But she was surprised to see that it was not: there stood a lone figure, standing inside the doorway, erect, with her posture perfect, as always. She walked slowly and stately towards Gwen, stopping a few feet from her bedside, staring down at her, expressionless.

Her mother.

Gwen was surprised to see her standing there, the former Queen, as stately and proud as ever, looking down at her with an expression as cool as ever. There was no compassion behind her eyes, as there were behind the eyes of other visitors.

"Why are you here?" Gwen asked.

"I've come to see you."

"But I don't want to see you," Gwen said. "I don't want to see anyone."

"I don't care what you want," her mother said, cool and confident. "I am your mother, and I have a right to see you when I wish."

Gwen felt her old anger towards her mother flare up; she was the last person she wanted to see at this moment. But she knew her mother and knew that she would not leave until she had spoken her mind.

"So speak then," Gwendolyn said. "Speak and leave and be done with me."

Her mother sighed.

"You don't know this," her mother said. "But when I was young, your age, I was attacked in the same way as you."

Gwen stared back, shocked; she'd had no idea.

"Your father knew of it," her mother continued. "And he did not care. He married me just the same. At the time, it felt as if my world had ended. But it had not."

Gwen closed her eyes, feeling another tear roll down her cheek, trying to block the topic out. She did not want to hear her mother's story. It was too little too late for her mother to give her any real compassion. Did she just expect she could waltz in here, after so many years of harsh treatment, and offer a sympathetic story and expect all to be mended in return?

"Are you done now?" Gwendolyn asked.

Her mother stepped forward, "No, I'm *not* done," she said firmly. "You are Queen now—it is time for you to act like one," her mother said, her voice as hard as steel. She heard a strength in it she had never heard before. "You pity yourself. But women every day, everywhere, suffer far worse fates than you. What has happened to you is nothing in the scheme of life. Do you understand me? It is *nothing*."

Her mother sighed.

"If you want to survive and be at home in this world, you have to be strong. Stronger than the men. Men will get you, one way or another. It is not about what happens to you—it is about how you *perceive* it. How you *react* to it. That is what you have control over. You can crumple up and die. Or you can be strong. That is what separates girls from women."

Gwen knew her mother was trying to help, but she resented the lack of compassion in her approach. And she hated being lectured to.

"I hate you," Gwendolyn said to her. "I always have."

"I know you do," her mother said. "And I hate you, too. But that does not mean we cannot understand each other. I don't want your love—what I want is for you to be strong. This world isn't ruled by people who are weak and scared—it is ruled by those who shake their heads at adversity as if it were nothing. You can collapse and die if you like. There is plenty of time for that. But that is boring. Be strong and live. *Truly* live. Be an example for others. Because one day, I assure you, you will die anyway. And while you're alive, you might as well live."

"Leave me be!" Gwendolyn screamed, unable to hear another word.

Her mother stared down at her coldly, then finally, after an interminable silence, she turned and strutted from the room, like a peacock, and slammed the door behind her.

In the empty silence, Gwen began to cry, and she cried and cried. More than ever, she wished all of this would just go away.

CHAPTER SIX

Kendrick stood on the wide landing at the Canyon's edge, looking out over the swirling mist. As he looked out, his heart was breaking inside. It tore him up to see his sister like that, and he felt gutted, as if he himself had been the one attacked. He could see in the faces of all the Silesians that they viewed Gwen as more than just a leader—they all viewed her as family. They were despondent, too. It was as if Andronicus had hurt them all.

Kendrick felt as if he were to blame. He should have known his younger sister would do something like that, knowing how brave, how proud she was. He should have anticipated that she would try to surrender herself before any of them had a chance to stop her, and he should have found a way to prevent her from doing so. He knew her nature, knew how trusting she was, knew her good heart—and he also, as a warrior, knew, better than she, the brutality of certain leaders. He was older and wiser than she, and he felt he let her down.

Kendrick also felt to blame because all of this, this dire situation, was too much to put on the head of a single person, a newly crowned ruler, a 16-year-old girl. She shouldn't have had to bear the brunt of it alone. Such a weighty decision would have been hard even on his own head—even on his father's head. Gwendolyn did the best she could do in the circumstances, and perhaps better than any of them would have. Kendrick had had no ideas for how to deal with Andronicus himself. None of them had.

Kendrick thought of Andronicus, and his face reddened with anger. He was a leader with no morals, no principles, no humanity. It was clear to Kendrick that if they all surrendered now, they would all meet the same fate: Andronicus would kill or enslave each and every one of them.

Something had shifted in the air. Kendrick could see it in the eyes of all the men, and he could feel it in himself. Silesians were now no longer intent on just surviving, just defending. Now they wanted vengeance.

"SILESIANS!" bellowed a voice.

The crowd quieted and looked up. In the upper city, at the edge of the Canyon, looking down at them, there stood Andronicus, surrounded by his henchmen.

"I give you a choice!" he thundered. "Turn over Gwendolyn, and I will let you live! If not, I will rain down fire on you, starting at sunset, a fire so intense that not one of you will live."

He paused, smiling.

"It is a very generous offer. Do not ponder it long."

With that, Andronicus turned and stormed off.

The Silesians all gradually turned and looked back at each other.

Srog stepped forward.

"Fellow Silesians!" boomed Srog, to a huge crowd of growing warriors, looking more serious than Kendrick had ever seen him. "Andronicus has attacked our very finest, our most cherished leader. The daughter of our beloved king MacGil, and a great Queen in her own right. He has attacked each and every one of us. He has tried to put a stain on our honor—but he has only stained his own!"

"AYE!" screamed the crowd, the men stirring, each grasping the hilts of their swords, fire in their eyes.

"Kendrick," Srog said, turning to him. "What do you propose?"

Kendrick slowly looked into the eyes of all the men before them.

"WE ATTACK!" Kendrick screamed, fire in his veins.

The crowd screamed back in approval, a thicker and thicker crowd, fearlessness in their eyes. Each and every one of these people, he saw, was ready to fight to the death.

"WE DIE LIKE MEN, AND NOT LIKE DOGS!" Kendrick screamed again.

"AYE!" screamed back the crowd.

"WE WILL FIGHT FOR GWENDOLYN! FOR ALL OF OUR MOTHERS AND SISTERS AND WIVES!"

"AYE!"

"FOR GWENDOLYN!" Kendrick screamed.

"FOR GWENDOLYN!" the crowd screamed back.

The crowd roared in ecstasy, growing thicker with each passing moment.

With one final shout, they followed Kendrick and Srog as they led the way up the narrow landing, higher and higher, for Upper Silesia. The time had come to show Andronicus what the Silver was made of.

CHAPTER SEVEN

Thor stood with Reece, O'Connor, Elden, Conven, Indra and Krohn at the mouth of the river, all of them looking down at Conval's corpse. The mood in the air was somber. Thor felt it himself, the weight of it on his chest, pulling him down, as he stared down at his Legion brother. Conval. Dead. It did not seem possible. There had been six of them, together, on this journey, for as long as Thor could remember. He had never imagined there would be five. It made him feel his mortality.

Thor thought of all the times that Conval had been there for him, remembered how he had always been there, every step of his journey, from the first day Thor had joined the Legion. He was like a brother to him. Conval had always stuck up for Thor, had always had a good word for him; unlike some of the others, he had accepted Thor as a friend from the very first day. To see him lying there dead—and especially as a result of Thor's mistakes—made Thor feel sick to his stomach. If he had never trusted those three brothers, perhaps Conval would be standing alive today.

Thor could not think of Conval without Conven, the two identical twins, inseparable, always completing each other's thoughts. He could not imagine the pain Conven was feeling. Conven looked as if he was not in his right mind anymore; the happy, carefree Conven he once knew seemed to have departed in a single stroke.

They all still stood at the edge of the battlefield where it had taken place, the Empire corpses piled up around them. They stood there, rooted, looking down at Conval, none of them willing to move on until they had given him a proper burial. They had found some choice furs on some Empire officers, had stripped them, and had wrapped Conval's corpse in them. They had placed him on a small boat, the one they had used to get here, and his body lay in it, long, stiff, facing the sky. A warrior's burial. Conval already seemed so frozen, his body stiff and blue, as if he had never lived.

They had been standing there for Thor did not know how long, each of them lost in their own sorrows, none wanting to see his body go. Indra moved her palm over Conval's head in small circles, chanting something in a language that Thor did not understand, her eyes closed. He could tell how much she cared for him as she conducted the solemn funeral service, and Thor felt a sense of peace at the sound. None of the boys knew what to say, and they all stood there glumly, silent, letting Indra lead the service.

Finally, Indra finished and took a step back. Conven stepped forward, tears running down his cheeks, and knelt down beside his brother. He reached out and lay a hand on his, bowing his head.

Conven reached out and gave the boat a shove. It bobbed out into the still waters of the river, and then, as if the tides understood, they suddenly picked up, pulling the boat away, slowly, gently. It drifted farther and farther away from the group, Krohn whining as it went. Out of nowhere there arose a mist, and it consumed the boat. It disappeared.

Thor felt as if his body, too, had been sucked into the underworld.

Slowly, the boys turned to each other and looked out, past the battlefield, and to the terrains beyond it. Behind them was the underworld from which they came; to one side was a vast plain of grass; and to the other side was an empty wasteland, a hard-baked desert. They stood at a crossroads.

Thor turned to Indra.

"To reach Neversink, we must cross that desert?" Thor asked.

She nodded.

"Is there no other way?" he asked.

She shook her head.

"There are other ways, but less direct. You would lose weeks. If you hope to beat the thieves, it is your only way."

The others stared long and hard at it, the sun baking off it, rippling in waves.

"It looks unforgiving," Reece said, coming up beside Thor.

"I know of no one who has ever crossed it and lived," Indra said. "It is vast, filled with hostile creatures."

"We don't have enough provisions," O'Connor said. "We wouldn't make it."

"Yet it is the way to the Sword," Thor said.

"Assuming the Sword still exists," Elden said.

"If the thieves have reached Neversink," Indra said, "then your precious Sword is lost forever. You would risk your lives for a dream. The best thing you can do now is turn back to the Ring."

34

"We will not turn back," Thor said, determined.

"Especially not now," Conven added, stepping forward, his eyes alight with fire and grief.

"We will find that Sword or die trying," Reece said.

Indra shook her head and sighed.

"I didn't expect any other answer from you boys," she said. "Foolhardy to the last."

*

Thor marched side by side with the others through the wasteland, squinting into the harsh sun, gasping in the relentless heat. He'd thought he would be thrilled to be rid of the underworld, of its ever-present gloom, of being unable to see the sun. But he had gone from one extreme to the other. Here, in this desert, there was nothing but sun: yellow sun and yellow sky, all beaming down on him and nowhere to go. His head hurt, and he was feeling dizzy. He was dragging his feet, and felt as if he had been marching a lifetime; as he looked over, he saw the others were, too.

They had been trekking half a day, and he did not know how they could possibly continue to keep this up. He looked over at Indra, holding her hood over her head, and wondered if she had been right. Maybe they had been foolhardy to attempt this. But he had vowed to find the Sword—and what choice did they have?

As they went their feet stirred up clouds of dust, swirling everywhere, making it even harder to breathe. On the horizon there sat nothing but more sunbaked dirt, everything flat as far as the eye could see. There wasn't the slightest glimmer of structure, or road, or mountain—or anything. Nothing but desert. Thor felt as if they had come to the very end of the earth.

As they went, Thor took solace in one thing: at least now, for the first time, he trusted where they were going. No longer was he at the mercy of listening to those three brothers and their stupid map; now they listened to Indra, and he trusted her more than he had ever trusted them. He felt certain they were being led in the right direction—he just didn't feel certain they would survive the journey.

Thor began to hear a subtle whooshing noise, and as he looked down, he saw the sand all around him swirling in circles. The others saw it, too, and Thor was confused as he watched the sand slowly gather, the circles growing more intense at his feet, then lift up into the sky. There soon arose a dust cloud, lifting off the desert floor, rising higher and higher.

Thor felt his entire body suddenly getting drier. He felt as if every drop of water was being pulled from his body, and he ached for water; he had never been so thirsty in his life.

He reached out in a panic, fumbling for his water sack, and raised it and squirted it towards his mouth. But as he did, the water turned and went upwards, towards the sky, never reaching his lips.

"What's going on?" Thor yelled to Indra, gasping.

She watched the skies with fear, retracting her hood.

"A reverse rain!" she yelled.

"What's that?" Elden yelled, gasping as he grabbed his throat.

"It's raining upwards!" she yelled. "All the moisture is being sucked up to the sky!"

Thor watched as the rest of his water shot upwards from his sack, and then watched the sack itself crackle and turn dry, dropping down to the ground as a dry crisp.

Thor dropped to his knees, grabbing his throat, barely able to breathe. All around him, the others did the same.

"Water!" Elden pleaded beside him.

There came a great rumble, like the sound of a thousand thunders, and Thor looked up to watch the sky blacken. A single storm cloud appeared, racing towards them at incredible speed.

"GET DOWN!" Indra screamed. "The sky is reversing!"

She had barely finished speaking when the sky opened up and a wall of water came gushing down, knocking down Thor and the others with the force of a tidal wave.

Thor went rolling over and over in the wave of water, tumbling he did not know how long. Finally, he surfaced back on the desert floor, the wave rolling right past them. This was followed by sheets of pouring rain, and Thor threw his head back and drank and drank, as did the others, until finally he felt hydrated again.

Slowly, each of them regained their feet, breathing hard, looking beaten up. They turned to each other. They had survived. As their shock and fear subsided, slowly they burst out laughing.

"We're alive!" O'Connor yelled out.

"Is that the worst this desert can give us?" Reece asked, joyful to be alive.

Indra shook her head, somber.

"You celebrate prematurely," she said, looking very worried. "After the rains, the desert animals come out to drink."

An awful noise arose, and Thor looked down and watched in horror as an army of small creatures arose from the sand and scurried their way towards them. Thor checked back over his shoulder and saw the lake of water the rains had left, and he realized that they were right in the path of the thirsty creatures.

Dozens of creatures which Thor had never laid eyes upon before raced his way. They were huge, yellow animals, resembling Buffalo, yet twice as large, with four arms and four horns, and they stood on two legs as they ran towards them. They charged in a funny way, running on two legs, but every once a while pouncing down on all fours, then bouncing up again. They roared as they came for them, their vibrations shaking the ground.

Thor drew his sword, as did the others, and prepared to defend. As the first of the animals neared, Thor rolled to the side, out of the way, not striking it, hoping that it would just run right past them and go for the water.

The creature lowered its head to gouge Thor, and just missed as Thor rolled. To Thor's dread, it was not content—it circled back, in a rage, and charged right for Thor. It seemed it wanted him dead more than it wanted water.

As it charged again, lowering its horns, Thor leapt high into the air and swung his sword, chopping off one of its horns as it rushed by. The animal shrieked, jumping up on two legs, and spun around, clipping Thor and knocking him to the ground.

The creature lifted its feet and tried to stomp Thor, and Thor rolled out of the way as its feet made an impression in the sand and stirred up a cloud of dust. The creature raised its feet again, and this time Thor raised his sword and plunged it into the creature's chest.

The beast shrieked again, the sword plunging to the hilt, and Thor rolled out from under it right before it collapsed down to the ground, dead. He was lucky he did: the weight of it would have crushed him into the earth.

As Thor gained his feet another beast charged for him, and he leapt out of the way, but not before its horn grazed his arm, slicing it, making him scream out in pain and drop his sword. Swordless, Thor extracted his sling, placed a stone and hurled it at the beast.

The beast staggered and screamed as the stone impaled its eye—but still, it charged.

Thor ran to the left and to the right, trying to zigzag out of the way—but the creature was too fast. There was nowhere left to run, and he knew that in moments he would be gouged. As he ran he glanced over at his Legion brothers and saw they were not faring much better, each on the run from a beast.

The beast neared, just inches away, its awful snorting and smell in Thor's ears, and it lowered its horns. Thor braced himself for the impact.

Suddenly the beast shrieked, and Thor turned to see it being lifted high into the air. Thor looked up, puzzled, not understanding what was happening—when he saw behind it a huge lime-green monster, the size of a dinosaur, a hundred feet tall, with rows of razor-sharp teeth. It held the beast in its jaw as if it were nothing, and leaned back scooped it up in its mouth. It held it there, squirming, then chewed it and gobbled it down in three huge bites, swallowing and licking its lips.

All around Thor the yellow creatures turned and ran from the beast. The beast chased after them, sliding and whipping its huge tail as it went; the tail caught Thor from behind, and sent him and the others landing hard on the ground. But the beast continued charging past them, more interested in the yellow creatures than in them.

Thor turned and looked at the others, who all sat there, dumbfounded, and looked back at him.

Indra stood there, shaking her head.

"Don't worry," she said, "it gets much worse."

CHAPTER EIGHT

Kendrick walked slowly through the burnt-out courtyard of Upper Silesia, at his side Srog, Brom, Kolk, Atme, Godfrey and a dozen Silver. They all marched slowly, deliberately, hands clasped behind their heads in a show of surrender.

The small group worked its way past the thousands of watching Empire soldiers, towards the waiting figure of Andronicus at the far city gate. Kendrick felt all eyes on them as they went, the tension thick in the air. The courtyard, despite being occupied by thousands of troops, was quiet enough to hear a pin drop.

An hour before, Kendrick had yelled up his surrender to Andronicus, and this group had ascended together, making a show of not carrying weapons as they had marched between the parting crowd of Empire soldiers, on their way to formally kneel before Andronicus. Kendrick's heart was pounding as they went, his throat dry, as he saw how many thousands of hostile enemy surrounded them.

Kendrick and the others had rehearsed a scheme, and as they approached Andronicus, and Kendrick saw firsthand how huge and savage he looked, Kendrick prayed the scheme worked. If it did not, their lives were over.

They marched, spurs jingling, until finally one of Andronicus' generals stepped forward, an imposing creature with a deep scowl, and stuck out a rough palm, jabbing Kendrick in the chest. They were stopped about twenty feet away from Andronicus, presumably out of caution. Their soldiers were wiser than Kendrick had predicted; he had hoped to march all the way to Andronicus, but clearly that was something they would not allow. Kendrick's heart beat faster, as he hoped it did not put a wrinkle in their plan.

As they all stood there, silent, facing off with each other, Kendrick cleared his throat.

"We have come to surrender before the Great Andronicus," Kendrick announced, his voice booming, trying to use his most convincing tone as he stood with the others, unmoving, looking up into Andronicus' eyes.

Andronicus reached up and fingered the shrunken heads on his necklace, looking down at them with something like a snarl, or perhaps a smile.

"We accept your terms," Kendrick continued. "We admit defeat."

Andronicus leaned forward, just slightly, seated on a huge stone bench, and looked down at them with something like a smile.

"I know that you will," he said, his voice booming back across the courtyard. "Where's the girl?"

Kendrick was prepared for that.

"We have come as a contingent of our most senior and decorated officers," Kendrick responded. "We came first, to profess our surrender to you. When we are finished, the others will follow, with your permission."

Kendrick thought that adding "with your permission" was a nice touch, would help it seem even more plausible. He'd learned a great lesson long ago, from one of his military advisors: when dealing with a narcissistic commander, always appeal to his ego. There was no limit to the mistakes a commander might make when you flattered them, when you played up their greatness.

Andronicus leaned back just a bit, barely responding.

"Of course they will," Andronicus said. "Otherwise the group of you would be very foolish to appear here."

Andronicus sat there, staring down at them, as if trying to decide. He seemed as if he sensed something awry. Kendrick's heart pounded.

Finally, after a long wait, Andronicus seemed to decide.

"Step forward and kneel," he said. "All of you."

The others all looked to Kendrick, and Kendrick nodded.

They all took a step forward and knelt down, before Andronicus.

"Repeat after me," the commander said. "We, representatives of Silesia...."

"We, representatives of Silesia...."

"Do hereby surrender to the Great Andronicus...."

"Do hereby surrender to the Great Andronicus...."

"and vow allegiance to him for the rest of our days and more...."

"and vow allegiance to him for the rest of our days and more...."

"And to serve as slaves to him for as long as our days endure."

The final words were hard for Kendrick to get out and he swallowed hard, until he finally repeated them, word for word:

"And to serve as slaves to him for as long as our days endure."

It made him nauseous to do so, and his heart was thumping in his ears. Finally, the pain of it was over.

A tense silence followed, and Andronicus finally smiled.

"You MacGils are weaker than I thought," he snarled. "I shall take great pleasure in enslaving you, and in making you learn the ways of the Empire. Now go and fetch the girl, before I change my mind and kill all of you on the spot."

As Kendrick knelt there, he felt his entire life flash before his eyes. He knew that this was one of those defining moments in his life. If all went as he hoped, he would live to tell the tale of this day to his grandchildren; if not, he would, in moments, be lying here a corpse. He knew the chances were stacked against him, but it was a chance he had to take. On behalf of himself; on behalf of the MacGils; and on behalf of Gwendolyn. It was now or never.

In one quick motion, Kendrick reached behind his back, grabbed a short sword hidden beneath his shirt, stood, and screamed as he hurled it with all his might.

"SILESIANS, ATTACK!"

Kendrick's sword hurled end over end, heading right for Andronicus' chest. It was a mighty throw, with true aim, a throw bold enough to kill any other warrior.

But Andronicus was not any other warrior. Kendrick was just a few yards too far, and Andronicus was just a touch too quick; Andronicus managed to duck out of the way with a moment to spare. He still screamed out in pain, as the blade grazed his arm, drawing blood. It then continued through the air and killed the general standing beside him, lodging in his stomach instead.

On Kendrick's scream, chaos erupted. All around him the others reached back and drew their hidden swords and decapitated the soldiers standing amidst them. Brom pulled a dagger from his belt, stepped to the side, and slashed it backwards through the throat of a soldier standing close by. Kolk removed a short sling from his waist, placed a rock, and hurled it, hitting a distant soldier, holding a bow, in the head, right before he could fire. Godfrey threw a dagger; his aim was not as true as the others, and the dagger missed its mark, impaling instead the leg of a young soldier.

All around them, screams erupted of the wounded Empire soldiers, none of them expecting the surprise attack.

On cue, at the same moment, on all sides of the courtyard Silesian soldiers suddenly emerged from the ground, from the walls.

They came up with a great battle cry, aiming arrows, darkening the air with them. Thousands of arrows crossed the courtyard, felling Empire soldiers in every direction. They were attacked from so many sides, the soldiers were at a loss as to which way to turn; many of them, in their panic, ended up attacking each other.

Kendrick was thrilled to see his plan was working perfectly. Srog had informed him of the hidden tunnels connecting lower Silesia to the upper city, built in the case of a siege, for a last-resort element of surprise. All the soldiers had waited patiently, all of them in place, waiting for Kendrick's cue.

Thousands of them now emerged, firing with such speed and aim that it gave the Empire soldiers no time to react. Kendrick charged forward and entered the fray, snatching a sword from a dead Empire soldier and attacking the soldiers nearest him, joined by his friend Atme and the others. The Empire soldiers, panicked in the chaos, turned and ran in every direction, not even sure which way to go.

The Silesians were gaining the advantage. Kendrick felled a dozen men before he even had to raise a shield in defense. Atme fought back to back with him, as he always had, doing equal damage. With every stroke he thought of Gwendolyn, thought of revenge.

The thousands of Empire soldiers were so flummoxed that they all ran back, heading for the set of gates to the outer courtyard. The mob rushed Andronicus and his men, stampeding them, who tried to stand firm but were forced back by the sheer numbers. Like cattle, they were all herded through the far gate, all desperately trying to get away from the arrows, which continued to hail down from all directions. As the Silesian soldiers ran out of arrows, they all drew their swords and charged, at their brothers' sides.

The number of Empire soldiers was vast, yet they were not well-trained warriors—most of them were just bodies, enslaved peoples in the service of Andronicus. The Silesians, on the other hand, were few in number, yet each and every one of them was an elite warrior, a hardened, well-trained soldier, each worth the weight of ten Empire men. They also had the element of surprise—and most of all, they had fire in the veins. Their backs against the wall. An urge to live. An urge to protect their loved ones. Fury for Gwendolyn. After all, this was *their* city. And they knew that if they did not win, it would be there their deaths.

Scores of Silesians sounded horns, the noise terrifying, sounded like a limitless army, and more and more of them emerged from the tunnels. They all charged forward as if their lives depended on it, thousands of them meeting the thousands of Empire soldiers.

The fighting was thick and fierce, blood covering the courtyard as sword met sword, dagger, dagger, as men grappled and looked into each other's eyes, struggling hand to hand and killing each other face to face. Quickly, the tide turned in the direction of the Silesians.

Another horn sounded, and out from the lower gates came charging the Legion, hundreds strong, screaming a fierce battle cry of their own. They raised slings and arrows and spears and swords, and charged into the fray, killing Empire soldiers left and right and helping to turn the tide. The Legion were hardened warriors already, even at a young age, and as they ran, they all screamed out for Gwendolyn, and for Thor.

The Legion did as much damage as the others as they all joined forces seamlessly, pushing the Empire farther and farther back towards the outer gate. Soon the tide of battle turned in their favor, as Empire corpses fell in every direction, and the ones who remained grew panic-stricken and ran. A million Empire soldiers awaited beyond the gates—but there was a bottleneck of soldiers fleeing, and they could not get in.

Andronicus rose in a rage, jumping into the mix, fighting back the fray of soldiers charging him, attacking his own people, grabbing soldiers with his bare hands and smashing their heads together, twisting their necks, killing them on the spot.

"WE DO NOT RETREAT!" he screamed.

He grabbed swords from soldiers' hands and stabbed them in the hearts with their own weapons. He was a one-man wave of destruction, ironically, helping the Silesians.

A few others of his closest generals fought, too, as viciously as he.

But there was nothing they could do against the stampede, the endless tide of soldiers racing for them. Despite their efforts, they were forced back, pushed all the way through the outer gate.

Soon there was not a single Empire soldier left within the inner courtyard. The Legion rushed the gate, fighting valiantly, and as they reached it they yanked on the heavy ropes with all they had. More than one Legion member died as they pulled the ropes, exposed, but they did not back away. Finally, the great iron gate lowered and slammed shut, sealing the city from the Empire army.

It landed with a thud, and after that thud there came a momentary silence. It was a silence of shock. A stunned silence of victory. The Silesians had won back their city.

They all erupted in a shout of triumph. Kendrick embraced the others, who were ecstatic, hardly believing it. They had won the battle. They had really won.

*

As the iron gate slammed, Kendrick turned to the others; he had never seen these brave warriors, who he had fought with through so many conquests and battles, ever as elated as they were on this day. They could all now breathe a collective sigh of relief. Against all odds, they had pushed back Andronicus's men. Their risky plan had worked.

For the first time in as long as Kendrick could remember, he actually felt optimistic. Maybe, he thought, they could hold this city after all; maybe they could actually hold out against Andronicus. Here they stood, in the last remaining free sliver of the Empire. Right now, it was theirs. And no matter what happened in the future, on this day, Andronicus could never nullify the victory they had achieved.

As the men fanned out across the courtyard, relaxed their guard, collected their wounded, celebrated, embraced, as more and more citizens of lower Silesia ascended to see for themselves the victory that had been achieved—suddenly, something happened. Their world was shaken by a tremendous crash, one strong enough to make the ground beneath them shake. It was the sound of metal meeting metal. Followed by an animal's enraged scream.

Kendrick turned and was horrified to see that the Empire had wasted no time in regrouping, this time with a huge iron battering ram. They were smashing it into the gates, the only barrier left to defend the city from the masses. The gate bent in half, and the ram bent it again and again, and before their eyes it buckled and gave way.

The Empire cheered.

But they did not charge through. Instead, even more ominously, they stepped aside. They made way, and their came another animal scream.

Kendrick was awestruck to watch an elephant charge through the gates. It raised its huge feet and trampled Silesians as it went, shaking the ground.

44

His men, stunned, quickly regrouped and did their best to fight back; they fired arrows and threw spears. But these all bounced helplessly off the animal's hide. Silesians died left and right.

Following on the elephant's heels were the Empire soldiers, racing through the open gates.

"ATTACK!" Kendrick yelled to his men, trying to rally them to meet the Empire's men before they got too deep into the courtyard, while dodging the racing elephant.

It was a futile effort. This time, Andronicus's men poured in fast and furious, and Kendrick's men were too busy dodging the animal. Within moments, Empire soldiers fanned out across the courtyard, killing Silesians in every direction.

Still more soldiers continued to pour in, an endless stream, unstoppable.

Kendrick raised his sword as an Empire soldier slashed down at his face, blocking and spinning around and slashing the soldier in the stomach. He stepped forward and blocked two more blows—but then felt himself kicked hard in the small of the back. He fell to his face.

Kendrick spun to see a soldier raising his boot to bring it down on his face. As it was halfway down, his friend Atme arrived and jabbed a spear in the soldier's stomach, preventing him from crushing Kendrick's face with his boot.

Kendrick gained his feet, grabbed his sword, and spun around and faced off with two more soldiers. But before he could even swing, he was tackled from behind by a third. Then a fourth.

The Empire men came from everywhere, descending like a swarm of locust. So outnumbered, there was little Kendrick and the others could do. Beside him, Atme, too, fell. All around them, he watched his men share similar fates.

Kendrick did not go down easily: he fought viciously, killing two of the four men pinning him down. But yet another one raised his gauntlet and smashed it down on Kendrick's face, connecting with his temple. There came a great ringing of metal in Kendrick's ear as he hit the ground, his head splitting. The soldier came down for another blow but Kendrick grabbed a mace from the ground and spun around and managed to crack the soldier across the head, knocking him back.

But no sooner had he finished this blow when he felt a hard jab in his ribs, and fell face-first again. He looked up to see himself pinned down by a soldier who looked different than the others, one of Andronicus' elite.

45

The man stepped on his ribs, nearly crushing the life out of him, and he held a short metal point to the back of his neck. Kendrick reached around and managed to clutch his dagger and raise it just enough to stab his attacker in the foot. The man screamed out in pain, stepping off of him.

But as soon as he had, he watched from the corner of his eye as another soldier swung for him with a hammer. Kendrick was too slow to dodge it, and the blow smashed Kendrick's helmet, knocking him back down with a clang of metal, ringing in his ears.

His head hit the ground, and this time he knew it was for good.

CHAPTER NINE

Thor, on his last legs, staggered with the others deeper into the desert, each step feeling like a thousand pounds. Covered in sweat, he gasped for air, the heat from both suns radiating down on him with more strength than he thought possible. All around him he heard his fellow Legion gasping for breath, the scuffling of their feet, as it became harder for them to lift them off the ground. He could not help but feel as if they were all shuffling their way deeper into nothingness, deeper towards death.

Even Indra, the native, struggled with every step, and Krohn, beside him, had finally stopped whining; he was too exhausted for that now. He merely panted, his mouth open, his tongue hanging low, his eyes squinting, his head lowered. It did not bode well for any of them.

Thor scanned the horizon, raising his chin with one last effort, squinting into nothingness, into the harsh blinding light, hoping for the millionth time he might spot something—anything—in any direction. But there was nothing but emptiness. The desert floor was becoming increasingly hard, cracked, baked, and Indra's warning rang in his head. She had been right all along. There was no way to cross this desert. They had been foolish to try. He was leading them all towards their deaths.

Thor felt weaker than he ever had, parched, and he lifted his empty sack, opened his mouth, and squeezed it for the millionth time. Of course, nothing came out. It had dried up long ago. He didn't know why he kept trying; some part of his brain still hoped that maybe there was a drop left.

The only one who had any water left at this point was Indra. Despite himself, Thor could not help turning and looking at her, allowing his eyes to rove down to the sack of water dangling at her waist. He licked his dry lips, then forced himself to turn and look away immediately. It was hers. She had rationed better than the rest of them, and being smaller and lighter, didn't need as much. She also knew these lands better. He wondered if she would be the lone survivor of the bunch.

Suddenly there came a loud sound, like a log falling, and Thor turned with the others to see Elden collapse. The biggest of them, he hit the ground hard, landing on his shoulder, stirring up dust. Then he just lay there, on his back, immobile.

The others lethargically gathered around him and looked down as if looking at themselves. There was no surprise in their eyes. Thor was only surprised that one of them had not collapsed sooner.

"Elden," Indra called out, kneeling beside him. She was always so hardened, so guarded, so careful to let others know that she did not care. So Thor was surprised to see concern and worry in her face.

She reached down and wiped the sweat from his brow, stroking his hair. Elden's eyes were half closed, and he licked his parched lips again and again. Indra removed the water sack from her waist, and in an act of supreme generosity, lifted Elden's head and gave him all of her remaining water. He drank it greedily, lapping his lips, the water running down his cheeks, as he drank and drank. Within moments, her sack was empty.

She lowered his head, and Elden leaned back, coughing and gasping.

Thor saw for the first time how much she cared for him; he could also see how much he had underestimated her. They had taken her for just another slave, a thief—but it turned out that she had been the most resourceful and most generous of them all. Without her, surely Elden would have been dead.

"You do great honor upon your race," Thor said to her.

She shook her head humbly, looking down at Elden.

"It is no honor," she said. "Soon, we will all go the way of flesh. What I did will be inconsequential in the wheel of time."

Indra reached over to pick up Elden, and the others crouched down to help her. She and Reece lifted him to his feet, then Thor came over and helped, draping Elden's arms over their shoulders.

Thor and Reece walked, dragging him, continuing through the desert, Elden's immense weight dragging them down. Elden was half-conscious, barely walking, more dragging his feet. As hard as it had been to march before, now, with Elden, it was unbearable. Thor did not know how he could make it.

But they all plodded on, marching together, one step after the next, deeper and deeper into nothingness. With every step, the sun seemed to grow stronger.

Finally, Reece's legs gave out. He went tumbling down, bringing Elden and Thor with him. Thor's legs were too weak to resist. He lay there, helpless. He looked around to see if the others would come to his rescue.

But Thor was surprised to realize that the others had already collapsed, some time ago, all of them laying prone on the desert floor in various positions, far away. He'd been too exhausted and delirious to even know he had been the last one standing when finally he went down.

Now they all lay there, motionless on the desert floor, beneath the sun of a hostile sky, waiting for nothing, except to die.

*

Thor found himself standing alone, in a small boat, drifting out to sea in the midst of a vast and empty ocean. Far off in the distance were soaring cliffs, and atop one, at the very edge, sat a castle. It seemed like a magical castle, a fantastical place, perched on the very edge of the world, high in the clouds. It seemed like a place protected from every danger of the world, a place in which anything was possible. Thor could feel the tremendous energy radiating from it, even from this great distance, and more than he had ever wanted anything in his life, he wanted to be there, inside.

Most of all, Thor sensed that up there, high up in that magical place atop the cliff, his mother lived. He knew that he was approaching the Land of the Druids.

Thor's boat was suddenly pulled by a strong current, bringing him towards the rocky shore at the very base of the cliff, lined with jagged black rocks. The boat deposited him there and he staggered off, collapsing face-first into the rocks, too exhausted to lift his head. He knew that somewhere, high up on those cliffs above, was his mother. But he did not have the energy to get there.

"My Thorgrin," came a voice.

It was a woman's voice, the sweetest and most reassuring voice he'd ever heard in his life.

Thor knew it was the voice of his mother. He knew that she was standing over him now, and he could feel the intense light and energy radiating off of her. He knew that he only needed to lift his head to see her. But he was too exhausted to do even this.

"Mother," he gasped, it coming out as a whisper.

"My son," she added. "I have been watching over you. I have been waiting for you. It is time for you to come home. It is time for us to meet."

"I want to," he said. "But I can't reach you. I can't cross the desert. I can't find the Sword."

"You can," she said, her voice resounding with confidence. "And you *will*. It is not yet time for you to die, brave warrior. Death will come for you soon enough. But not now. Now, it is time for you to live. Rise, and meet your destiny."

Thor felt a hand, the softest touch of his life, under his chin, felt it slowly lift his face, so that he looked up, higher and higher, towards his mother. He wanted desperately to see her face, but the soft blue light shining off of her was so intense that he was blinded by it. It was like looking into the sun.

"I am with you, Thorgrin," she said. "Arise, and make me proud."

Thor suddenly opened his eyes and found himself looking at the desert floor. He blinked and turned and looked for the others. But there was no one in sight. He lay there, all alone, confused.

Thor felt a new energy course within him, and slowly, he rose to his hands and knees. He felt the presence of someone over him, blocking out the suns, and he looked up and was surprised to see Argon. He stood there, holding his staff, looking down at him with an intensity that even outshone the sun.

Thor rose to his feet, feeling renewed, and looked back, wondering where everyone else was.

"You have passed many tests," Argon said slowly. "Yet there are always more tests. The greatest quest requires the greatest travail. And behind each quest, for the warrior, there always waits another."

"Where are my friends?" Thor asked.

Argon shook his head.

"They live somewhere between the land of life-and-death. It is the land you walk in now. You have not died. But you are not alive. You would have died on this day if it were not for the grace of your mother. You have powerful beings watching over you, and you have been given many chances at life."

Argon turned and stared out at the desert.

"Before you can return to the others," Argon said, "you must further your training. You cannot go any further in this quest unless your training is deepened. The desert is vast and deep, and only a skillful spiritual warrior can cross it. Are you ready to reach the next level?"

Thor nodded back earnestly.

"I wish for nothing more. Tell me what I must do."

"Walk with me," Argon said.

Thor walked side-by-side with Argon, deeper into the desert, wondering where they were going. He felt an intense energy radiating through him with each step, felt as if he were slowly coming back to himself. He also felt more powerful than he ever had.

As they were walking, Thor looked down and stopped short, shocked at what he saw. The ground fell away, and he found himself standing at the edge of the Canyon.

He looked down, overwhelmed at the depth and scope of it. It seemed to stretch forever. Its strange mist swirled all around him, and Thor looked over to see Argon standing beside him, looking out, too.

"How did we get here?" Thor asked. "How did we make it back to the Ring?"

"We are everywhere and nowhere," Argon replied. "We travel through the crack between the realms. You see, place and time are but an illusion. We now transcend these illusions. I want you to look into the Canyon, into its mist. What do you see?"

Thor squinted into the expanse, but saw nothing but swirling mist, lit with every color.

"I see nothing," Thor responded.

"That is because you look with your eyes, and not with your mind," Argon responded. "Now close your eyes," he said firmly, "and look."

Close my eyes and look? Thor wondered. He did not understand.

But he did as he was told, closing his eyes, facing out in the direction of the Canyon, feeling the swirling mist stroke his face. The moisture felt so good in the heat.

"In your mind's eye, see it," Argon said. "Allow it to come to you."

Thor breathed deep and centered himself, trying to understand. And as he stood there, for he did not know how long, slowly, he began to see it.

Below him, Thor saw a red city, built on the edge of the Canyon. Its stone sparkled red, and it was divided into two cities, a lower and upper one.

"I see a red city," Thor said.

"Good. What else?"

Thor's heart started to pound as he saw fires raging through it. Destruction. Bloodshed. People dying.

"I see an army," Thor said, "as fast as lightning, covering the Ring. Entering the city. Destroying it."

"Yes. What else?"

Thor struggled. At first it was obscured, but then it came into focus.

His heart plummeted as he saw one last thing. It was too horrible, and he wanted to look away. But he could not. He saw Gwendolyn, lying on a sickbed. Close to death. He saw her surrounded by several black angels of death, waiting patiently, as if ready to take her away.

Thor opened his eyes and spun and faced Argon.

"Is it true?" he asked. "Gwendolyn? Is she dead?"

"There are many forms of death," Argon said.

"She needs me. I must return to her."

"No," Argon said firmly. "Her destiny is her own."

"I must return to her!" Thor insisted.

"The time is not now," Argon said. "You must complete your quest. You must complete your training. If you returned to her now, she would die, and so would you."

"What must I do?" Thor asked, desperate.

"Up until now, you have fought with your hands, sometimes, with your heart, and sometimes with your spirit. But you are uneven. This is because you are still stuck in human nature. You still cling to this planet, to all the physical things around you, as if they are real. On one level, they are real. But on another, they are not. They are just energy forms. Until you understand that, your powers will never be complete."

Argon turned.

"There," he nodded, "do you see it?"

Thor heard a hissing noise and spun to find himself standing back in the desert. Racing towards him was a huge snake, with three heads, raising them and sticking out its tongues. It slithered right for him.

"Stop it!" Argon said.

Thor reached for the hilt of his sword.

"No!" Argon commanded. "Not with your sword! Use your mind. Draw on your inner force."

Thor's heart was pounding as the beast approached, too quickly; a part of him wanted to rely on his human side, to grab his sword and chop it in half. It took all his will to force himself to let go of the hilt, to stand there, hands at his side, and reach out a single palm, directing it towards the snake.

Thor tried to direct energy to it—but nothing happened. The snake was getting closer.

"Argon!" Thor screamed, frightened.

"Stop trying to direct your force," Argon said calmly. "You must understand that the force to stop this creature does not come from within you; it comes from within the creature itself. Let go of you. Become one with the creature. Feel its muscles, its three heads, its tail, its tongue, its venom. Feel how it moves on the floor. Feel how much it wants to kill you. Feel its hate. Appreciate its hate."

Thor closed his eyes and lowered his hand, and tried to do everything Argon said. As he focused, as the hissing grew louder and the animal closer, Thor began to feel something; it was slow at first, but then he felt it more and more strongly. It was the energy of this beast. Fast and slick, filled with venom and hate. It was intent on destroying Thor. Thor felt it clearly, as if he were the beast itself.

"Very good," Argon said. "Now you are the snake, too. Change your nature. Change the nature of the snake."

In his mind, Thor commanded the snake to stop.

Thor opened his eyes, and looked down to see the snake, twenty feet long, stopped before him, its three heads hissing but unable to reach him, as if frozen. Each of the three heads snapped towards Thor.

"You have stopped the beast," Argon said. "But you have not changed its nature."

Thor could feel the energy of the animal coursing through him, and as much as he tried to will it to turn around, it would not. He was stopping it, but nothing more, and it was taking a tremendous effort. His whole body shook from it, and he didn't feel he could hold it back much longer.

Suddenly, one of the beast's three heads extended and sank its fangs into Thor's arm.

Thor screamed out in pain as the venom shot through him; its two long fangs remained lodged in his forearm, burning, and it was the most painful thing he'd ever experienced. He felt as if his whole arm were on fire.

"Your power is wavering," Argon said.

"Help me!" Thor gasped, in agony.

"Not until you send away the beast," Argon said. "Stop opposing it. You are still opposing it, even while it is biting you."

Thor closed his eyes, in extreme pain, covered in sweat, and did everything he could to focus on Argon's words. He tried to center himself, to calm himself, even in the midst of such pain, even in the midst of being attacked.

Finally, something within him shifted; he stopped resisting the creature. He allowed it to be what it was. And then he willed the beast to lift its teeth from his skin.

The beast listened, and as it did, Thor felt the awful pain of the fangs leaving his skin, then the release of the burning. And then, suddenly, the beast turned and darted away, across the desert floor, as Thor collapsed.

Suddenly, Thor understood. He had been resisting the beast. Resisting all the forces around him. He had failed to see that they were all one. One huge life force. He had only been seeing the separation between them; and it was the separation that was making him weak.

"Excellent," Argon said.

Thor opened his eyes and saw Argon standing over him, reaching out his staff, and touching the golden end of it to Thor's wound. A moment later the wound healed, his flesh returning to normal, as if he had never been bit.

"You are a fast learner," Argon said. "Like your father."

"My father?" Thor asked. "You know him? Who is he?"

"Of course I know him," Argon said. "I trained him."

"Trained him?" Thor asked. "Tell me," he pleaded, "who is he?"

Argon shook his head.

"All will be revealed when the time is right. The question you must ask yourself now is if you want to live. Do you choose to fulfill this quest? To save Gwendolyn?"

"I do!" Thor yelled back enthusiastically.

"Your destiny is a great one," Argon said, "but it is also a dark one. With anything great comes light, and darkness. You must be prepared to accept both."

"I am!" Thor yelled back.

Argon stared at him for a long time, as if summing him up, then finally he nodded back in approval.

"Arise, brave warrior," Argon said. "It is time to live."

Thor blinked several times, opening his eyes to find himself lying face-first in the desert floor. All around him were his Legion brothers, lying near him, just as he had left them. They all lay there as the second sun grew long, the heat of the day beginning to cool, exactly as they had been.

Thor slowly rose to his hands and knees, feeling a new energy, a new strength, course through him. He felt different, in every fiber of his being. He rubbed his head and wondered. Had it all been a dream? How much of it had been real? His mother? Argon?

And who was his father?

Thor rose to his hands and knees, and he realized he was the only one awake. All the others were either unconscious or dead, he was not sure which.

Thor heard a shuffling of feet, and he looked up to see a person standing over him. He wore a brown and yellow robe, with a large white sash, and he looked down at Thor with curious and gentle eyes. This man was of a race Thor had never encountered before: he had green skin, a very narrow nose, wide lips, and huge eyes, disproportionately large for his face.

He pulled back his hood and peered down at Thor, as if examining a curiosity. From behind him, there appeared several more, just like him. They were short people, and they each held a long ruby staff.

"Help them," said the leader.

The men scrambled, each running to one of the Legion and to Indra and Krohn and picking them up. Thor felt his arms draped over two of their shoulders, and allowed himself to be dragged.

"Who are you?" Thor asked.

"Desert dwellers," the man responded. Thor sensed a positive energy from him, and he did not resist.

"Where are we going?" he inquired.

"Young warrior," the man said. "It is time for you to recover."

Thor felt himself dragged along for he did not know how long, in and out of consciousness as they went. The sun grew darker, until finally the ground beneath him, to his amazement, turned to a soft, lush grass.

There came the sound of gurgling water, of a flowing spring, and Thor opened his eyes fully, to his utter delight, to see that they were in a desert oasis. For a large perimeter, perhaps a hundred yards, there was a circle of the most lush grass and palm trees and fruits that he had ever seen. In its center was a crystal blue lake, and Thor stumbled towards it, sinking to his knees with his brothers and falling face first at the edge of the water.

They all drank and drank, and with each sip, Thor felt his life force returning.

When he drank until he could drink no more, he rolled onto his back, the water cooling the back of his neck. He looked up at the sky, the palms swaying above him, casting shade, and wondered if he'd arrived in paradise.

"Who are you?" Thor asked again, as the man smiled down.

"We have been watching you for a long time, brave warrior," he said. "And we have decided we are not going to let you die."

CHAPTER TEN

Andronicus rode triumphantly through the sacked city of Silesia, reveling in his victory. Sprawled out on either side of him were the hundreds of corpses of MacGil's army, of Silesian soldiers, piled in heaps where they had been slain. Amidst these were thousands more Silesian captives, bound to each other in long lines, being whipped and led throughout the city. There was the omnipresent sound of hammers striking pegs, and all around him, he saw enormous crosses being erected, tall enough to hold even the largest Silesian warriors. They were getting ready to crucify the leaders.

Already several soldiers screamed out, as pegs were driven through their wrists and ankles, nailing them to the crosses. Already many had died. Those who survived, screamed and moaned. Andronicus smiled. This was always his favorite part: basking in the suffering of those he crushed and making them learn the sting of the long arm of the Great Andronicus.

Some captors learned the lesson quickly; for others, it took longer. The Silesians were proud, hardheaded people, and they had surprised Andronicus, holding out much longer than other peoples he had subdued. For that, he admired them; yet for that, he would also have to make them pay.

These were a people who did not seem to want to be broken. No matter how much he enslaved them, tortured them, none of them would pledge allegiance to him. Ever since their ruse, since that initial, fake pledge, they had remained silent, even in the face of torture and death. But everyone had a weak spot, and he would find a way to break them, no matter what, or how long, it took.

As he rode through the town, a cold winter gale rushing through, Andronicus breathed deep, finally satisfied, finally having conquered all of the Ring. All of the Empire. Finally, there was not a place left on the globe his foot had not touched. Finally, he was supreme master of the universe.

Andronicus passed rows of women and children, chained to each other, already being led to the new camps being erected all around them. Already they were setting them to work on rebuilding the city's rubble, shaping the city in a new way. Andronicus' way. Already dozens of slaves were hard at work erecting the emblem of

57

Andronicus' kingdom, a lion with a bird in its mouth. And another group was hard at work on erecting a statue of Andronicus himself. It would be a tall and wide statue, right in the center of the city square, fifty feet at its base, and rising one hundred feet into the air. It would be coated in gold when they were done, a gleaming reminder to all who they now served.

Andronicus reveled as he saw prisoner after prisoner led past him, so many Silesian officers, so many MacGils. He would find out who was who, one at a time, and torture each one himself. On all sides of him the city was ablaze, fires being lit to the remaining dwellings, setting the rest of the city ablaze. All that once was would be destroyed, replaced with the new.

The most pressing and final piece of business would be his descent to the lower city, to deal personally with that MacGil girl. Gwendolyn. His people had already flushed out nearly all of the lower Silesians, had taken them onto captivity; there remained only that Gwendolyn girl to find, who was well-hidden. His men had identified where she was, hidden inside a castle in the wall, and in a matter of hours, they would find her and bring her to him. This time, she would not escape. This time, he would make a public spectacle of her, make sure that all the men had their way with her, and that everyone was made to watch. And then, when he was done with her, he would kill her himself.

Andronicus smiled and breathed deep at the thought.

His horse marched towards the outer gate, towards the open expanse of the Canyon, the descent to Lower Silesia just feet away. He was getting closer with every step to finding Gwendolyn, to making his victory complete. This was one of the great moments of his life, and torturing her was all he needed to make it complete.

*

Kendrick's eyes, heavy from exhaustion, injury and loss of blood, struggled to open. He felt heavy ropes binding his arms tightly behind his back, wrenching his shoulders to the point of agony. He felt himself being dragged, grabbed by the back of the hair, and as he went, he felt every ache and pain in his body from the battle.

Kendrick had killed many Empire soldiers, but had sustained countless kicks and punches and elbows all over his body, a sword slash on one arm and on one thigh, and welts on his face and head.

His hair hung over his face, matted with blood—he wasn't sure whose. One of his eyes was swollen halfway shut, and it was an effort to see. But see he did. And he wished he hadn't.

All around him he saw comrades, members of MacGil's army, dead. Members of the Silver, people he had grown up with, fought with through countless battles, dead. And what hurt the most, what made him close his eyes and try to shake it away was the sight of hundreds of Legion members. Dead. They had been killed in their first rush of glory, boys, taken before their time.

At the sight, Kendrick wished that he had died with them. It was a curse that he been left to live.

As Kendrick was led, one of countless prisoners dragged across the courtyard, he saw the fires, the women being attacked. Even children were bound. Empire soldiers were everywhere, and the city had been thoroughly sacked. Already, they were beginning to rebuild it as a slave city, as another monument to the conquests of the Great Andronicus. Already slavemasters were whipping prisoners, setting them to work on piles of rubble. The cracks of whips filled the city.

Kendrick was kicked from behind, and he shuffled forward with the others. He wanted to just close his eyes and collapse. But he saw another prisoner collapse, a few feet away, and as soon as he hit the ground, an Empire soldier raised a sword and stabbed him through his heart. The prisoner was too tired—or didn't even care enough—to cry out, as he met his death in silence, another nameless corpse.

Kendrick wanted to die. But he was determined not to. That was not his creed. He was a fighter to the last, and he would live, in whatever form that took.

Kendrick was led to a huge cross along with several others, falling in and out of consciousness. He felt himself lifted and opened his eyes to see Empire soldiers lifting him up high overhead, holding him up against a crooked wooden cross. Beside him he heard a horrific scream, and he looked over to see a member of the Silver being crucified, an Empire soldier nailing a peg through his wrists and ankles. Kendrick struggled, wanting to help his friend, but he couldn't budge.

Kendrick looked to his other side, and his heart fell to see on the other cross beside him, one of his beloved comrades. Kolk. Crucified long ago, his head hung low, barely clinging to life.

On the cross beside Kolk hung Atme. Kendrick was relieved to see he was still alive, and close by, though Atme looked as if he were clinging to life, his body covered in bruises and wounds.

As Kendrick was hoisted, he braced himself for the same awful fate. But the Empire soldiers began arguing with each other. He felt himself tied and bound to the cross, but he could tell from the soldiers' arguing that they had run out of pegs. Luckily for him, they could not hammer a peg through his skin.

Instead, they tied his ropes tighter as they bound him to the cross. It was still horrifically painful, as he felt all of his limbs stretching, about to burst.

Kendrick closed his eyes and thought of all he held dear in life. He thought of those closest to him. He prayed silently that each had made it. Most of all, he shook his head as he shut his eyes tight and prayed for his younger sister. Gwendolyn.

Please God, he prayed. *Of all of us, let her live.*

*

Gwendolyn paced the floor of her dim chamber, walking to the window for the millionth time that day and watching the unfolding chaos in lower Silesia. From her hidden spot she could look down on the lower plaza and witness the devastation being wrought by the Empire soldiers. They were descending like goats down the side of the cliff, hundreds of them, terrorizing her people. There were few people left now, most of them already bound together as captives and led away by the Empire to the upper city.

All that remained in the emptying streets were the vacant echoes of their screams, echoing off the Canyon walls, carried by the howling wind. The Empire had made it down here, and that could only mean one thing: Kendrick's final stand had failed. There was no one left to fight Andronicus. This was what defeat looked like. The defeat they had all known was inevitable.

Gwendolyn watched the Empire troops canvassing the lower city, and she knew they were looking for her. She was lodged in a secret hiding place in this secret castle, built into the cliffs, yet she knew it was only a matter of time until they found it. Until they brought her back up there, back into Andronicus' arms. She shuddered at the thought.

Gwen knew that Argon would not be here to save her, would not mettle in human affairs a second time—nor would her amulet be able to save her again. She knew that this was it. Thor was gone from her, far away in a land she did not know where, and she had no one else left to help her now. Now, she would be facing death all alone.

Gwen watched a group of Empire head her way, and she knew she had even less time than she thought.

As she looked out, Gwen felt sorry not for herself, but for all the people she had let down. She closed her eyes and a tear fell, as she pondered what tragedies must have befallen them. Kendrick, Godfrey, Srog, Brom, Kolk, Atme and the others, all up there, probably all dead by now. It left a pain in her chest.

She thought of Thor and her heart sank. She loved him more than she could ever express, and she could not imagine life without him. A part of her didn't want to live without him. Nor could she imagine life as Andronicus' slave, as his play thing. She felt that if she were going to die, better to die with dignity.

Gwen came to a decision.

She turned and called out to the attendant standing by her door.

"Bring me Illepra—now!" she called

"Yes, my lady," he said and ran from the room. She heard his footsteps echoing the distance.

Gwen paced and paced, her heart thumping in her chest, and in moments the door opened and Illepra burst in, holding her basket in her arms.

"My lady, I am glad to see you up and walking about! The color has returned your cheeks. You are healing well."

"Too well, I'm afraid," Gwendolyn replied.

"My lady?"

"I need a special vial," Gwen said. "It is a vial that no person should wish to take. But that some must take when no other herbs suffice."

Illepra looked at her carefully, and her perceptive eyes widened.

Slowly, she shook her head.

"You ask for poison," she said.

Gwen nodded.

"The vial of choice for Kings and Queens," she said.

Illepra shook her head vigorously.

"I will not do it, my lady. I practice the healing arts, and I took a vow."

Gwendolyn was determined.

"I am your Queen and I *command* you!" she said firmly.

Illepra stared back, unmoving, and Gwendolyn took a step forward and clutched her hands.

"I beg you," she added. "Give me the vial."

Gwendolyn felt tears running down her cheeks.

"Andronicus's men will come for me," she added. "Do you imagine a life for me with them? Everyone and everything we know and love is dead. I don't want to live like this."

Illepra stared back long and hard, silent, then finally lowered her chin, a tear rolling from her cheek, and reached deep into her basket, past all the herbs, and rifled around until she brought out a single small vial of black liquid. She held it up to the light.

"Blackroot," she said. "Sip this, and you will be no more. Be careful, my lady. Do not touch it to your lips unless you want it to be the last time you sip again."

Illepra turned her back and hurried from the room, slamming the door behind her.

Gwendolyn watched her go, then raised the vial, examining its liquid in the light. She watched its viscous, black liquid move as she turned the hour-glass shaped vial. It was both sinister and beautiful. Gwen recalled her history books, all the stories she'd read of kings and queens taking it. She had never imagined holding one herself.

"The drink of kings and queens," came a voice.

Gwendolyn's heart raced as she recognized the voice.

She spun to see Argon standing there, staring back at her, his eyes shining. He seemed to see right through her, to penetrate her darkest thoughts. She felt ashamed, and immediately hid the vial in her pocket.

She lowered her head and blushed.

"You saved my life today," she said. "On the battlefield. I don't know how to thank you."

He remained expressionless.

"Though it appears, from the vial you hold, you will be dead soon enough," he responded coolly, disapproval in his voice. "Was it all for nothing then?"

Gwendolyn blushed, feeling guilty.

"It is never for nothing," she said. "Whether in this life, or the next, I owe you a great debt."

"The debt you owe me is to live," he answered.

Gwen furrowed her brow.

"I still do not understand," she said. "How did you do it? I thought you can never intervene in human affairs? That sorcerers are forbidden?"

"You are correct," he said, walking slowly to the far window. He looked weary as he went. "What I did was forbidden. I broke the sacred sorcerer's vow. It was the first and only time I have ever done so, the first and only time in a thousand years that I have interfered in human affairs. I violated our code, and for that I must pay a very dear price. What I did sapped my powers, and I will have to sleep a long time. You will not see me again for quite a while. At least not in the way you once did."

Gwendolyn felt overcome with emotion.

"I am sorry that you did that on my account," she said. "And touched that you would do such a thing for me, of all the kings and queens you've ever known."

"You are different than all of them," he said. "You have a bigger heart. You are more pure. More courageous. You are noble. You are a leader. And that his how I know you will not drink from that vial in your pocket."

Gwen flushed.

"Would you leave me at the mercy of Andronicus, then?" she asked, indignant.

"Even in death, you must set an example," he said. "It is not about whether or not you die. It is about *how* you die. That is what lives on for others."

"How can I live after what he has done to me?" she asked, pained. "Even if nothing more happened?"

"You can live just as easily as anyone else," he said. "There is no shame in what happened to you. There is only shame in being too much of a coward to carry on. In not realizing that *what happened* to you is not *you*. *What happened* is not the same as *who you are*. Your body and spirit and soul are distinct from the events in this world that happen to you. You are looking at the world now through a very narrow, physical lens. But the world is not only physical—it is also spiritual. Looking at things physically is the lowest form of all.

"Do you think you entered this world through the physical alone? You were also conceived spiritually. That is the highest level in which we all live. And that is why physical occurrences to the body do not mean a thing. They do not touch, and cannot reach, our spirit, our essence. It would be the same if you scraped an elbow, or lost a finger. You, Gwendolyn, have not changed."

She flushed, embarrassed. She knew there was truth to what he was saying, but it was hard to take it in right now. She was finding herself feeling defensive.

"I am not a coward," she said, bunching her fists.

"I know you're not," he said. "And I also know that you pay your debts."

"Debts?" she asked, confused.

"Don't you remember, that day, when you begged me to save Thor's life? I told you it was not meant to be, yet you insisted, you said you would give anything. I told you you would pay a debt, you would die a small death. You have now paid that debt. That was your small death. A small death of the spirit. But not of the body. And not of the soul."

Gwen remembered it all, and hearing his words gave her comfort. It gave meaning to the horrors she had endured. Now it all made sense, at least.

"You should be grateful," Argon continued. "You are still alive. You have your health. You have Thor's child, within you. Would you sacrifice the child to kill yourself? Just out of cowardice? Are you that selfish?"

"I am not selfish," she said defiantly, knowing he was right.

"Right now, from where you are standing, it seems in your eyes that the future will only bring you more pain, more sadness," Argon said. "It seems in your eyes that you have suffered a humiliation from which you can never recover. But your vision is limited; you look at time from only one perspective, and it is a very narrow one. This is the lens of all who have been through suffering. And it is a distorted lens. The future will surprise you; it may just be bright, brighter than you ever imagined. And what happened to you today will fade in your mind, fade so much that you may never even remember it, as if it never was. Life is not just one life: it is many lives. And your new lives will wash away whatever pain and regret there was in the old ones. When we have tragedy in life, we get stuck, like getting stuck in the mud. When we are in the mud it feels as if we can never get out. But these come to us as great life lessons: it is up to us to pull ourselves out of the mud. Not just once, but time and time again. This is your moment to pull yourself out. To show life that you are bigger than your fears. Unless you are too afraid."

"I am *not* afraid," she answered, determined.

Argon smiled back, the first time she had ever seen him smile.

"It is not me you must convince," he said. "It is yourself."

Gwen turned and paced herself, walking slowly back to the window, breathing deep, feeling better. She felt that maybe everything he said was right. But there was still one thing bothering her.

"But what about Thor?" she asked. "After what has happened to me, Thor won't love me anymore. I will be lowered in his eyes."

"Do you think so little of Thorgrin?" Argon asked. "He may love you even more."

Gwen hadn't considered that.

"He may," she said, "but deep inside he might feel differently. I don't want to put that burden on him. I don't want him to feel that he *has* to be with me. I want him to *want* to be with me."

Argon slowly shook his head.

"You vastly underestimate our friend Thor," he said. "His love for you is as for himself."

Gwendolyn lowered her face and felt a tear roll down her cheek. As he spoke the words, she felt them to be true.

"So what now?" she asked. "I can't stay here. I will be captured. Do I just surrender?"

Argon sighed.

"You are well-read," he said. "Do you remember what women would do in times of old if they were attacked? Where they would go?"

"Go?" she asked, puzzled. As he said it, she was dimly aware, and it began to come back to her.

"The Tower of Refuge," Argon said.

As he said it, she began to recall.

"At the southern end of the Ring," she said, remembering. "A place where women go to heal. A monastery. They take a vow of silence. Some return to society, some don't."

"It is a sacred place," Argon added, "a place where you cannot be touched by anyone. Not even Andronicus. Take time to heal, to reflect. And then make a decision. Better to go there, and retreat from the world, than to die."

As Gwendolyn pondered it, she looked out of the window and watched Andronicus' troops closing in. It slowly came back to her, stories she had read of the Tower of Refuge, the place where women fled in ancient times, to regroup and heal themselves. The more she thought about it, the more it felt like the right thing to do. Her people did not need her now. What they needed was for her to survive.

"But what if—" Gwen turned to talk to Argon, but he was already gone.

She searched the room, baffled. But he was nowhere to be seen.

Gwen knew it was only a matter of minutes now. She took out the vial and examined it once again, struggling with herself.

Suddenly, she came to a decision. Argon was right: she was stronger than that. She would never give in to cowardice. *Never.*

Gwen reached back and hurled the vial, smashing it into the wall. The liquid stuck to the wall with a hissing noise, then dripped slowly down it like tar.

"Steffen!" Gwen called, hurrying towards the door.

In moments Steffen arrived, rushing into the room, looking at her with panic in his eyes.

"The secret tunnels you told me of. Do you know them?"

"Yes, my lady," he said in a rush. "Srog instructed me. He commanded me to stay by your side, and if you ever needed them, to show you the way."

"Show me now," she said.

His eyes lit in excitement.

"But my lady, where will you go?"

"I will cross the Ring, to the South, to the Tower of Refuge."

"My lady, I must accompany you. It is not a journey you should make alone."

She shook her head, anxious, hearing the footsteps of the soldiers outside the gates.

"You are a true friend," she said, "but it will be a perilous journey and I will not endanger you."

He shook his head, adamant.

"I will not show you the way unless you allow me to accompany. My honor forbids it."

Gwendolyn heard the distant footsteps of the approaching men, and she knew she had no choice. And she was, as ever, grateful for Steffen's loyalty.

"Okay," she said, "let's go."

Steffen turned and fled the room and she followed him down corridor after corridor, twisting and turning, until they came to a hidden door at the end of a hall, camouflaged in the stone. Steffen opened it, and she knelt down beside him and peered in.

It was a tunnel of blackness, cold and dank, insects crawling inside, a chill running through her at the feel of the draft. They exchanged a worried look, and she gulped at the thought. But she had no choice. It was that, or death.

As the soldiers' footsteps grew ever louder, the two of them hurried inside and began the long, hard crawl towards freedom.

CHAPTER ELEVEN

Thor opened his eyes and felt a sense of content and peace that he hadn't known in a long time. He felt rested, rejuvenated, and he lay on his back in soft luxurious grass, cool breezes caressing his face. He sat up and looked all around, wondering if this were all a dream.

The early morning light spread over the desert, illuminating the oasis in which Thor lay. Slowly, it all came back to him. His dream, his mother, seeing Argon, then awakening to find that man, the desert dweller, who had led them here. He had been in and out of consciousness, and he immediately looked around, making sure the others were with him.

He breathed a sigh of relief to see that they were. They all lay comfortably on the grass, by the edge of the lake, sleeping contentedly and looking better than he had seen them in a long time. All around them were palm trees, laden with fruits, swaying slightly in the cool morning breezes.

They had been saved by these desert dwellers, Thor realized, and he turned and looked for them, to thank them. He spotted the group of them, seated beside the waters, holding out their palms, eyes closed, chanting in some sort of ritual. Their image reflected off the still waters, and it was a beautiful sight. The soft sound of their chanting lifted and carried on the air, making the place feel even more surreal.

Beyond the perimeter of the oasis, in every direction, there was desert. Yellow, baked desert, sprawling endlessly, cruelly, to the edges of the horizon. It was too early in the day for the heat to be rippling, but Thor knew it would be soon enough.

"You have awakened," came a voice.

Thor turned and saw one of the desert dwellers, the one who had saved him, standing over him, looking down with kind, compassionate eyes.

"You slept a long and fitful sleep."

Thor wracked his brain, trying to remember. Thor looked around and saw his brothers rousing.

"I owe you a great debt," Thor said. "We all do. You saved our lives."

The man shook his head.

"You owe us nothing," he said. "The debt is ours."

Thor looked back, confused.

"You see," the man said, "our legend tells of you. It tells of this day. The day when you would pass through here. We have been waiting for you for generations, waiting for this moment to help you on your journey. Your quest is not just for you—it is one that will free us all, even here in the Empire."

"Waiting for me?" Thor asked, confused. "I don't understand. You must have me mixed up with someone else."

But they shook their heads.

The others crowded around, and Thor felt Krohn rubbing against his leg, and reached down and stroked his head.

"Where are we?" O'Connor asked

"You are deep in the Great Desert," the man answered, as his people finally rose and joined them. "Right in the center. No human being has ever made it this far. Those of us who live here know this oasis. The desert is an unforgiving place. You are lucky to be alive."

"I warned them," Indra said, shaking her head.

"We are on a quest," Reece responded.

"For the stolen Sword," O'Connor chimed in.

"We were told it is being taken to Neversink," Elden added.

The desert dwellers turned and looked at each other, eyes wide in surprise.

"It is just as the prophecies foretold," said their leader, turning and looking at Thor.

"Can you lead us there?" Thor asked.

"Of course," the leader responded. "We must. It is our duty. Follow us closely. And grab as many fruits as you can carry," he said, as they all lowered their hoods, raised their staffs and began hiking, "it will be your only source of life."

Thor and the others turned and examined the thick yellow fruits hanging from the swaying palm trees and they each picked as many as they could carry, then turned and hurried off after the desert dwellers, who were moving surprisingly fast, already becoming obscured in the morning mist.

As they all fell into line, Thor marching beside his brothers quickly to keep up, Thor raised one of the yellow fruits out of curiosity and bit into it. As he did it exploded with water, water gushing down his face, his chin, his throat and spilling down to the desert floor. He tried to catch as much of it as he could in his palm, upset that he wasted it.

"You must be more careful," Indra said. "Waterfruits are delicate. They are mostly water, and just a tiny bit of skin. Inside is not just water—it is a special water, which gives you energy. More energy than food."

Thor drank the water, which was sweet and gave him a burst of energy. It also tasted a little bit tart. He looked at the fruit with a new respect.

"You must bite into them slowly and carefully," Indra added. "You have already wasted one."

Thor leaned over and put the remainder of the fruit to Krohn's lips, allowing him to lap from it. He drank it greedily, eager for more.

Thor and the others walked closely behind the desert dwellers as they weaved, following some sort of inscrutable path that Thor could not detect. As they trekked, the sun grew higher and hotter in the sky, and Thor could feel himself breathing heavily. It didn't help that every now and again a cloud of dust blew through; Thor raised his hands to his eyes, trying to keep the sand out. The desert dwellers merely lowered their long hoods, and seemed immune to these distractions.

When Thor got thirsty, he bit into another waterfruit, slowly this time, and was so grateful for the liquid, which he shared with Krohn. All around him, his brothers were doing the same. Unlike their first desert trek, this fruit gave him the energy to keep him going. At first, when he had gathered them, he had resented the extra weight—but now he was so glad he had them. He actually feared how light he was getting, as he ate more and more of them.

"Hey, more fruits!" O'Connor yelled.

Thor turned and saw, to their side, a sole swaying palm tree in the middle of the desert, filled with low hanging red fruits. O'Connor headed towards it, when suddenly a desert-dweller grabbed him roughly by the shirt, and yanked him back.

Thor and the others exchanged looks of wonder, not understanding.

"Let me go!" O'Connor yelled.

But then, suddenly, the earth opened up beneath a tree, into a massive and spreading sinkhole, swallowing the tree and everything around it.

O'Connor stood there and stared at it, wide-eyed; if he had taken just one more step, he would be dead.

"The desert is filled with its own seductresses," the desert dweller said to O'Connor. "As I said, stick closely to our trail."

They continued trekking, O'Connor shaken, all of them with a new respect for this place, following the trail of the desert dwellers as closely as they could.

They marched and marched, silently, deeper and deeper into the desert, until their legs and feet grew weary. It was feeling more and more like a pilgrimage.

Hours passed, and Thor needed a break in the monotony; he ambled up and fell in beside the lead desert dweller.

"Why do you dwell here?" Thor asked.

"Like you, we want to be free. Free from Andronicus' long reach. Our freedom is more dear to us than where we live."

It seemed to be a recurring theme that Thor was hearing throughout the Empire.

"If you can defeat Andronicus, you would free not only yourselves, but all of us," he added.

"But this desert seems like such a hostile and unforgiving place," Thor said.

The man smiled.

"The Empire is filled with hostile and unforgiving places," he replied. "It is also filled with places of unimaginable beauty, abundance, prosperity. Ocean cities. Cities made of gold. Stretches of green, of farmland, as far as the eye can see. Waterfalls that have no bottom. Rivers packed with fish. These are the places Andronicus' has claimed. One day, still, they may be ours again."

They trekked and trekked, Thor's feet throbbing, until the second sun already fell low in the sky. Their waterfruits were long ago exhausted, and Thor did not know if he could make it any longer. Just as he was going to speak, up ahead, in the rippling waves of heat he saw the outline of something. He blinked several times, wondering if it was another mirage. But as they neared, he realized it wasn't.

"Neversink," Indra called out.

Thor's heart soared with relief.

"Yes," the leader said, "the Lake borders the desert. It is where one terrain ends and another begins."

Rejuvenated, they marched until the sand gradually gave way to grass, until they reached the edge of the desert, the grass becoming thicker and greener. There, perhaps a hundred yards in the distance, surrounded by grass, sat Neversink. On one side it was framed by a tall wood, and on the other, rolling green hills.

"This is where we leave you," the lead desert-dweller said, stopping and facing Thor.

"I don't know how we shall ever repay you," Thor said.

"Find your Sword," he answered. "Defeat Andronicus. That is repayment enough."

He leaned forward and embraced Thor, and Thor embraced him back.

"Remember us," the man said.

With that, the desert dwellers all turned, covered their faces with their hoods, and headed back into the desert. Thor and the others watched them go; they had not gone far when a desert storm kicked up sand, enveloping them, making them disappear.

Thor and the others exchanged a look of wonder, then all turned and surveyed the bottomless lake before them. Neversink. It was larger than Thor had imagined, seeming to stretch miles in each direction. It glowed a light blue, and Thor could sense an intense energy coming off of it. It did not seem like a normal lake.

Thor looked every which way for any sign of the Sword, of the thieves. He was on guard, as were the others, grasping the hilts of their swords, bracing for a confrontation. If they had beat the thieves here, they could arrive at any moment.

But as much as Thor scoured the shorelines, he could not see a thing, no evidence that they were here. He only prayed that they had not been too late.

"Maybe we were too late," O'Connor said. "Maybe they already cast the Sword and left."

"Or maybe they haven't arrived yet," Reece said.

"If they did come and cast the Sword, there's no way we can check the waters," Elden said.

"If the Sword is in there," Indra said, "then it has sunk to the bowels of the earth. Your only hope is if you have arrived here before they and can stop them before they cast it."

"We must find out if they were here," Thor said. "If they were here, they left a trail. We must find it. We must know for sure what has happened. Let's check the shoreline."

As one, they all set off, trekking along the white, sandy shores of the lake, scouring the shoreline for any tracks, any sign of disruption. Thor took off his shoes and walked with bare feet in the grass, then along the sand, dipping his feet into the icy waters; it felt good, cooling him, especially beneath the shade of the towering trees. The others did the same.

They walked for hours, nearing the far shore of the lake, its waters glistening, when Reece called out: "Over here!"

They all turned excitedly and followed Reece as he pointed to footprints in the sand; they were the prints of a large group of people. They all stood there, studying them.

"They came from the wood," Reece said.

"That means they have beat us here," Elden said.

Thor's heart dropped as he looked up and saw the trail of prints in the sand. It did not bode well.

They all followed the prints along the white sands, following the contours of the lake. Suddenly, abruptly, they ended.

They all stood there, scratching their heads, looking down at the sand, then out at the waters.

"The water is darker here," Reece said.

"This must be the deepest part of the lake," O'Connor said.

"It is," Indra said, stepping forward, peering into the water. "If they were to cast the Sword anywhere, it would be here."

Thor gulped. She was right. Could the Sword be lost forever?

"But why do their footsteps end?" Thor asked.

They all looked out at the still waters, wondering. The only sound was that of the whipping wind off the water, as they all watched. Thor felt a sinking feeling.

"Have we come all this way then," O'Connor asked, "to find a Sword that is lost forever?"

They scanned the waters, but they were impenetrable.

"If it is in there, there is no way to retrieve it," Elden said.

"So then what now?" Reece asked. "Return to the Ring as failures?"

Indra turned her backs on them and meandered over to the edge of the wood.

"I'm not so sure," she finally said.

They all turned and looked at her; she was kneeling, examining branches.

"Do you see those trees?" she said. "Look at the branches. The angle of them. It looks like maybe somebody had retreated from this spot, back into the wood."

Thor turned with the others and followed Indra, walking away from the lake, into the towering pines. They had all learned enough not to doubt her, and they followed her without question as she led them into the wood. As they continued further, Thor began to see it, too; at first it was faint, but then it came into view. There was a subtle trail, a series of broken branches. A pattern. It was beginning to look like a trail. She had been right.

The trail wound its way through the forest, then finally, it opened up, back onto the sandy shores at a different part of the lake. This part of the shore was obscured, covered in shade, long, heavy branches of pine curving over it. Thor had to look closely to see that there was something on the sand, hidden in the shade.

As they got closer, Thor suddenly stopped and stood frozen in place, as did the others, shocked at the sight before them.

There, lying on the sand, at the edge of the lake, where the bodies of the thieves who had stolen the Sword from the Ring. The whole group of them, all lying in the sand, dead.

Blood trickled from their bodies, onto the sand, still wet, staining it red, and lying amidst them, were the bodies of several dozen Empire soldiers, all dead.

Thor and the others stood there, baffled, trying to make sense of the sight. Clearly a great conflict had happened here. But why? How? And what had happened to the Sword? There was no sign of it anywhere. Had the thieves cast the Sword into the water before they were killed? Had any Empire soldiers survived and ran off with the Sword after the conflict?

"It looks like they all killed each other," Elden said.

They all began to walk slowly through the carnage, trying to understand.

"No," said Indra, finally, kneeling and examining the marks on their bodies. "They were attacked. All of them. By something else."

"Attacked?" Elden asked. "By what?"

Indra ran her hand along the chest of one of the soldiers, then looked up ominously:

"Dragons."

CHAPTER TWELVE

Godfrey slowly peeled open his eyes, his head throbbing. He hurt more than he could remember, his body feeling as if it bore the weight of the earth. Every muscle ached and throbbed, and as he lay there, face first in the grass, he slowly tested his limbs, trying to move each one. He felt as if he had rigor mortis settling in.

He shook his head, and tried to remember. Where was he? What had happened?

Godfrey looked out and saw not far from him, the dead face of a corpse staring back, eyes wide open as if looking right at him. He opened his eyes with a start, leaned back, and looked all around: there were hundreds of corpses sprawled out on the battlefield all around him. He turned his neck, and saw the same view in every direction.

Then he remembered. The battle against Andronicus. At first, the victory; then, the defeat. The slaughter.

Godfrey was amazed to see he was alive. He also could not help but feel proud of himself that he had actually had the courage to fight, to stand side-by-side with his brother Kendrick and the others. He did not have their skills, but ironically, perhaps that was what had saved him. He had thrown himself clumsily into the thick of battle and embarrassingly, he did not have their agility either—as he had charged, Godfrey had slipped on the slick blood of a soldier, and had slipped before he could wield his sword. He remembered lying face down on the ground and trying to get up, but being trampled by soldiers and horses.

Godfrey recalled receiving a solid kick to the head from a horse that had knocked him out. After that, all had been blackness.

Godfrey raised a hand to the side of his side, and felt a huge welt where the horse had kicked him. He was embarrassed to have been taken down by a horse and not to have gone down with his sword raised high, by another knight. But at least, unlike the others all around him, it had spared his life.

It was the next morning and as a cold mist blew in off the Canyon, Godfrey shivered, realizing he had been out all night. He sat up amidst the sea of dead bodies, a stark scene in the first light of morning. In the distance he spotted Andronicus' troops, patrolling. There came the distinctive noise of a sword cutting through air and impaling flesh; Godfrey craned his neck to see an Empire soldier, about fifty yards off, walking from one body to the next, raising his sword and plunging it through each corpse to make sure it was dead. He was methodical, going from corpse to corpse—and he was heading in Godfrey's direction.

Godfrey swallowed hard, eyes opening wide, realizing that he had escaped death once—but was not about to escape it again. He had to think quick, or he would end up *truly* dead.

What Godfrey lacked in fighting skills, he made up for in wit. He did not have the training of his brothers, but he had a unique ability to survive. Growing up, he had always found a way out of everything, and now, more than ever, it was time to draw on his skills.

Godfrey quickly scanned the corpses around him and spotted a dead Empire soldier about his size and height. He checked back over his shoulder, making sure the patrolling soldier was not looking, then crawled forward on his hands and knees to the corpse. He quickly stripped it of all its armor, moving as discreetly as he could, praying he was not detected.

Godfrey removed his own armor, his body freezing as it was exposed to the winter air, and reached over and dressed himself in the enemy's armor from head to toe, even taking his belt, which had a short sword and a dagger on it; he then reached over and grabbed his shield. He even reached over and took his helmet, which luckily concealed half of his face in its semi-circular shape. He managed to do all of this as quickly as he could, checking over his shoulder every few seconds to see if the other Empire soldier was getting closer. Luckily, while he made his way closer, he was not looking his way.

Godfrey quickly turned and lay on his back, holding the shield of the Empire soldier above him so that the crest—a lion with a bird in its mouth—was clearly visible. He closed his eyes, feigning sleep. And prayed.

The patrolling soldier approached him, and stopped. Godfrey, eyes closed, prayed that he bought it. He knew the next second would define whether he lived or not. If he heard the sound of steel slicing through the air, he knew he would be killed, his ploy discovered. But if he felt the soldier nudge him in some other way, he knew his ruse had worked.

Godfrey waited for what seemed like forever, as the soldier stood over him, debating.

Finally, he felt the tip of a boot, nudging him on the shoulder.

Inwardly, Godfrey sighed with relief; outwardly he feigned being awakened, opening his eyes, fluttering them slowly, pretending to be disoriented.

"You're alive," the Empire soldier said. "Good. Are you wounded? Can you walk?"

Godfrey sat up slowly, and it wasn't too hard to feign pain, since his pain was real; he reached up and felt the welt on his face, and allowed the Empire soldier to drag him to his feet. His legs were stiff, as was the rest of his body, but he could walk.

"I am sorry, sir, I did not see your stripes," the soldier said in awe, suddenly stiffening at attention.

Godfrey looked back in surprise, not understanding. Then he realized: the uniform he stole. The soldier he raided must have been an officer.

Godfrey immediately fell into the role, for fear of being discovered.

"I will forgive you this time," he said, "but next time you will address your superior appropriately. Do you understand?" Godfrey said, mustering as harsh and authoritative tone as he could.

"Yes, sir!" the soldier replied.

Godfrey stood there, staring back, and had to think quick. He knew he had to continue playing the role well; one false move and he would be discovered.

"Shall we get a nurse for you, sir?" the soldier asked.

"No. I have no need of one. I am an officer, lest you forget. We suffer minor wounds."

"Yes, sir," the soldier said.

Godfrey thought quick. He could not just walk away. It would be too risky. What if something he did gave up his ruse?

"There you are," came a voice.

Godfrey turned to see several Empire officers approaching. With his helmet low and his visor lowered, they must not have recognized him.

"Officer's meeting," came a voice.

The group of Empire officers approached, and one put a hand on his back and led him along with the others.

Godfrey found himself walking with the group of Empire officers, making their way through the field of corpses, towards the outer gate of Silesia, towards Andronicus' camp. He was afraid to check back over his shoulder, to check and see if that soldier was watching him, giving him a second glance, wondering if he made a mistake. So instead, he doubled his pace and went with these men, marveling at this odd turn of fate. He wondered how long he could keep this up. A part of him wanted to turn and run—but if he did, he knew he'd never make it. Besides, where was there to run to? The entire city was enslaved. There appeared to be no safe place anywhere.

They soon passed through the outer gate, away from Silesia, and as they did, before them there was revealed the huge expanse of Andronicus' million-man army, camped out in tents. Godfrey swallowed hard, in awe at the sight. He was led deeper and deeper behind enemy lines, blending in with the others, and as he headed deeper and deeper into the heart of Andronicus' camp, no one seemed to look twice.

He had survived. He had tricked them all. He was maintaining the ruse.

But how long could he keep it up?

CHAPTER THIRTEEN

Erec rode with Brandt and scores of the Duke's men, all of them charging out the gates of Savaria, the portcullis slamming down behind them, the city left secured only by the few soldiers remaining to stand guard. They all charged down the road heading east, hundreds of them, raising up dust in a great noise as they began the journey for the Eastern Gulch.

They rode as one, a fearless, determined group, riding for their very lives in the light of dawn. They all knew what was at stake, and were all fully prepared to throw themselves into the impossible: to try, with but a few hundred men, to defend their homeland against Andronicus' million man army. Erec knew they were all likely riding to their deaths. But that was what they had all been born and bred to do: risk their lives, every day, to protect and defend those left behind. In Erec's mind, it was a privilege. It was what he—what all of them—had lived their lives for: valor.

Erec was grateful that they were charging to meet the enemy face-first, instead of waiting with trepidation within their own gates for the enemy to approach. He did not know if they would live or would die, and in some ways that didn't matter. What mattered most was that they have a chance to meet the enemy with honor, with courage, and in a clash of glory.

Erec felt a sense of assurance this time knowing that Alistair was safe in Savaria, behind the Duke's gates, secure in the castle, hundreds of miles behind the front lines. He could throw himself into battle with peace of mind, knowing he would not have to worry about her.

They rode and rode, the only sound that of the trampling of their horses, the ever-present clouds of dust in Erec's face, his hair, his nose, until the sun grew high in the sky. Erec lost himself, as he often did, in the great cacophony of hundreds of horses' hooves, of spurs jingling in his ears, of swords rattling in their scabbards. It was a sound he had been accustomed to since his youth. It felt like home.

As the sun grew long in the sky and Erec's legs began to ache, the road elevated and they reached the top of the Eastern Hill; they paused, and from this strategic vantage point they were able to look down at the eastern countryside spread out below.

As they all came to a stop, the Duke and Brandt beside Erec, he pointed.

"There!" Erec said.

Before them lay a huge mountain range, stretching as far north and south as the eye could see. It created a natural barrier, blocking East from West, and there was but one way through: a narrow gulch, a slice of a divide, large enough to fit maybe six men side-by-side, and perhaps a hundred yards deep, amidst the mountain range. It was the only way those approaching from the West could reach Savaria without scaling the steep mountain. It was a passageway for travelers. And a chokepoint for soldiers. It was the quickest and most direct way for an army to travel—that is, if an army had nothing to fear. A cautious army, in the midst of a conflict with a strong enemy would not attempt it; but a huge army, with nothing to fear, just might. It was the perfect place for an ambush.

They could not see beyond the mountain range, and had no idea how close Andronicus' army was—or if they were even traveling this way.

Erec was invigorated; they had beat Andronicus here. Now, they had a fighting chance.

"FORWARD!" Erec screamed.

As one the Duke's men screamed and kicked their horses, and they all went galloping down the hill, covering ground quickly.

Soon, they reached the base of the gulch.

"What now?" the Duke asked Erec, breathing hard, as they all sat there on their horses.

"We must split our men," Erec answered. "Half on one side and half on the other. Then we must split these groups again, half taking positions high atop the mountain, and half down below. Those up high can create an avalanche on our signal. Then, when the fighting is thick, they can join us down below."

The Duke nodded in approval.

"We must also stage archers along the way," he added. "Every twenty feet, at every elevation, to cover all the angles."

Erec nodded in approval.

"And spears and pikes below," Brandt chimed in, "to create a wall of blood."

The Duke screamed out orders and as he did, his men all dispersed with a great cheer, galloping and taking up positions up and down the mountain face, all along the edge of the gulch, and down below, right at its edge.

Erec dismounted and took the opportunity, before the storm, to walk inside the empty gulch, Brandt and the Duke joining him. Erec went slowly, looking up at its walls, feeling its rock, examining it. It was darker in here, and his footsteps echoed. He craned his neck, looked hundreds of feet high, and saw their men beginning to take up positions. It was a steep drop from there, and even the smallest rock cast from that height would be deadly.

Before Erec was the long and narrow tunnel formed by the gulch, and in the distance, the sunlight shone from the far end, perhaps a hundred yards off. As of now, all was eerily quiet; Erec saw no sign of Andronicus men. He wondered how a place could be so peaceful that would soon be filled with bloodshed.

Apparently, Brandt and the Duke, beside him, were feeling the same way.

"Maybe they shall not come this way," Brandt said, his voice echoing in the silence.

"Maybe they will take another route," the Duke added.

But Erec stood there, hands on his hips, feeling the smell of battle in the air, a smell he had known since childhood. The hairs on his arms rose just slightly, as they always did before a conflict. He had a sixth sense for battle, ever since he could walk.

He slowly shook his head.

"No," he said, "if there is one thing you can be sure of, it is that war is coming our way."

CHAPTER FOURTEEN

Romulus stood on a high knoll north of Neversink, watching the horizon in a fit of rage. Commander of all Empire forces in Andronicus' absence, number two general only to Andronicus himself, Romulus was known to suffer no fools. He stood just a bit shorter than Andronicus, but nearly twice as wide, with a stocky face, a wide jaw, and shoulders so large that his neck nearly disappeared. He had wide, brutal lips, blazing black eyes, huge ears, and smaller horns than Andronicus. He did not wear a necklace of shrunken heads, like Andronicus did. He did not need to. When he encountered his enemies, he snapped their heads off with his bare hands, and was known to hold them in the air and stare into the corpse's eyes long enough to memorize each face. He branded the face of his enemies into his mind that way, and he never forgot a single one. He held in his head a vast catalog of all the faces of the men he had killed, and sometimes, in the middle of the night, he would lay awake for hours picturing the contours of their faces, and he would smile wide. It gave him a warm feeling inside, and sometimes it helped him fall asleep.

But Romulus was not one to sleep much. He lived for battle, for ambushing his enemies in the middle of the night, on their own turf, and he was famed, deservedly, to be at least as ferocious as Andronicus. Most people knew him to be even more brutal. And that was what irked Romulus: he was greater than Andronicus, he knew this in his heart. So did the people. There was not a single person in the Empire he answered to—except for Andronicus. And if it weren't for Andronicus, he would be leader of the Empire.

Romulus hated being number two. He had suffered being number two only because he had been biding his time, because the time had never been right to stage a coup. Andronicus was too paranoid and kept too many spies, too many checks to save himself from his own men.

But now that Andronicus had left the Empire to invade the Ring, Romulus sensed an opportunity. For now at least, he, Romulus, was the de facto ruler of the Empire at home; now all the forces were looking to him while Andronicus was out there waging his silly war, following his obsession to dominate the Ring. It had been a foolish misstep, and Romulus was determined to make him pay dearly for it.

Romulus smiled wide: he was preparing his coup, and when Andronicus returned, he would have his head on a plate. First, he would make Andronicus kneel to him, admit his superiority. Admit for the entire Empire to hear that Romulus was the fiercer of the two.

For now, though, Romulus had more pressing matters on his mind. That stupid Sword, the ancient Destiny Sword that had been a thorn in the Empire's side for centuries, had been so close to his grasp. He had sent a contingent of men to kill the thieves from the Ring before they could cast into the lake. But it had all gone terribly wrong. His men had caught them in time, but they had all been ambushed by the dragons. There was nothing Romulus had been able to do but to stand there, at a distance, and watch as the hideous beasts carried away his treasure, the Sword, flapping their wings, flying high into the horizon, the Sword gleaming in their claws.

As Romulus stood there now, in a rage, still rooted in place, he watched the dragons fly away, farther and farther north, their victorious screeches cutting through the air. Hundreds of men stood behind him with bated breath, all knowing better than to utter a word until he was ready to move.

As he watched the last of the flock of dragons disappear into the horizon, Romulus took a deep breath. It would be a long and hard march to follow them, deep into the Land of the Dragons, and he would lose tons of men confronting these beasts. He might lose them all. It had been centuries since the Empire had dared face off with the dragons.

Yet he had no choice. That Sword was what he needed to establish his legitimacy, to make all the Empire see that he, Romulus, was the one and only great leader; it was what he needed to oust Andronicus. With it in hand, he could make the case that he, not Andronicus, was the one; without it, though, he feared his people would not rally behind them. He had only chance to oust Andronicus, and he could not take any chances.

"MARCH!" Romulus screamed, and as soon as he did, his men began to follow, in unison, without question, on the long trek north to the Land of the Dragons.

The chanting began, the symphony of armor, of weapons, clacking their way down the mountain, as they all marched as one. Romulus searched the horizon as he went, watching the final vestige of dragons in the sky. He would find that Sword. Or have all of his men die trying.

CHAPTER FIFTEEN

Thor stood beside the shimmering waters of Neversink, the others beside him, staring at the corpses, and he wondered. Dragons. All of these men, slaughtered by dragons. The Sword, stolen, carried far away. On the one hand he felt relieved that it was not lost in the lake; yet he also felt an even deeper sense of dread knowing where it went. It was lost, just in a different way. The dragons were an indomitable force, and they lived so far away. How could they possibly wrest it away from them? Had their mission here failed? A part of him could not help but feel as if it had.

Yet, at the same time, Thor knew they had no choice. They were on a quest, and they had taken a vow to fulfill it. There was no backing down, their honor prevented it. They would have to do whatever it took to track the Sword and bring it home.

"So what now?" Reece finally asked, on behalf of all of them, who stood there, silent.

Thor turned to his old friend.

"We have no choice," Thor answered. "We follow the Sword."

"To the Land of the Dragons?" O'Connor asked, nervous.

Thor nodded back gravely.

"You are crazy," Indra said.

They all turned to her.

"Crossing that desert was craziness. But this—what you propose—it is a guaranteed death sentence. Why not just throw yourselves off a cliff now and be done with it? The Land of the Dragons is a land of ash and fire. A land of death. You will never succeed in reaching it. And if you do, what will you do? Confront an entire nest of dragons? Even one of them will eviscerate you in the blink of an eye. Do you really presume you can just waltz in there and take back from them their most valued treasure? Dragons are greedy about their treasure, and they will not part with it without death."

Thor sighed.

"You might speak the truth," he acknowledged. "I do not argue with you. But it matters not. We are on a quest. We have taken a vow, and we must fulfill our vow, wherever it should take us. It is not about life or death. It is about valor."

Indra shook her head again and again.

"There is a limit to your craziness that I can put up with. I came with you as you followed your silly map; I even followed you through the desert. But that is all. I value my life. I am sorry. I will not venture to a sure death."

Thor nodded back.

"I understand," he said. "We are not keeping you."

Elden looked at Indra, and Thor could detect a sadness cross his face.

"Are you leaving us, then?" he asked. "Is that it?"

She nodded back, and Thor could detect the same sadness in her eyes.

"You don't have to do this," she said. "You don't have to kill yourselves."

"We *have* to do this," Elden responded. "It is our way."

She looked at him long and hard, and finally, she said:

"I understand."

Indra stepped forward, reached out a hand and touched Elden's cheek, then surprised them all by leaning in and kissing Elden.

She let her palm rest on his cheek, then slowly pulled back, turned, and walked away. Within minutes she was lost in the woods, gone from view. She never looked back.

Elden looked crushed, and flustered from embarrassment.

Thor and the others looked away, giving him his privacy. They had all lost something on this journey; they all understood.

They each stood there, lost in their thoughts, the gravity of the final step of their journey weighing on them.

The Land of the Dragons, Thor thought.

He wondered if they could ever reach it. And if they could ever make it out alive.

*

Thor, Reece, O'Connor, Elden and Conven—just the five of them now—marched with Krohn at their side. With Conval dead and Indra gone, they felt their absence, and Thor could not help but feel as if their group was ever shrinking. He'd had an ominous pit in his stomach ever since they'd left Neversink, just the five of them, ever since they'd parted ways with Indra; she was as fearless a girl as he'd ever met, and yet even she was afraid to go this way. It did not bode well.

As Indra had instructed, they had headed north, following a rough trail through rolling hills; they had been marching for hours, heading ever north, the hills dipping and rising in ever-higher rows of false peaks. Each time they reached the top of another one, Thor was sure there would be no more peaks; yet always there came another on the horizon. They continued like that, rising and falling for hours, all of them breathing hard, exhausted.

At this point, Thor wasn't even certain they were following the right trail. All they had to go on was spotting the occasional carcass by the side of the road. The road was dotted every so often with skeletons, whether of people or animals Thor did not know, and each one put another pit in his stomach. The farther they went, the more skeletons they encountered, and the feeling of ominousness deepened. With every step, Thor felt more certain that they were all marching towards their deaths.

The gloom lay heavy on everyone. Conven was distraught with grief, out of his mind, unlike Thor had ever seen him. His eyes were bloodshot from crying, and while his tears had finally stopped, now they were replaced with a silent sense of devastation. He looked like a man ruined by grief; he looked unhinged. Thor was scared when he looked into his eyes: Conven did not seem to be quite there with them anymore.

Elden was despondent, too, ever since Indra had left. Clearly, he had cared for her, more than he had let on, and he walk with his jaws locked, a frown on his face. He, too, seemed lost in another world. That left just Reece and O'Connor, walking on either side of Thor, gripping their sword hilts, on-edge. Their endless trekking had taken a toll on them too, their eyes sunken into their heads from constant fear and exhaustion, and they did not look like the same boys who had set out on this quest. They all looked aged. Thor wondered if he looked as weary as they did.

With every step they took, Thor's knees shaking, he could not help but wonder if this journey would ever end, if it had been a mistake to venture to begin with.

The Land of the Dragons. He could hardly believe the craziness of the five of them, in their state, marching to confront an army of dragons, daring to somehow wrest the Sword from their grip. It was a mission not even an armored army could hope to achieve. How they would succeed, he had no idea. His honor, though, demanded that he see it through. Whether he lived or not, in his mind, that was not what mattered. He would not return a failure. And he would not return a coward. A lesson Argon once taught him rang in his mind, like a mantra: *sometimes, it is harder to retreat than to move forward. Sometimes, the only way out is THROUGH.*

The one thing that gave Thor solace was thinking of Gwen. He felt his mother's ring, deep in his shirt pocket, and he reached up and assured himself it was still there. He thought of Gwen constantly, more and more these days, and it kept him going. He wanted to be away from this awful place, from all these awful creatures and monsters and soldiers and slaves, to just be back in the Ring, back by her side. Now it felt, more and more, like a distant dream, like a fantasy that had never been real to begin with. He could hardly imagine being back in a world of peace, being together with Gwen, laughing, carefree, just lying there in a field of flowers and staring up at the sky. It seemed like another lifetime.

They all ascended yet another peak, this one steeper than the rest, huffing as they made it to the top, nearly climbing straight up as grass turned to rock. It had become more of an exercise in rock-climbing than hiking, and the higher they got, the stronger the gusts of wind became, and the colder the air. As they reached the top of this one, Thor prayed this would be the final ascent; he did not know how they could dip and rise one more time.

They reached the top and they all stopped, taken aback by the sight before them. They had reached the summit, and the view before them was astounding. The ground dropped off steeply below them at a sharp angle, plummeting hundreds of feet below. And down there, spread out below, was an entirely new landscape. There was no longer grass in sight—or rocks or mountains or hills or trees. Instead, the landscape was entirely, shockingly, white. It positively glowed. It looked like a desert, or beach, made up of tiny, white gravelly rocks, the light shining off it so brightly that Thor had to squint. It seemed to stretch to the end of the world.

The only variety in this endless landscape were massive holes in the earth, dotting it every hundred feet or so. Gaping black holes, scarring the landscape, like a minefield, making the landscape look like a giant game of checkers.

Thor turned to the others in wonder, and they all bore looks of surprise. No one knew what to make of it.

Thor knelt down, grabbed some of the fine white pebbles in his palm, felt them, and watched as they crumbled beneath his fingers. On a hunch, he raised them to his mouth and touched them to the tip of his tongue.

As he suspected.

"Salt," Thor said. "It's all salt."

They all looked down at the landscape below them with a new sense of respect and wonder.

"That's what Indra said," Reece said. "The salt fields lie on the way to the Land of the Dragons."

"But it stretches forever," O'Connor said, looking out. "It's like a desert. If we enter that, how can we ever possibly cross it? It's vast. And we're exhausted. And there's no shelter anywhere."

"And what of all those holes?" Reece asked.

"I, for one, am not in the mood to enter another desert," Elden said.

"What choice do we have?" Thor asked. "There's no turning back."

Thor closed his eyes and heard Argon's voice.

Sometimes the only way out is through.

Thor was feeling the same way the others were, but he knew he had to be strong. Confident. For all of them.

Thor looked down at the steep drop off and knew they wouldn't be able to climb down on the fine sediment. They would have no choice but to slide down. It was a steep drop, and while it eventually curved off, as he stood there, he was reluctant, he had to admit, to take the first step. He could see the expressions on the others' faces, and realized they were reluctant, too. It was so steep, it was almost like stepping off the edge of a cliff.

Conven stepped forward and without hesitating, he suddenly jumped, right off the edge. Thor could not believe it: he did it with no emotion and no hesitation, as if he were suicidal.

Conven did not even scream as he plummeted straight down the side of the salt cliff. His feet and back rubbed against the fine sediment, like sand, raising a huge white cloud of dust and making Thor lose sight of him. The dust cloud continued all the way down the mountain, hundreds of feet, until eventually the cliff began to curve and finally, Conven slid to a stop.

There were a few moments of silence, as Thor and the others looked to each other in wonder, waiting for the huge cloud of dust to evaporate, to see if Conven had survived.

As Thor peered into the dust, suddenly, there came motion. Conven stood, brushed himself off, and began to march, his back to them, as if nothing had just happened.

Thor gulped. He feared for Conven; he seemed unhinged.

Thor didn't like heights, and he wavered as he looked straight down below.

Thor reached over and picked up Krohn, whining, and held him in his arms.

"I guess it's now or never, old friend," Reece said.

Thor nodded back, but neither of them moved.

"Remember that time you dove into the red sea," Reece reminded him, and then laughed. "It was full of monsters."

Thor smiled at the thought; it felt like a lifetime ago.

"It was quite a way to start The Hundred," Thor said back.

As one, they all suddenly stepped forward and off the ledge.

They all screamed as they plunged through the air; Thor felt the wind rushing through him, pushing up his cheeks, feeling as if he were plummeting down to the very core of the earth.

Finally, Thor felt his feet, then his back, make contact with the fine salt sand as the cliff began to curve gradually outward. Luckily he was wearing thick clothes, otherwise he was sure it would have burned his skin. He felt a rubbing against his whole body, and it became more intense as gradually the mountain curved outwards.

Thor felt himself tumbling head over heels, as the mountain curved more and more; he started coughing as he was caught up in a huge cloud of salt, salt in his eyes and hair and mouth. For a moment he felt like he couldn't breathe.

Finally, Thor tumbled and came to a stop, shaken and scraped, but unhurt. All around him, the others tumbled to a stop, too, not too far away. They all settled there in a huge cloud of white dust, and it took several seconds for it to clear enough for Thor to realize that everyone else had made it alive and unhurt, including Krohn

Slowly, they all began to dust themselves off and gain their feet. Thor rubbed his head as he fell in with the others. He turned and looked back up and was shocked: it looked impossibly high, as if they had just fallen off a mountain.

They turned and began the long march through the salt fields, trying to catch up with Conven, already far ahead and not looking back.

*

They trekked across the monotonous landscape, heading ever farther north, weaving in and out between the gaping holes. They passed more and more skeletons now, strewn haphazardly, and Thor could not but help but wonder how all these animals—or people—had died. He wondered what had killed him—and when. Most bones looked old, but some looked fresh. It did not put him at ease. He couldn't help but shake the feeling that they were all walking into a big trap.

Thor looked over at one of the gaping holes in the ground and walked over to its edge. He stopped and looked.

The others gathered around and they all leaned over and looked down, and saw only blackness.

"What is it?" O'Connor asked.

As he voiced the words, they echoed and reverberated.

"It looks like some sort of tunnel," Reece said.

"Perhaps they are the salt mines Indra spoke of," Thor said.

"But who would mine this place?"

Thor turned and surveyed the landscape and realized that at some point some industry must have been here, tore up the land, then abandoned it. These holes were all that remained.

They continued their trek, marching through the endlessly landscape. As the sun grew long and Thor was overcome with hunger and thirst and exhaustion, he wondered, once again, where on earth they could take shelter in this place. Clearly they could not rest in one of the caves, which seemed to drop straight down to a bottomless pit, and he doubted they could sleep on the salt floor, wondering what creatures might roam here at night.

Before he could finish the thought, Thor suddenly heard an odd hissing noise, and his stomach dropped as he turned and saw, approaching them in the distance, a group of strange creatures. There were perhaps ten of them, and as they got closer, their appearance became more distinct: they looked like miniature alligators. They alternately slithered on their stomachs, then rose up on their forelegs, sometimes crawling and sometimes slithering. They had long tongues,

91

as long as their bodies, and an armored skin, and every few feet their skin blew up, like a blowfish, the sharp points at the end of it protruding, then retracting. They had four eyes, and everything about them was colored white, camouflaging them perfectly with the salt terrain; except for their eyes, which were a bright, glowing purple.

"What the hell is that?" O'Connor asked.

Krohn snarled back, the hair rising on his back, as the boys all stopped in her tracks—all except for Conven, who kept walking casually towards them as if he had not a fear in the world.

"Conven, I wouldn't do that," Thor said.

But Conven kept marching. He casually drew his sword, the sound cutting through the air, and went out to meet the closest creature, who charged towards him.

Conven raised his sword—but before he could lower it, the creature closest to him suddenly looked up, opened its mouth, and extended its jaw revealing several sets of fangs.

"Conven, look out!" Reece screamed.

The creature craned back its neck, opened its jaws and sprayed a liquid from the back of its throat; it shot up through the air and doused Conven's eyes.

Conven screamed, clutching his eyes as he dropped his sword and stumbled back.

"I can't see!" he cried out.

The creatures approached, and Thor gulped, realizing they had a battle on their hands.

Watching what had just happened to Conven, Thor knew they had to act quickly or else all be blinded.

"Raise your shields!" Thor yelled.

He grabbed his shield and the others did, too, all of them crouching down and covering their faces. The creatures leaned back and hissed at them, and the liquid sprayed against the metal, just missing their eyes. Thor could hear the acidic venom eating into the metal of the shield.

When the spraying stopped, they all lowered their shields and charged forward. Thor sliced his sword down at the closest one, severing its head, while Elden swung his axe high and brought it down on the one before him, chopping off its head; Reece drove his spear through the head of another, and O'Connor raised his bow and shot one right in its open throat.

But as quickly as they killed the first four, four more appeared, darting forward and spraying venom at their eyes. They all quickly raised their shields, then attacked again.

But these creatures were smart; this time, they retreated, slithering backwards as Thor and the others swung down at empty air. Krohn leapt forward, snarling, and the creatures sprayed him. Krohn was too fast, though, dodging the venom, ducking low, then leaping high and pouncing, clamping down on one of the creature's throats with his fangs, snarling as he killed the writhing creature on the spot.

Another creature leapt for Krohn, whose back was exposed, and began to bite him on his rear leg; Krohn yelped, and Thor leapt forward and slashed it—though the creature was too quick, and retreated before Thor could get it. Krohn, enraged, turned and pounced on several more creatures, killing three more—but he was not fast enough to avoid the tail of another creature, which whipped him hard on the back of his other leg, making him shriek and roll over several times, whining, limping. Thor realized that the tails of these creatures had stingers.

Finally the blinding effect of the spray seemed to wear off on Conven, and he, blinking tears from his eyes, reached down and grabbed his sword, and charged for the remaining creatures. He raised the shield, blocking the spray of several of them, and charged madly.

But they were too fast for him, all of them retreating from his wild sword slashes. They had learned too quickly.

Thor realized they had an intense battle on their hands. He did not know how they would kill the remaining group.

That was when he heard the noise. It was a tremendous hissing noise, and as he looked to the horizon, Thor's heart dropped to see hundreds more of these creatures appearing, all slithering their way. Thor suddenly realized why there were so many skeletons on the road: these things must have killed everything in their path.

Conven backed up to their side, and the five of them faced off with the creatures, holding their ground, bracing for the destruction to come.

"Now what?" O'Connor asked.

Before Thor could respond there came a great rumbling from beneath the earth, stronger and stronger, until it shook the ground beneath them, making them all stumble. As it grew more intense, suddenly, all the creatures before them turned and scurried away in the other direction, slithering off as one unit, in a great cacophony of hissing noises. In moments, they disappeared from view.

"An earthquake?" Reece asked.

Thor was relieved the creatures had gone, but he had a sinking feeling as to what might have scared them away. They all looked at each other, baffled.

There came a great shriek, one so loud it nearly shattered Thor's eardrums, and beside him there emerged from one of the holes a beast unlike anything Thor had ever seen. It looked like a monstrous snake, its body fifty feet wide and ten times as long. White in color, it had a flat head, slits for eyes, and its face was consumed by rows and rows of razor-sharp teeth. It roared and shrieked as it rose up from the ground, so high it blocked the sky. Then it arched down, opening its jaws impossibly wide and nose-diving to the ground as it caught and devoured dozens of those creatures. The creatures hissed and screamed as the beast picked them up in the air, dangling them from its mouth, squirming, and chewed on them. Their purple blood dripped down its mouth and body.

The snake must have eaten a dozen of them at once, and Thor could see the outline of their bodies writhing within as they slid down the creature's throat.

Thor looked up with real fear, realizing now that they probably would have been better off facing hundreds of those creatures than this single huge monster.

The monster twisted its awful face and turned and set its sights on Thor and the others, as it opened its throat and screeched.

It came plummeting down, blocking out the sun, opening its mouth and diving downward to swallow them all at once. It came down impossibly fast, and Thor realized that in moments, they would all be dead.

Thor felt a tremendous heat rise through his body, and he stood in place, raised a palm, closed his eyes, and let the energy flow through him. He recalled Argon's words.

Do not fight nature. Do not resist anything. Allow it to be what it is. Do not try to control it. Become one with it. Do as it would do.

Argon's words rang through Thor's mind and finally, he felt as if he was gaining some control over his powers. He noticed that whenever his back was truly to the wall, whenever he had no choice but to use his powers or die, they returned to him.

Thor raised his palm higher, trying to stay calm, and he felt the creature's nature; it was an intense, monstrous nature, intent on killing them all. Thor did not try to resist it. Instead, he felt his energy morphing with the creature's, and as he held up his hand, an orb of light suddenly shot up from his palm, rising into the air, as a stream of white light went forth from him, heading right for the creature's face.

The light met the creature and it managed to hold it at bay, stopping it just feet from them, holding it frozen in mid-air right before it swallowed them. Thor felt his entire body shaking from the effort, and he did not know how much longer he could hold it back.

Conven screamed and charged forward, leaping into the creature's mouth, raising his sword and stabbing it in the roof of its mouth. The creature shrieked.

The others followed suit, Reece jabbing it in the nose with his spear, Elden chopping it in the cheek with his axe, and O'Connor firing arrow after arrow into its eyes. The creature seemed more annoyed than hurt, and it was not even close to dead.

Thor's arms were shaking, as he felt his control of the beast waning quickly. Finally, Thor felt himself lose control; his power was just not strong enough, and he could hold it back no longer.

The light ceased from Thor's palm and the beast pulled back immediately, lifting its head high in the air. Conven was still standing there, inside its mouth, jabbing his sword into the roof of its mouth, and as the beast rose higher into the air and tried to swallowed him, the only thing keeping Conven alive was the sword thrust vertically into the roof of its mouth. As the beast clamped down, trying to squash Conven, the sword was beginning to bend.

Conven finally had fear in his eyes, as he hung there high in the air, between the beasts rows of teeth, his sword bending before his eyes and the beast's mouth closing.

Thor was exhausted from his exertion, yet he forced himself to try again; somehow, he summoned some last part of himself, drawing on whatever energy reserves he had. He did not know if he could have done so for himself—but to see his friend in danger brought out another burst of energy in him.

Thor screamed and raised his other palm, and another light, a yellow light, came streaming forth. Just as the beast snapped the sword in its mouth, the light struck it, and Thor used his power to force the beast to open its jaws all the way. As they kept opening,

Conven, spared from death, tumbled out of the beast's mouth and went hurling through the air, landing on the salt floor with a thud.

The beast, enraged at losing a meal, raised its neck and shrieked, then turned and zeroed in on Thor. It plummeted down, right for him, clearly wanting to crush him.

Thor closed his eyes and raised both palms, summoning his last bit of strength. This time, a blue light shot out, covering the beast's entire body. Thor raised his palms higher and higher, and as he did, he hoisted the beast high into the air, higher and higher, until its entire body exited the hole. It extended to its full length, hundreds of feet long and covered in a slimy ooze that had probably not seen the light of day. It wiggled furiously in the air, like a worm pulled out from beneath its rock.

In one last exertion of effort, Thor threw his hands forward, directing its energy with all that he had; as he did the beast, shrieking, went sailing through the air and came crashing down sideways, smashing on the ground. It shrieked an awful noise as it squirmed on its back, until finally it stopped moving.

Dead.

Thor dropped to his knees, collapsing from the exertion of strength. His powers were stronger than they had ever been, yet at the same time, he did not have the endurance to maintain them.

Suddenly, there arose a tremor all around them, the same tremor they'd heard when the beast had emerged from its hole. All around them, as far as they could see, the ground began to shake. They turned and exchanged a panicked look, and realized that monsters were about to emerge from every hole in the landscape.

Thousands of them.

"Are you going to just stand there all day?" came a voice Thor recognized.

Thor turned to see, with immense relief, Indra. She was galloping towards them on an orange beast that looked something like a camel, but was taller and broader, and had a wide, flat head. She led, by a rope, five more of them, stirring up dust as they charged right for them.

"GET ON! NOW!" she screamed.

Without hesitating Thor and the others mounted the animals, Thor grabbing Krohn with him. They all took off, together, at a gallop, racing through the salt field, narrowly avoiding the holes.

As they went, one by one, thousands of monsters emerged from the holes, shrieking, rising into the air, aiming for them. But the creatures they rode were fast—faster than any horse Thor had ever ridden, so fast, he could barely catch his breath as they rode. And clearly they had been trained to navigate this terrain to avoid these holes, these monsters, which they did deftly. As they rode, Thor holding on for his life, the monsters snapped down all around them and just missed each time, the animals faster than they, zigzagging every which way to avoid the strikes.

They narrowly dodged strike after strike, monster after monster, as they all charged through, taking them farther and farther from the salt fields.

As they finally cleared the perimeter, leaving the monsters behind them, Indra turned and smiled.

"Did you really think I would let a bunch of fools like you die in my own backyard?"

CHAPTER SIXTEEN

Sarka sat there in her cottage, cross-legged, her back against the wall in her humble living room, and watched Gareth. Bleary-eyed, she had been watching him all night, while he held his dagger to her sister's throat. She had been waiting for her chance. She knew that at some point he would give into weakness and doze off. She, though, would not.

Sarka adored her sister more than anything, and it sickened her to sit here, helpless, and watch this excuse of a King burst into her home and hold her kid sister hostage. It had been one of the worst feelings of her life, and she sat there, determined, whether he was king or not. She would not cower in fear and deference like her father; she would be bold and risk her life to save her sister's.

Her father, an oaf of a man who had never been too bright and who had always been too hard on her, had always insisted that he knew the right way and that she did not. He had chastised her earlier, after Gareth had taken her sister hostage, warning her that she better not do something rash. He had argued that if she made a wrong move her sister could die—and so could she. Plus, her father had argued, it was sacrilegious to raise a hand against the King—whether he was corrupt or not.

Sarka, as usual, disregarded her father's logic, and his threats. He'd been wrong one too many times in her life, and even though she was just a peasant, she still had her pride and she was not about to sit by passively, waiting for Gareth to make up his mind. After all, waiting was risky, too—Gareth might break his word and kill her sister. It might be a chance her father was willing to take, her stupid father who had always trusted everyone; but it was not a chance that she would take. He had taken her sister hostage by the blade, and he would pay for it. She would not give him a chance to make a decision.

The first light of dawn crept through the window, and as it did, Sarka could see clearly that Gareth's eyes were shut, that the dagger which she had been watching all night, was slipping. She held secretly the hemp rope which she had taken from her father's stables in the middle of the night, just enough to do the trick. She was young, and perhaps not as strong as this man, and perhaps naïve to believe she could bring down a King, a man who had evaded every sort of assassination attempt—yet she was determined. And she would have the element of surprise on her side.

Sarka sat there, heart pounding in her chest, and knew her moment had come. It was now or never.

"Pssst!" she hissed at her sister.

There came no response.

"Pssst!" she hissed again.

Larka finally opened her eyes, and looked up at her. There was fear and terror in them as she sat there in Gareth's lap.

Sarka motioned for her to stay calm and not move. She slowly held up the rope, and gestured what she was about to do. She hoped she understood. Her younger sister cried, tears rolling down her cheeks, but she slowly nodded, seeming to understand.

The time had come.

Sarka leapt to her feet, her limbs more stiff than she had anticipated, not working as quickly as she would have liked, and she felt as if she were moving in slow motion as she bounded across the simple cottage, rope held out in front of her. She moved quickly, and as she ran across the cottage, her sister took her cue and leapt forward, out of Gareth's arms.

Gareth's eyes opened wide, startled, but before he could reach out and grab her, Sarka was already on top of him, not giving him time to react. She kicked the dagger from his limp hand, and it went flying across the cottage floor; as Gareth turned to grab it, she descended on him with the rope, wrapping it tightly around his upper body, again and again, tying it tight.

Gareth struggled and squirmed, his weight nearly too much for her, but she managed to hold on, the coarse hemp rope digging into her palms, as she pinned him down face first. His legs buckled beneath her, and it was all she could do to hold him in place.

"Help me!" Sarka yelled out.

Her mother and father came running over, standing over her, her father looking down wide-eyed in fear, shaking his head.

"What have you done?" he asked her. "You know better than to lay a hand on the King!"

"Shut up and help me!" she yelled.

His father just stood there, though, hands on his hips, shaking his head, cowering to authority as he had always done.

"I cannot lay a hand on the King. Nor should you."

Sarka flushed with rage, but luckily Larka came running over and helped her, grabbing the other end of the rope and helping her secure it. Sarka immediately made a tight knot, binding Gareth's arms behind his back. Then she took her other piece of rope and handed it to her sister, who ran it around Gareth's ankles and crafted a knot no man could undo. He moaned and whined and began cursing them, and she reached around and tied another piece of rope in his mouth, muffling his noise.

The two of them leaned back, breathing hard, surveying their handiwork: Gareth was secure.

Sarka was thrilled. She had succeeded. Here was Gareth, her King, bound by her hand, in *her* control. And her sister was free—and safe. She was elated.

Her sister turned and hugged her, weeping, and Sarka hugged her back, rocking her, not wanting to let her go.

"I was so scared," Larka said, again and again.

"You're okay now," Sarka said.

Sarka leaned forward, dug a knee into Gareth's back, and scowled down at him. She retrieved the dagger from the floor and raised it. The time had come for him to pay, and she was determined to put an end to him for good.

"You dare hold a blade to my sister," she hissed down at him. "Now you see what it feels like," she said, digging the blade into the back of his neck. Gareth grunted, his cries muffled by the rope.

Sarka raised her hand to finish him off when suddenly she felt a strong beefy palm grab her wrist; she looked over to see her father standing there, scowling down.

"You are a foolish girl," he said. "The former King is worth much more to us alive than dead. I can sell him for ransom to Andronicus' army. They would pay a hearty price for it. The money I earn can keep us all clothed and fed for years. You almost ruined a glorious future for all of us."

Sarka's heart pounded in anger.

"You don't know what you are talking about," she said. "Andronicus will not pay anything for him. They will either kill him or let him free. We have him now. This is our chance. We must kill him before he wreaks any more havoc."

But her father yanked her back roughly, so hard that he yanked the dagger from her hand and pulled her to her feet.

"You are too young to understand the affairs of men," he scolded.

Then her father reached down, grabbed Gareth by his ropes, and yanked him to his feet. He looked Gareth up and down, as if he were an item for sale.

"You shall fetch a hefty price," he said.

"No Papa!" Sarka screamed, in a rage, as she watched them cross the cottage, leading Gareth out the door. "Don't let him go!"

Sarka ran to the door and watched her father walk out, leading Gareth proudly to the closest group of Empire soldiers, on patrol.

The soldiers all stopped at the sight, then turned and looked Gareth up and down.

"I've caught the former MacGil King," her father announced proudly. "Give me one hundred dinars of gold, and he is yours."

The soldiers turned and looked at each other, then broke out into a grin. Finally, the lead soldier stepped forward, pulled back his sword, grabbed Gareth, pulled him close and inspected him. Satisfied, he turned and threw him to the others, who caught him.

The soldier turned and smiled at her father.

"Why don't I pay you a fistful of steel instead," the man said.

Before her father could react, the man stepped forward, and plunged his sword through his heart.

"Papa no!" the girls screamed in horror, as they watched their father's face contort in shock, then blood pour from his chest as he sank to his knees.

"But thanks for the gift," the soldier added. "I can't wait to tell Andronicus who I just caught."

CHAPTER SEVENTEEN

Godfrey, dressed in the enemy's ill-fitting armor, walked awkwardly, feeling conspicuous, trying to look natural. He realized, too late, that the corpse he had stripped was his same height, but thinner than he; he cursed himself for drinking one too many cups of ale in his life as he felt his belly and shoulders bulge against the armor. He only hoped it did not give him away.

Other than that, Godfrey looked at himself and at the others, and was amazed at how much he resembled an Empire soldier. Especially with his face plate pulled down, he couldn't even tell the difference between himself and one of Andronicus's men. The weapons on his belt were of fine quality, too, a long and short sword, a dagger, a short spear and a flail, all a glossy black and yellow, bearing the markings of the Empire. As he marched, at first he'd braced himself to be discovered; but the farther they went, the more he realized that no one looked twice—and the more he began to relax. He was sweating inside, despite the cold, and he had no idea where he was going, but at least he was still alive and succeeding in his ruse.

If anything, soldiers looked at Godfrey with a sign of respect, several stiffening to attention as he passed and they saw his officer's stripes. As he went, he could not help but feel more and more inflated, and he actually started to relish the idea of being paid respected. He actually began to get swept up in it and to feel like an officer himself. It was a fun role to play, and it never took much for Godfrey to get into character. He wasn't a good warrior, but he had always been a great actor; one too many tavern plays had taught him well. In fact, he had always wished he had been born the son of actor instead the son of a King.

"Sir," said a soldier, hurrying up to him, "now that the siege has been won, all the officers are being shipped out. The carts are being loaded as we speak, and I've been ordered to round up the remaining officers. Right this way, sir."

Godfrey gulped behind his faceplate, realizing he had no choice but to go along or else blow his cover. He turned and marched with the soldier, weaving his way in and out of the busy camp, thousands of soldiers milling about in every direction, wondering with each step what to do.

Godfrey found himself led to the back of a long troop cart, open in the back, drawn by several horses. In the back there sat dozens of officers, all jostling and bantering with each other, in high spirits. Godfrey hesitated at the base of it, as the soldier gestured for him to board. As he stood there, slowly the banter subsided and all eyes fell on him. He knew that if he did not make a move soon he would be discovered.

He turned to the soldier.

"And where is this cart going exactly?" he asked the soldier.

"To take us home, finally," one of the officers said. "Back to the ships, and back to the Empire. We're finally done with this horse dump."

Godfrey gulped. He couldn't get on that cart, couldn't allow himself to be taken across the sea, to the Empire. The thought of it left a pit in his stomach. He had to think quick.

As he stood there, immobilized in panic, an officer leaned down from the cart with an open palm, grabbed Godfrey's forearm and yanked him hard, hoisting him up three steps and onto the back of the cart. The officer smiled back and patted him on the back.

The rear door of the carriage was slammed behind him, there came the sound of a horse whipped, and soon they were off, their cart moving and bumping along the dirt road.

As Godfrey was swept away, he began to panic; it had all happened so quickly, he hardly knew what was happening. He sat there at the edge of the cart, sweating, looking about at the other soldiers, who all seemed to be ignoring him, passing around a sack of wine, drinking long and hard and laughing with each other. All around him, the Empire camp was flying by.

Godfrey had to think quick. He had to get off this cart. It was taking him farther and farther away from Silesia, with every bump.

They passed two Empire soldiers dragging a Silesian captive, and Godfrey was struck with a plan. It was risky, but he had no other choice. It was now or never.

Godfrey suddenly stood, leapt off the moving cart, landed in the mud beside it, rolling, then jumping to his feet. The cart stopped, all the officers staring, and Godfrey made a show of hurrying over to the two soldiers and, in his most authoritative voice, he screamed at them, loud enough for the others to hear:

"And just where do you think you're bringing this slave!?" he screamed.

Behind him he could feel all the officer's eyes digging into his back. He knew he had better play this well; if not, it would be his head.

The two Empire soldiers turned and looked back at him, confused.

"We have orders to bring him to the slave mill, sir," they said.

"Nonsense!" Godfrey screamed. "That is no ordinary slave. I captured this one myself! He's a Silesian officer. Can't you tell by his markings?"

The two soldiers looked at the captive, confused.

"What markings?"

Godfrey stepped forward, grabbed the captive roughly, spun him and pointed at a small spot on his back.

Then, before the soldiers could examine it too closely, Godfrey reached back and smacked the soldiers across the face.

"Didn't they teach you anything in training?" he yelled. "This slave was supposed to be brought inside Silesia, for interrogation. Must I do everything myself?"

Godfrey felt the stares of the officers behind him, on the cart, and prayed this worked. He turned to them, peremptorily, and he waved his hand, and in an annoyed voice, he said:

"Move on without me. I'll take the next one. I must return my captive to his proper place and rectify the errors of these ignorant soldiers, or else it will be on my head."

Godfrey didn't wait for a response: instead he turned, grabbed the two soldiers by the arms, along with the slave, and led them all, marching firmly back towards the gates of Silesia.

Godfrey's heart pounded in his chest as he took the first several steps, hoping and praying he had played it off well, that he didn't hear the soldiers chase after him. He also hoped that the two soldiers didn't fight him, that they were stupid and intimidated enough to go along with it.

Please God, he prayed. *Let this work.*

This was the ultimate test of his acting skills, the ultimate role he had ever played.

After what felt like forever, to Godfrey's immense relief, finally, he heard the sound of the cart taking off behind him. The officers resumed their laughter, and the wheels began to disappear.

And the two soldiers before him did not even look back.

"I'm sorry, sir," one soldier said. "I had no idea."

Godfrey smiled inwardly to himself, doubling his pace, and then shoving them even more roughly.

"Of course you didn't," he said. "That is why you are a soldier—and *I* am an officer."

*

Godfrey marched with the two Empire soldiers and their captive back through the gates of Silesia, past thousands of Empire soldiers, some of whom looked their way but most of whom were preoccupied. The city was mostly rubble, and as Godfrey re-entered it, getting a good glimpse of it for the first time, his heart sank. All around him, for the first time, he saw the devastation, the oppression of his people. The extent of their defeat hit home. Everywhere were smoldering flames, the city in ruin, slaves bound together and being whipped as they sorted through the rubble.

Godfrey saw the crosses, high up, and he was aghast to spot Kendrick, up there on a cross, beside Atme, Brom, Kolk, Srog and several others. It made him sick. He wanted to run to them, to free them all at once. But now was not the time.

Most pressing on Godfrey's mind was getting rid of these two soldiers he was accompanying, especially before they figured out that something was not right. He had to finish playing his role, and as he went, a plan came to him.

"Where to now, sir?" one of the soldiers asked.

"Don't ask questions!" Godfrey snapped. "You answer your superior only when talked to!"

"Yes, sir. I'm sorry, sir."

"Just follow me and shut your mouth," Godfrey added. "We are going to deliver this slave exactly where he belongs."

As they passed, Silesian slaves looked over at Godfrey in fear, and Godfrey realized that he was playing the role too well, especially as Empire soldiers all around them continued to stiffen in salute. He found himself standing taller, walking straighter, really immersing himself in the role. He blinked and for a moment he almost forgot that he was not an Empire officer.

Godfrey realize that this was all he'd needed his entire life: a good suit of armor and an officer's role. Maybe if his father had given it to him, he would have avoided the taverns altogether.

Which, ironically, was where he was going right now. Godfrey weaved in and out of the back alleys of Silesia, which he had memorized in but a few days' time, and led the group towards the tavern he had frequented with Akorth and Fulton. If he knew those two—and he knew them like brothers—they had found a way to avoid the conflict, and to survive. They had probably snuck around corners, hidden in trash cans, done whatever they had to do to make it, and if he knew them, they would have somehow found their way right back here, to the pub, drowning themselves in ale and shrugging it all off as if war had never happened. In Godfrey's experience, even in completely sacked cities, pubs were left untouched by soldiers. After all, conquering soldiers wanted a drink, too. It was usually the *first* thing they wanted, and it only hurt their cause to destroy the taverns.

Playing his role well, Godfrey stepped forward, before the soldiers, and kicked the door open to the pub hastily, his face plate down, and feeling a rush of authority. He was getting lost in the role, and he really felt as if he were an Empire officer, storming down an illegal pub in the conquered city.

Godfrey stepped inside, and just as he suspected, he found the place jam-packed with Silesian survivors, slackers who had found a way to survive. The slovenly fringe sat hunched over the bar, which, as Godfrey suspected, had been left untouched by the conquerors. This place was a bit less crowded than it had been before the war— but not much. Godfrey's storming out of there and joining the army clearly had not been an example for any of them. These people who where they were. Godfrey did not blame them: he felt his knees grow weak at the smell of the strong ale and wanted a pint more than he'd ever had in his life.

As Godfrey and his group stormed into the room, it grew dead silent, everyone turning and looking at him in fear, cowering. They hurried out of his way as Godfrey marched forward with the others, right to the bar. Godfrey's heart soared with relief as he spotted who he was looking for. He saw from here the figures of Akorth, way too fat, and Fulton, tall and skinny, both hunched over the bar with their backs to them.

At the commotion they turned, and their eyes opened wide with fright as Godfrey approached.

Godfrey smiled to himself. Clearly they had no idea it was their old friend.

"Stop here!" Godfrey commanded the Empire soldiers, as loud and authoritative as he could be, and they both stopped and stiffened at attention, holding the slave.

"These two men are wardens to the slave," Godfrey said to the Empire soldiers, gesturing at Akorth and Fulton.

Akorth and Fulton stared back, confused.

"Wardens?" Akorth asked. "Us?"

"Sir?" one of the soldiers asked. "I don't understand."

"It is not for you to understand!" Godfrey screamed back at the soldier. "Unshackle the slave, and you will understand."

The two Empire soldiers exchanged a confused look, and they hesitated. Godfrey's heart pounded as he hoped they did not realize that something was awry.

But finally they each followed orders; they reached into their pockets, extracted their keys, and began to unshackle the slave.

As they did, Godfrey suddenly turned to Akorth and Fulton, who stared back at him in wonder, and he quickly lifted his visor. As he did, their eyes opened wide in shock.

Godfrey silently motioned with his eyes, telling them what to do. Thankfully, they were quick to understand.

Akorth and Fulton each immediately reached over, grabbed their mugs from the bar, and stepped forward and smashed them over the heads of the Empire soldiers. The soldiers collapsed to the ground, and as they did, all the other Silesian patrons joined in, kicking them until they finally stopped squirming.

Godfrey removed his helmet, and all the other patrons recognized who he was. They let out a cheer.

"Son of a bitch!" Akorth said.

"You are even craftier than I thought," Fulton added.

"There are many ways to win a war," Godfrey smiled.

"But I don't understand," Akorth said, looking down at the soldiers. "Why did you bring them here?"

"I figured these two were about your size," Godfrey said.

They looked back at him, baffled.

"Don their armor," Godfrey said. "I need your help. And you two are coming with me."

CHAPTER EIGHTEEN

Thor rode the camel-like animals, Krohn in his lap and Reece, O'Connor, Conven, Elden and Indra riding beside him, the group of them charging through the vast expanse of salt fields, stirring up clouds of white dust, as they had been for hours. Driven by adrenaline, by fear of those monsters, none of them had even thought about slowing as they galloped for hours, zigzagging in and out of danger, narrowly avoiding hole after hole as one monster after the next had emerged to snap at them. Luckily, the animals they rode were well-trained and just fast enough to save their lives. Thor looked at Indra with appreciation once again; they would have not survived if she had not shown up when she did.

It had been hours since they'd passed the final hole in the desert floor, and yet still none of them had slowed, driven by fear. But now the second sun was beginning to set, there had been no sign of danger for hours, and finally, up ahead, they saw the first structure on the horizon, the first shape in this empty landscape to break up the monotony of nothingness.

They all stopped together and sat there on their animals, breathing hard, staring out at it together.

"What is it?" O'Connor asked.

"A town," Indra answered.

"But who would live out here?" Elden asked.

Indra smiled.

"Me," she said.

They all turned and looked at her, shocked.

"Not anymore, of course," she said. "But it's where I grew up."

Thor looked at it with wonder, this small town on the horizon in the midst of nothing.

"I would extend you all a formal invitation," she said, "but I don't have a quill and parchment."

Indra screamed and kicked her animal, and she charged forward. They all kicked, too, and raced to catch up with her.

As they closed the distance, Indra's town came into view. Thor was excited to encounter an actual town in this desolate landscape, and his mind raced imagining what the town could be like, who lived there, what her people were like. He also wondered how they could survive out here, in the middle of nowhere.

That question was answered as they all approached the town wall, and Thor saw for himself: the town was abandoned. A small town, it was comprised of but a few dozen small cottages, all built of a white, hard substance that looked like dried salt, most of them dilapidated and crumbling. The town did not have a soul in it.

A lonely wind whipped through, sending large thorn bushes tumbling end over end, and they all slowed to a walk as they followed Indra through, Thor looking for any sign of life.

"There's no one here," Elden finally said.

"There was once," Indra said. "The Empire came and took us all away, as slaves. I vowed to never return. This place was bad enough, even when we were free. It was terribly boring, another suffocating small town on the edge of the Empire. It was the most dull and monotonous life you could imagine. In some ways, the Empire did us a favor to clear us all out of here. Not that being a slave was fun. It sucked. But living here was worse."

Thor was taken aback by Indra's candor, and by her strength. She called things for how she saw them, and she never minced words.

"The only saving grace of this place," Indra said, as they all continued to walk through on their animals, "is that these walls keep the insects out at night and they slow the wind. At night, the wind can get really bad. And the dwellings provided shade overhead. Otherwise, there's nothing to redeem this place."

"But I don't understand," Elden said, as they continued to walk through, doors hanging crookedly off their hinges, items left in the streets, clearly showing a people who had left in haste. "Why was this town ever here to begin with? I mean, we're in the middle of nowhere. What justification could there be to live out here?"

"Right over there," she said, gesturing with her chin.

They all turned and looked and there, beside the town, were several dozen small caves. Large crops of rock rose from the ground, into which were carved huge holes, disappearing somewhere inside. The overhangs were all white, and it looked as if they had been covered in years of salt.

"The salt mines," Indra explained, dismounting from her animal and leading it by the reigns.

They all followed and dismounted, too. Thor let Krohn down gently, then he stretched his aching legs. After so many hours, it felt good to be on his feet again.

"People moved here for the same reason they move everywhere," Indra added, as they all walked on foot. "Money. There was a salt boom, back when I was young. People came here and mined until their fingernails fell off. They used pickaxes, shovels, chisels, anything they could get their hands on. This was where the finest salts were. They made more money than you can imagine."

She shook her head.

"When the mines dried up and salt became cheap, life became harder and harder. Most people moved away. Not my family. My father," she said, shaking her head, "was stubborn to the end. He kept insisting that good times would come back here, that things would be like they once were. He refused to see the reality before him. He refused to leave. I was about to run away. Until the Empire came along."

Indra walked forward and kicked an empty bowl, sending it across the landscape.

"Ironic that I should find myself back here. It is also the only town between here and the Land of the Dragons. I told myself I'd never step foot in it again. But for you knuckleheads, here I am."

They followed her lead as she tied her animal to a post, each of them securing theirs. Thor came over to her.

"You saved our lives back there," Thor said, as the others gathered around. "We owe you a great debt."

"And it is not the first time," Reece added.

"We shall find some way," O'Connor said.

Indra shook her head.

"You don't owe me anything," she said. "After all, you saved me from boredom. What would I be doing back there? Figuring out somewhere else to go, something else to do. I've been a slave so long I don't even remember how to live life. At least you guys are interesting. You're all just reckless enough to be fun. Even with that stupid quest of yours."

Elden stepped forward and lowered his head, bashful. Thor could see him blush.

"I, for one," he said to her softly, "am very happy you returned."

He looked up at her and smiled, and for the first time Thor could see the little boy inside him. It was jarring, juxtaposed with his huge muscular frame.

Indra smiled, then turned away.

"You are not so bad yourself," she said.

Indra suddenly strutted across the small courtyard in the center of town, looking flustered, and quickly changed the topic.

"The sun will set soon," she said. "It will be blacker than black out here. Help me gather wood, and milk. The sun sets fast out here, so follow me."

They followed her out the other side of the town and back into the desert, which, on this side of the town wall, was dotted with strange, cactus-like plans, each about ten feet tall, in all different colors.

"What are these?" O'Connor asked.

"Qurum," she said. "The wood inside the qurum is dry, perfect for burning." She approached one as they followed. "If you can get past the thorns. Can I borrow your axe?" she asked Elden.

Elden stepped forward without hesitating and, too proud to let her do it and wanting to show off, he raised his axe and chopped off one side of the qurum, cutting all the thorns off at once and making one side flush and flat. It exposed the dark brown wood inside—but it also began leaking a white liquid all over the floor.

Indra shook her head.

"You are too impatient," she said. "Now you've ruined it."

"What do you mean?" he asked. "I cut off its thorns, like you said."

She shook her head.

"You cut too deep into it. See that liquid? That's qurum milk. We want to collect that. Now it's wasted. When you cut the thorns, cut just enough."

The qurum slowly stopped leaking, then before their eyes it wilted, collapsing down to the floor.

She walked to another, a few feet away, and this time she snatched the axe from Elden's hand, raised it high, and sliced one side of a qurum herself. She did it with perfect aim, slicing only the thorns, and this time the qurum did not wilt.

Indra then went expertly around the qurum, chopping off the thorns on all four sides, then chopped off its base, separating it from the earth. She handed Elden back his axe, then reached down and hoisted it. It looked like a large log.

"Your dagger," she said, holding out a hand.

Thor stepped forward and placed a dagger in her hand, and she reached up and poked a small hole in it; as she did, white milk began to bubble up.

"Your helmet, quick," she said.

She grabbed O'Connor's helmet and turned it upside down, and collected all the milk as it flowed. Soon she had a large bowl full of milk.

"Can you drink it?" Thor asked, examining it.

She nodded.

"It's sweet," she answered. "And filling. It's a complete meal in just a few sips. It also has qualities. It relaxes you. It puts you in a bit of an altered state, if you have too much. Kind of like drinking wine. You'll feel good," she said, smiling. "We call it truth serum. Because usually when people drink it, they say what's on their mind. Whether they mean to or not."

She turned and handed Elden the qurum.

"It's heavy," she said. "You can carry it back."

"This isn't heavy," he said. "I can carry more of these."

She smiled.

"Good, then get to work. We will need about ten of them to make it through the night."

The boys fanned out, each going to another qurum and using their swords and daggers to strip the thorns and bring the logs back.

As Thor worked on his, he looked over at Conven standing beside him, and saw how red his eyes were; he could tell how distraught he was. Conven had barely spoken a word since his brother had died, and his actions seemed desperate and reckless, and Thor feared for his state of mind.

Thor came up beside him, ostensibly to assist him on his qurum, but really to see if he could help him.

Thor stood there for a while, scraping the thorns on the other side of Conven's qurum; Conven barely seemed to notice, or to care. After some time passed, Thor asked: "Are you okay?"

Conven nodded, not meeting Thor's eyes as he continued to cut away at the qurum.

Thor cleared his throat. He wondered what to say to make him feel better.

"I loved Conval, too, like a brother," Thor said.

Conven kept cutting, with no reaction.

Thor tried again.

"I'm sorry he's gone," Thor said. "I can't imagine the suffering you're going through. I just want you to know that I am here. We are all here for you."

Conven continued to look down, refusing to meet Thor's eyes. He kept cutting away, and for a while Thor thought he would not respond. Then, finally, he said, in a quiet, raspy voice:

"He liked you."

Thor looked at Conven, surprised, and Conven finally raised his eyes, fiery red, and stared back into his.

"You were one of the few people he admired," Conven added.

Thor shook his head.

"I feel like I let him down," Thor said. "I never should have trusted the three brothers. If I hadn't, maybe he'd be alive today."

Conven shook his head.

"You didn't let him down," he said. "*I* did."

Thor did not understand what he meant by that. Conven reached up and played with his dagger, watching it gleam in the last light of the sun.

"But that's okay," Conven added. "Because I'll be joining him soon enough anyway."

Thor looked back at him with concern; he was about to say something, when Conven suddenly turned and hurried off, making his way to another qurum.

Thor figured he shouldn't press him any further; clearly, Conven wanted to be left alone.

Thor turned and headed over to another qurum, a yellow one, and raised his sword to chop it as he had the others—when suddenly Indra's voice rang out:

"NOT THAT ONE!" she screamed, panicked.

All the others stopped and looked at Thor, and he turned, sword in mid-air, and looked at Indra. She came running over to him and yanked back his wrist, looking at him in fear.

"Don't touch the yellow ones," she said, looking from him to the qurum with worry.

"Why not?" he asked.

"Poisonous," she said. "If it's cut, it sprays a liquid. The person cutting it will die within about two seconds."

113

Thor turned and looked at the yellow qurum sitting innocently before him, and gulped. Would the dangers in this Empire ever cease?

*

Thor sat with the others around the raging bonfire, the flames moving every which way as the cold gusts ripped through the desert night. Thor was grateful for the warmth. Indra had been right: the desert grew oddly cold at nighttime, and the wind was much stronger. He had thought it was overkill to bring back all those logs—but now he realized it was necessary. The blazing bonfire was the only thing keeping them warm from the icy cold in this desolate wilderness.

The group of them all sat huddled close before the flames, elbows resting on their knees, each holding a small bowl of qurum milk in their laps. Thor had taken his first sip moments ago, and it had went straight to his head. Not only did the thick, sweet milk fill his stomach, satisfy all his cravings immediately, but it also made him feel relaxed. Even intoxicated. It was as if he had drank an entire sack of wine. He felt warm, and light, and his entire body felt soothed. Yet it was also a different feeling than wine: unlike being drunk, he also, oddly, felt clarity and presence of mind. It was a strange feeling of both being relaxed, drifting away, and being present.

Thor could tell by the glazed eyes of all the others that they were feeling the same. All of them leaned back a bit, relaxed, staring into the flames. Thor let Krohn drink from his bowl, and ever since then, Krohn lay at his side, resting his head in his lap, not squirming around as much as he usually did. His eyes were open, too, staring into the fire.

Elden sat beside Indra, close to each other, their legs almost touching, and Thor could see that Indra was beginning to feel more relaxed around him. Looking at them from here, the two already seemed like a couple, as if they fit perfectly together. Thor wondered if they would all ever make it back to the Ring, and if so, if Indra would come with them, and if she and Elden would end up together. He hoped that they would.

Only Conven seemed on-edge. He had abstained from the liquid. Instead he sat there, jaw set, staring into the flames with an intensity that scared Thor. He seemed as if he were lost in another world, deep inside a world of grief. Thor wondered if he would ever come back to them, ever be the same old Conven that he had been. The others saw

114

it, too, and Thor caught Reece looking at him with concern. They exchanged a look, but neither of them knew what to do or say to make Conven feel better.

Indra looked over at Conven, and she reached over and handed another bowl to Elden and whispered something in his ear. Elden nodded, leaned forward, and held the bowl out towards Conven, sitting beside him.

But Conven not even look over at it.

"You should drink," Elden said, his voice punctuating the silence amidst the crackling of the flames. "We have a big day ahead of us tomorrow. Now is time to rest."

But Conven, still staring into the flames, shook his head curtly, and Elden set the bowl down, clearly sympathizing with Conven's grief.

Elden cleared his throat.

"Conven," he said. "Did I ever tell you about how I joined the Legion? About how I left my village?"

Conven slowly shook his head, still not looking at him.

Elden cleared his throat several times, then took a deep breath, now staring into the flames himself.

"My father, you see, he was a blacksmith. I was his apprentice. He wanted me to follow in his footsteps. I didn't want to. I wanted to be a warrior. To train with the Legion. I could not imagine a life in my village, being a blacksmith my entire life, at the mercy of serving others. I enjoyed the hammer and the forge, but it was not enough for me. I needed something bigger.

"The problem was, my father was deep in debt to our landlord. A certain Mister Tribble. My father was a good and decent and hard-working man, and he always paid his debts. But our village was small, and there was a limit to the amount of business we had. We were not near any crossroads, and business rarely passed through. My father tried as hard as he could to be prosperous. He worked harder than you could imagine. But even so, it just was enough to pay for our food and our rent. But Mr. Tribble kept raising the rent, every year, exorbitantly, and we just couldn't keep up.

"Over time, my father fell deeper and deeper into debt to Mister Tribble. And when the time came for me to leave our village, to join the Legion, I was not allowed. Mister Tribble forbid my father to let me go. He insisted that I continue to work as his apprentice, to pay off the debts—or else he would kick my father out of our cottage.

"My father was furious. He told me to go—he wanted me to be happy above all. But I couldn't. He needed me. And I knew that it was my place. So I stayed behind, to help him pay off Mister Tribble, who already owned nearly all of the town and was richer than you could imagine. This was what stopped me from joining."

Elden fell into silence, staring into the flames.

"But I don't understand?" Conven said, finally snapping out of it and turning to Elden. "You did join. What happened?"

Elden stared long into the flames, cleared his throat, and finally continued.

"One day, Mister Tribble came to our house. It wasn't enough that he was squeezing every penny out of us, with interest. It wasn't enough that he forbid me to leave and join the Legion. It wasn't enough that my father did nothing but work to pay his rent. One day, he decided he wanted more. He decided he wanted to take over our house, and make it a bar. He showed up one day, and announced that we had to be packed up and out by morning light. On the street. He didn't care where we went. That was that. He turned and walked out.

"My father just collapsed before me. He wept and wept, like a broken man. And that was the moment that changed my life. I could not stand to see my father like that. I could no longer stand the injustice of it all.

"I charged out of our house, mounted our horse and chased after Mister Tribble. I overcame him on the road, on the outskirts of town, and I confronted him. I pulled him down from his cart, and my goal was to talk sense into him. To make him understand. Not to hurt him. But when I pulled him down, he reached for a dagger and sliced my cheek. He left me this scar," Elden said, pointing to the scar that ran beneath his eye, aflame against the blaze of the fire. Thor had always wondered about that scar, but had never asked.

Elden cleared his throat.

"Mr. Tribble then raised his dagger and aimed it for my heart. Even though I was weaponless, and had not struck him. My defenses kicked in. I redirected his hand away from me, and as it happened, he ended up stabbing himself in the stomach. I'll never forget his expression as he looked into my eyes, dying, on the way to the underworld. I held him in my arms for about a minute, until he collapsed at my feet. It was the first man I had ever killed."

Elden sighed, frowning, and it seemed he was reliving it as he spoke.

"It so happened that the law had been out patrolling, and they saw me, holding Mister Tribble, the knife in his stomach as he died. They blew their horn, and they came charging for me. If they caught me, I knew I'd be sitting in a jail right now."

"So what did you do?" Conven asked, finally snapping out of it and engrossed in the story.

"I didn't wait," Elden said. "I couldn't. No matter what I said, they would assume my guilt. So I jumped on my horse and continue riding and I never turned back. "I rode all the way to the next town, and it so happened that was the time they were coming through for the Selection. I stood with the other boys, and I stood a foot taller than all of them, and I made sure I was selected. Thank god I was. It saved my life. If I ever went back to my hometown, I'd probably be arrested."

There came a long silence as Elden finished and they all stared into the flames.

"And whatever came of your father?" Conven asked.

Elden shook his head.

"I do not know. I have not seen him since."

Elden sighed.

"I do not even know why I'm telling you this story," he added.

Indra smiled.

"I warned you all. It is the qurum milk. It quickens the blood, and urges people to speak their deepest thoughts."

They all turned and stared back into the flames, crackling in the night, as a silence fell over them. Conven did not necessarily seem happier than before, but hearing the story did seem to help snap him out of his gloom.

We all feel for your loss," Reece said to Conven. "But you are not the only one who has lost. Each of us here, we have all lost someone dear to us. I..." he said, then lowered his head, pausing as if debating. "Well...I...I never told anyone this before, but I lost my dear cousin."

"Your cousin?" Thor asked.

Slowly, Reece nodded, looking sadly into the flames.

"My father, King MacGil, was the eldest of three brothers. His younger brother, Lord MacGil, lives with his four children in the Upper Isles. The Upper Isles are part of the Ring, yet separated by the Tartuvian. They are not far, maybe fifty miles offshore. Have you ever been?"

The others shook their heads. Thor dimly recalled hearing of the Upper Isles, once, in school.

"They are a rough and desolate place," Reece continued. "Stormy seas. More rain than sun, and always a driving wind. Perched on the edge of cliffs, it is a beautiful terrain, but not for the weak of heart. They say the Upper Isles breed a different breed of man. And this is where the other MacGils live.

"When I was younger, we would visit. Many times. My father and his brothers used to be close. As close as brothers could be. And I was close to my cousins. Lord MacGil had three boys and one girl. The girl, Stara, is my age. She is the most beautiful and noble girl you have ever met. Inside and out. When I was young, we were raised as close as brother and sister."

Reece sighed, staring into the flames, seeming weighed down by the tale.

"At some point along the way," Reece continued, "my father and his younger brother had a falling out. Apparently, so the rumor goes, his brother became ambitious. He was next in line for the throne, after all, and he had new advisors whispering in his ear. He began to hatch a plan to oust my father. Or at least, that's what my father's spies told him.

"We visited less and less, and on our final visit there, the mood was already tense. It broke my heart. Because you see, I never told anyone, but I was in love with Stara. And she was in love with me. We had vowed that when we grew up, we would marry each other. And every year I saw her, we would renew that vow, and our love for each other never waned."

Reece took a deep breath.

"One night, in Lord MacGil's castle, while he was hosting us, his oldest son died. And that's when everything changed."

"How?" Thor asked.

"We were all at a feast, and a glass of wine was poured for Lord MacGil and his eldest son drank it in his stead. He keeled over, dead on the spot. The wine was poisoned, and it had been meant for Lord MacGil. Given the political climate, Lord MacGil assumed his older brother was behind it. He kicked us out, and after that night, he never spoke to my father again—and forbid his family to speak to us, too.

"We all left hastily, in the dark of night, and never returned to the Upper Isles, and I never saw my cousins again. Nor did they ever come to visit us."

118

Reece sighed.

"The irony is that I was close to my cousin who died; he was like an older brother to me. And as far as Stara...I still see her face every night. I want to talk to her again. To tell her that we had nothing to do with it. But I know I shall never be able to. That was the reason I have dated no other girl since. It wasn't until I met Selese that, for the first time, I was able to see another woman's face in her stead."

They all settled back into a heavy silence as the wind whipped through the desert, fanning the flames. Thor looked at his brothers and realized that each was burdened by his own quiet desperation. He was not the only one; neither was Conven. They were all young, yet they were all suffering in some small way, all already weighed down by life. Some, he realized, were just better at hiding it than others.

Thor wanted to ponder his further, but his eyes began to close on him, and he let them. Tomorrow, after all, would bring the toughest leg of their quest and, perhaps, his final day.

CHAPTER NINETEEN

Gwendolyn rode beside Steffen, the two of them alone on the winding forest trail, riding, as they had been for hours, through the deep wood. As they proceeded on their endless trek, slowing the horses to a walk, they passed beneath towering trees with gnarled branches, curving in tangled arches over their head, blocking out the sky. It was a surreal landscape, and Gwendolyn felt as if she were riding into a fairytale. Or into somebody's nightmare.

The only thing illuminating the forest was the dimmest streak of sunlight, somewhere in the distance. The Southern Forest. It was a forest of gloom, a place she had feared as a child. It was rumored to be thick with thieves and scoundrels, a place that even honorable knights feared to tread—much less a woman practically alone. Yet, at least, she kept reminding herself, she had escaped Silesia, at least she was alive.

"My lady?" Steffen asked for the third time.

She looked over, snapped out of her reverie, and saw Steffen. She was so grateful for his presence. He was like a rock to her, the one person left she could rely on to always be at her side.

"My lady, are you all right?" he asked.

She nodded back, dimly aware he had been trying to talk.

Gwen was amazed they had made it this far already. She closed her eyes and recalled their fleeing the castle, recalled Steffen's leading her through the secret tunnels. They crawled for she did not know how long, crouching low, brushing spiders off as she went, her back killing her. The blackness of the tunnel had seemed never-ending, and at many moments she was sure that Steffen had chosen the wrong path.

Finally, the tunnel had ascended, twisting up and up, and as they'd reached the very top, she'd been amazed to see them punch through soil and grass. They emerged to find themselves somewhere in a field of grass, miles away from Silesia. Steffen had done it. The two of them were far from anywhere, no Empire troops in sight. Gwen had been grateful for the sunlight, and grateful for the cold, fresh air on her face.

As they'd surfaced Steffen had whistled, and out from behind a cave emerged two beautiful gleaming horses.

"They are Srog's property," Steffen had explained, as they'd each mounted their stallions. "This was an escape hatch, meant for the King and Queen, in case of emergencies. Srog instructed me to use the horses. No one else can use them now: we are the only ones to get out."

They had galloped south for miles, heading towards the Tower of Refuge, somewhere on the other side of the Ring, the two of them alone charging across the plains. They charged and charged, while day turned into night, and night into day, hardly taking a break. They stuck to isolated terrain, riding in places they knew Andronicus' empire could not be. They crossed nearly the entire Ring, avoiding major cities and towns, traversing the plains until they had finally, but hours before, entered the great Southern Forest.

Now, finally, exhausted, they had slowed their hard riding to a walk. They finally felt far enough from Silesia, from Andronicus' reach, to slow down. They also felt extremely cautious in this forest, and wanted to go more slowly and be vigilant.

As they went, the two of them searched the gnarled woods, looking warily about at their surroundings, on guard. The woods were far too thick to peer through, and the hairs raised on the back of Gwen's neck. She imagined all sorts of creatures staring back at her. Winter birds cawed as they went, and Gwen had an increasingly bad feeling. She wondered if they had a mistake attempting this.

But Gwen realized she should be grateful they had escaped alive, had made it this far, and that Steffen was with her. They were close to the Tower of Refuge now, and they only had to stick to the course. Still, these last few miles were the hardest. With every step, she felt an increasing sense of danger. She had been in many woods in her life, and this wood did not feel safe to her. There was a reason that the Empire troops had not entered it, and a reason none of the King's men ever entered it. It was too thick, too susceptible to ambush. Everyone skirted it, even if that meant adding days to a journey. But not her: she couldn't afford to. It was most the direct route to the Tower of Refuge, and the safest route to avoid detection by the Empire.

"My lady, you don't have to do this," Steffen said.

Gwen looked at him blankly, lost in her thoughts.

"Do what?" she asked.

"The Tower of Refuge," he said. "To cut yourself off from the world. There are people who love you. Silesia is no longer safe, but there are other places you can hide, other places you can wait until Andronicus' men leave. But the Tower...that is forever. Those who enter never leave. It is a tower of nuns, doomed to silence."

Gwen shrugged. She felt her life was over anyway, that the best part of it had been stolen from her by Andronicus and McCloud.

"Whether it's this jail or another," she responded, "it's just a matter of choice. We all live in our own private jails."

They fell back into silence as the two of them walked, and Gwen could feel Steffen wanted to rebut her; but he held his tongue out of respect.

Gwen thought she heard a twig snap, and at the same moment Steffen suddenly held out a hand, stopping her and himself.

"What is it?" she asked.

"Shhh," Steffen said, looking all about, listening.

Gwen felt her heart pounding, as there came another twig snap.

She turned slowly, and froze as a large group of miscreants approached, more than a dozen of them. They emerged from all sides of the wood, each looking more desperate than the next. They wore rags, had dirt-covered faces and fingernails, were unshaven and missing teeth, men in their twenties, all equipped with crude weapons on their belts. They looked thin, and they had a frantic look in their eyes. They all had dark, soulless eyes, and Gwen could see that they all meant harm.

"That looks like Royal garb to me," one called out to the other. His accent was crude and rough, the accent of the South, and the tone of his voice sent a chill right through Gwendolyn.

"Sure does," answered another. "What have we here? Some sort of lady?"

"I swear I recognize that face," said another. "Looks like a MacGil."

"Can't be," said another. "The MacGils are all dead by now. Unless this one here's a corpse."

"Prettiest corpse I ever did see."

The crowd of ruffians broke into crude laughter, and Gwen's anxiety heightened as they got closer.

"I'm telling you it *is*," insisted one of them. "They're *not* all dead. The daughter. The girl."

They all studied her more seriously.

"Can't be," one said. "She's in Silesia."

"Maybe she escaped," said another.

Gwen felt increasingly uncomfortable as they scrutinized her. She wished she was not wearing the royal mantle that Srog had given her, the royal jewels, the rings on her fingers, her bracelets and necklaces. She realized she must be a walking target to these people.

"Come any further, and you will regret that you had," Steffen warned beside her, his voice steely cold.

The group broke into laughter.

"What have we here? A hunchbacked dwarf keeping guard of the lady, is it?"

"What happened, they ran out of ordinary guards?"

More laughter.

"My my, you must really be hard put if you're relying on this pygmy to do you any good," said another, shaking his head.

"I will not warn you again," Steffen threatened, his voice dropping in deadly seriousness.

Several of them pulled daggers from their waists.

"You can start by stripping all your clothing," one of them said to Gwendolyn.

Gwen hesitated, fear in her eyes, looking from Steffen to them, unsure what to do.

"Do it now or I'll do it for you," one of them said.

"Yeah, do it quick, so we can get past all this and have some fun with you."

They all, laughing, stepped closer, and finally, Steffen broke into action.

With lightning speed, so fast he surprised even Gwendolyn, Steffen reached back, extracted his short bow, and released four arrows, piercing four of them through their throats with perfect aim, killing them on the spot.

Gwen did not hesitate. She reached into her harness, grabbed the flail that she'd kept there, swung it high overhead, and watched as the chain flew through the air and the spiked metal ball connected with the face of a miscreant as he approached.

It impacted his eye and he shrieked and collapsed to the ground.

Before she could swing again, Gwen felt rough hands on her back, then felt herself being yanked backwards off her horse, flying through the air, and slamming to the ground, winded. Two more thieves pounced on her, tearing at her jewels, yanking off her mantle. She fought back, but it was useless.

Steffen rode up beside her and leapt through the air, landing on one, tackling him to the ground, rolling with him. The other thief, though, continued to hold Gwendolyn pinned down tight; he grabbed her arm, twisted it around her back, flipped her over and pushed her face down to the ground. He reached down, grabbed at her pants, and began to pull them down.

"I will have my way with you girl," he said.

As he let go momentarily to grab her pants, Gwendolyn used the opportunity: she reached into her waist, grabbed a small silver dagger that Godfrey had given her ages ago, and spun around and plunged it into her attacker's throat.

His eyes opened wide as blood dripped down to the ground. She thrust it in deeper, feeling rage course through her, feeling herself take revenge not only against this man but also against McCloud, Andronicus, Gareth—against all the men who had wronged her.

"No you won't," Gwen responded.

As he collapsed, dead, Gwen retracted her blade, wiped it on his clothing, and put it back into her waist, without even a thought of remorse. She wondered if she was becoming remorseless, or hardened—or both. She hoped not.

Gwen looked over and saw Steffen wrestling with a thief, rolling again and again, and she prepared to run over to him, to help.

But as she went to get to her hands and knees, she suddenly felt herself get kicked in the side of the temple with the metal-tipped toe of a boot. She screamed out and landed on her back, her entire world hurting, spinning, seeing stars.

The last thing she saw, before her world went black, was the ugliest face she ever saw, smiling down as he raised the back of his hand high and brought it down on her cheek.

CHAPTER TWENTY

Kendrick hung there, high up on the cross, feeling his life force drain out of him as the second sun grew long in the sky. His wrists and ankles were swollen from being bound with coarse ropes to the wood, the pain unbearable from his limbs stretching, from hanging there hour after hour. He had kept his head hung low and tried not to look up anymore, not wanting to see anymore destruction; but he heard a moaning and he couldn't help himself. He glanced around him, and saw all his friends hanging on the crosses beside him. Srog was on one side, Atme on the other, beside him Brom and Kolk and many other knights that Kendrick cared dearly for. At least, he told himself, they were still alive, or clinging to life. They were not dead, as the heaps of corpses were below.

Kendrick had tried to talk to them, but they'd been too weak or dehydrated to respond. They all seemed more dead than alive.

Kendrick heard the crack of whips, and looked out to see the picture of devastation that his beloved city had become: the survivors that remained were all enslaved, being led by Empire taskmasters, whipped, forced to lug huge rocks, moving one pile after another as they cleared rubble. Silesia had quickly morphed into an occupied slave city, a statute of Andronicus already rising into the sky, the Empire emblem—a lion with a bird in its mouth—already lodged above the city gates, and the Empire banner raised above that. All traces of the independence this city once had were gone. It was now subsumed, completely part of the Empire.

There came a commotion and Kendrick, licking his chapped lips, turned to see a group of Empire soldiers making way through the crowd; behind them, he was shocked to see, was none other than Andronicus himself, towering over the others. The soldiers before him held in chains a man who Kendrick, after several moments, recognized. It was his half-brother.

Gareth.

Kendrick's eyes opened wide and he did a double take, wondering if he were seeing things. He was not. There, in the flesh, was Gareth, emaciated, growing a beard, looking disheveled. He was led by Empire soldiers, chains rattling as he shuffled along.

They came to a stop before Kendrick. The crowd fell silent as Andronicus came up beside Gareth and lay a huge hand around his skinny neck, covering it completely, his long fingernails scraping down to the base of Gareth's throat.

Andronicus smiled.

"Identify who is who among these captives," Andronicus said. "And we will spare your life."

They all looked up at Kendrick and the others on the crosses.

"I will do it with pleasure," Gareth said. "I will identify everyone and more. I have no love for any of them; your enemy is my enemy, too."

Andronicus smiled down at Gareth.

"You are insolent," he said. "And cold-blooded, even towards your own family. You are a man after my own heart. I like you. Free him," Andronicus motioned to his guards, and they rushed forward and unshackled Gareth.

Gareth shook off the shackles, strutted forward, and walked right up to Kendrick, pointing a long, skinny finger in his face.

"That is Kendrick," he said. "My former brother. Or half-brother. He is a bastard, really. He is head of the Silver. An important man," he said, then turned and pointed elsewhere. "And that man beside him, he is Kolk, the head of the Legion; and that there is Brom, head of the army; and there is Atme, another hero of the Silver."

Gareth went on and on, rattling off the names; with each name he pronounced, a fire burned in Kendrick's stomach. He would kill Gareth for this, if he ever got the chance.

Finally, Gareth finished. He returned to Andronicus' side, a satisfied smile on his face.

Andronicus smiled, a deep purring coming from somewhere in his throat, and he placed another hand on Gareth's shoulder.

"You have done well," Andronicus said. "You will be rewarded."

Gareth stood there, puffed up.

"What position will you give me? Keep in mind that I am a King, after all. You could name me King of the Ring. That would be fitting."

Andronicus laughed, heartily.

"I am going to reward you with the position of slave. You will be king of the dung-heap shovelers."

Gareth's face fell in horror.

"But you said you would reward me!"

"That *is* a reward," Andronicus said. "I am not killing you."

Gareth, panic in his eyes, suddenly turned and bolted from the group; his skinny frame aided him, and he was able to weave in and out of the crowd.

"FIND HIM!" Andronicus screamed to his shocked soldiers.

His men took off after him, but within moments Gareth found a small hole in the stone wall and dove into it. He was just skinny enough to wedge his way through, into some sort of hidden passage, and as the Empire soldiers reached the wall, they could not fit inside.

"If you lose him, you will die!" Andronicus called out.

The soldiers took off, racing the long way around the wall.

Andronicus, red-faced, turned his attention back towards Kendrick and the others. He stepped forward, and eyed them all closely.

After an interminable wait, he stepped up to Kolk.

"We will start with him," Andronicus commanded. "We will kill just one a day." He smiled. "I like to prolong my pleasure."

Andronicus reached down, took a spear from the hand of one of his attendants, then stepped forward and suddenly pierced Kolk, right through the heart.

"NO!" Kendrick screamed out, as he watched Kolk's mouth gushing with blood. Kolk screamed out in pain, then finally slumped his head, dead.

Andronicus, leaving the spear impaled in him, turned back to his men, as they all began to walk away.

"Tomorrow, we will choose another," he said.

Kendrick struggled for all he had, but he could not loosen his ropes. He reached back and screamed out to the heavens, vowing vengeance for Kolk, for his people, for all of them. One day, somehow, he would kill Andronicus.

CHAPTER TWENTY ONE

Thor woke at dawn, squinting against the searing light of the first morning sun, a huge, blinding ball on the horizon with nothing in the landscape to shield it. He raised his hands to his eyes, and sat up slowly.

The desert was still cool in the early morning, the heat rising by the second; all around him were his brothers in arms, laid out asleep by the dying embers of the fire. Krohn lay with his head in his lap, fast asleep.

All were accounted for—except for one. Thor noticed that Conven was missing; he quickly turned and looked all around for him, and finally spotted him, about twenty feet away from the others, sitting cross legged, his back to them, looking out at the sun as it rose on the horizon.

Alarmed, Thor hurried over to him. As he walked around he saw his eyes staring right into the sun, bloodshot. He still looked grief stricken, as if he were not fully there with them. He stared into the horizon with a blank look, and Thor wondered at the depth of his sorrow.

"Conven?" he asked.

After several seconds, he finally, blankly, turned to look at Thor.

"It's time to go," Thor said.

Conven slowly rose, without a word, and walked to his beast, tied to a pole. Thor turned and followed him, and the others began to rise, too, all watching, wondering.

Conven was not the same person that Thor once knew, and despite himself, Thor was beginning to wonder if Conven would become a liability for them. He did not understand what Conven was going through. He was unpredictable. And he did not know how he would react in time of danger—or if he would endanger them all.

But he had no choice. As they all mounted their animals, bidding a hasty goodbye to this solitary town, they were off before the sun rose, needing to make time before they all became fried in the heat of the day.

*

The six of them rode their beasts at a walk across the salt landscape, all following Indra's lead. Thor was glad to be rid of that place, and he could understand Indra's anxiety at returning to her hometown. He would not want to be stuck there either.

Thor was still a bit lightheaded from that drink of the night before, and he tried to shake off the cobwebs. That qurum milk was powerful, and he had a hard time remembering exactly when he fell asleep.

"How much farther is the Land of the Dragons?" Reece asked Indra.

"We haven't even entered the tunnel yet," she said.

"Tunnel?" O'Connor asked.

"The only way to reach the Land of the Dragons is through the Great Tunnel. It connects the Salt Wastelands to the Mountains of Fire. The locals call it the Tunnel of Death. I've never heard of someone enter it and come out the other side." She sighed. "But this is the journey you chose. You knew it would not be easy."

They continued riding in silence and Thor felt the uneasiness among them as they headed across never-ending stretches of salt, as the sun rose ever higher. It felt as if they were trekking to their deaths.

After hours of absolute nothingness, on the horizon there cropped up before them a single huge mountain. At its base was the mouth of a vast tunnel, a hundred yards in diameter, a gaping hole into the blackness.

As they neared, their animals began to stomp and resist, and Thor could sense how uneasy they were.

Indra dismounted at the mouth of the tunnel, and the others did the same.

"What about the animals?" Elden asked, coming up beside her.

She shook her head.

"No beast will enter this tunnel," she answered. "They know better."

She stood there, holding the reigns and looking up at her animal wistfully. It leaned down with its huge head, made a moaning noise, and rubbed its nose against her neck.

She released the rope and slapped the beast on the back, and it turned and ran off, as the other beasts turned and ran off with him.

Thor turned with the others and watched them go, raising up a cloud of white dust as they faded into the horizon. He gulped. Now they were on their own.

Thor turned and faced the entrance of the tunnel, peering into the blackness. He knew they might not ever come out.

Indra raised a dagger and stepped forward to the wall of the cave and chipped off large pieces of yellow rock. She held one against the wall and smashed it with the butt of her dagger, and it revealed a glowing white core. She handed a rock to each of the men.

Thor held it in his hand, surprised at its weight, a rough yellow rock with a glowing core.

Indra took the first step into the cave, and as she did, Thor was shocked to see the rock cast a glow. It exuded the light of several candles.

"Hold yours high and the tunnel won't be as dark," Indra said.

"How long do they last?" O'Connor asked, as they all began to enter the cave.

"I don't know," Indra said. "No one's ever used them long enough to say."

*

The dim tunnel echoed with the strange noises of animals and insects, the fluttering of wings, the shrieks and cooing noises of hidden creatures echoing in every direction. They marched and marched, holding their glowing rocks out before them. Thor heard something crunching beneath his feet and as he lowered the rock it cast a light on millions of insects, crawling beneath his feet, crunching beneath his boots. Every once in a while he shook them off, as they tried to crawl up his leg.

Krohn, beside him, snarled at them, and he bent over and snapped at one or tried to catch it between his paws.

Thank god for the glowing rocks, Thor thought; without them it would be like hiking into utter blackness, and Thor was grateful to Indra, as always, as the rocks lit the way. Still, beyond their few foot radius, it was hard to see, and Thor could only wonder what was lurking deep in the corners of this place. He couldn't help but feel as if he were being watched, as if the creatures, whatever they were, were biding their time. A part of him was glad he couldn't see it.

They marched on and on, all of them breathing hard from exertion but more so from anxiety. Thor's legs grew weary, and he wondered when this would ever end.

There came a sudden fluttering of wings, and he felt something brush his face.

"Globas!" Indra screamed. "Get down!"

The cave was suddenly alight with thousands of small creatures glowing in the dark; they looked like bats, but were larger, and their heads were completely aglow in white. There were thousands of them, fluttering their wings in a great cacophony, and descending on them.

Before Thor could even try to dodge them he felt his cheeks get scratched, and he cried out in pain. He drew his sword and slashed frantically at them in every direction, and the others joined in. A few of the bats fell, but more and more scratched his face and neck and hands, and Thor finally gave up and followed Indra's lead: like her, he dropped and curved into a ball, hugging his knees, his face to the ground. The others followed, dropping beside him.

Thor felt a million claws scratching at the chainmail on his back, on the back of his hair and neck and arms—but he stayed down low, as did Indra, and prayed. For a moment, he felt as if he'd be scratched to death.

There came a sudden roar, echoing off the walls, and the animals suddenly flew off, the flock screeching and flying away.

After several moments, the fluttering of their wings finally faded, the awful flapping leaving Thor's ears, and he could hear himself think again. He heard himself breathing hard, as were the others, all in a panic. Gradually, they all stood, grateful to be alive.

But the roar rose up again, and Thor felt a pit in his stomach, as the roar sent chill up his spine; it was a deep, dark roar, like a lion.

"What was that?" Reece asked.

"I have no idea," Indra said.

"Whatever it is, it doesn't sound happy," O'Connor said.

The roar came again, louder and closer this time, now sounding like the roar of a lion. They all held their weapons out before them, sweating with fear. Thor felt the blood trickling down his neck and head from the scratches, and as he stood there, it was awful to wait, to stare into the blackness and see nothing.

Thor felt the ground beneath them shake, and he could wait no more. He reached back, placed his glowing rock in his sling, and hurled it as far as he could. It went soaring through the air, sending a blaze of light, illuminating the tunnel. After about fifty yards, finally, it lit up what was approaching.

Thor wished it hadn't.

Standing there was a huge beast, resembling a lion but three times as tall and as wide, with a trunk that hung down like an elephant's, but with fangs on either side of it, and a horn in his forehead. It was covered in yellow fur, and it stood on two legs, two huge muscular legs, with two claws for toes. It leaned back, raising its huge biceps, its body muscular, rippling, and it roared again, lifting its trunk and baring its fangs.

"A Cave Monger!" Indra whispered in awe.

"I take it it's not friendly," O'Connor said.

Indra shook her head.

"Not very," she replied.

The Cave Monger roared again, then suddenly charged, sounding like a herd of elephants.

They all stood there, frozen in fear, wondering what to do, when Conven suddenly rushed forward and charged the beast. Conven sprinted right for it, as if hoping to die.

As Conven raised his sword the Cave Monger, moving with deceptive speed, reached around and swiped him, sending him flying across the cave and smashing into the wall. Conven fell, limp, to the cave floor.

The beast ran over to him and raised a claw to finish him off, and Thor jumped into action. He knew there wasn't time to reach him, but he thought quick; he stepped forward, raised his sword, and threw it. It sailed end over end, crossing the cave and lodging in the monster's arm.

The Cave Monger shrieked, then turned and set its sights on Thor. It charged and leapt into the air for Thor, aiming for his throat.

As the beast came for him, Thor raised a palm, summoning his energy. A yellow light shot from Thor's palm, and he was able to stop the beast in midair, right before him. But Thor wasn't strong enough to stop it from swiping him. It reached out and smacked him across the side of his body, sending Thor flying across the cave and smashing into the other wall.

Krohn charged the beast and sank his fangs into its feet; the beast shrieked, then picked Krohn up high in the air, and opened its mouth to eat him.

O'Connor took aim and fired several arrows into the beast's open mouth, making it drop Krohn; Elden raised his axe, charged forward, and chopped off one of the beast's claws. The beast shrieked in rage, picked up O'Connor with one hand, squeezed him, and raise him high. O'Connor hung there, his legs flailing, looking death in the face.

Reece took his flail, swung it high, and impacted the beast's head, making him drop O'Connor. The beast shrieked and set its sights on Reece. It opened its wide jaws, its fangs protruding, and lowered them for Reece. Thor could see that Reece was about to die.

Thor shook off the tremendous pain in his head, and focused. He *had* to summon his power. He willed himself to become even stronger than he was. He saw Argon's face; he saw his mother's face; then he saw Gwendolyn's. He felt her energy rushing through his body, supporting him.

Thor stood, raised both palms, and willed for it to work.

A blue light radiated from his palms throughout the cave, and he hit the beast square in the chest. The beast stopped and screamed. Thor raised his arms, and as he did, he was shocked to see that he was managing to actually raise the beast into the air.

The beast screamed, flailing its arms and legs in mid-air. But it was off the ground, and there was nothing it could do.

Thor, in one last burst of effort, swung his arms—and as he did, the beast swung through the air. Thor pulled back his arms and threw them forward, and the beast went flying like a meteor through the cave, screaming, end over end, until finally it smashed into a wall and collapsed. A boulder came rolling down and landed on top of it, crushing it.

All was silent. It was Dead.

The others turned and looked at Thor, with a new look of respect and wonder.

Thor collapsed to his knees, weak from the effort. He was getting stronger, he could feel it. He could also control it more. But he still did not have the stamina he needed. That encounter had drained him. If another beast showed up right now, he would be helpless. He needed to become stronger.

Reece and O'Connor came over, and they each picked Thor up and draped his arms over their shoulders and held him between them as they walked. All of them wounded, stung, hobbled along as the group continued to slowly trek through the cave, into the blackness, and into whatever danger lay ahead.

CHAPTER TWENTY TWO

Night fell cold and black, and Kendrick hung on the cross, in and out of consciousness, plagued by troubled dreams. He saw his father, King MacGil, surrounded by white light, smiling down at him; he saw his sister, Gwendolyn, being dragged away; he saw his little brother, Reece, on a small boat drifting out to sea. And he saw King's Court roaring in flames.

Kendrick opened his eyes slowly, wincing from pain and exhaustion. He was disoriented and could not tell if he was asleep or awake. He blinked and made out before him, lit by sporadic torches, the inner courtyard of Silesia, what was once a shining, proud city, now a heap of rubble, littered with corpses, its citizens turned into slaves. With most people asleep, the activity was not as frenzied as it had been during the day, yet still Kendrick could hear the distant sound of his people being whipped by Andronicus' men, some of them driven to work even so late into the night.

The occupying soldiers sat around the courtyard in small circles, around bonfires that punctuated the night; they leaned over, rubbed their hands, shared wine sacks and laughed with each other as they tried to get warm. They wore expensive furs, furs they had looted from Silesians; as Kendrick hung there on the cross, bracing himself against another cold gust of wind, it made him acutely aware that he was wearing just a light shirt and pants. He, like the others, had been stripped of his best armor and furs, left to freeze to death, if the pain did not get him first. His teeth chattered, and his hands were blue—but none of that mattered anymore. He would be dead soon enough.

Kendrick mustered enough energy to turn, and he saw beside him the stiff figure of Kolk, now a corpse, eyes open in his death pang, his body still pierced with that spear. It inflamed Kendrick. It was disgraceful, the act of an enemy without honor. They should have had the decency to take down his body and give him a proper burial. Instead, they let him hang there, this fine warrior, like a common criminal, for all to gawk at. Kendrick knew he would be next, tomorrow, but he didn't care about that; what he cared about were his other friends up there, especially Atme, who hung just a few feet away and who he was helpless to do anything about. Kendrick looked over at them, but in the dim light he could not tell whether they were alive or dead.

Kendrick closed his eyes, trying to concentrate on making the pain go away. The pain would not listen. Sometimes it shifted in and out, so that he forgot for a few moments how much his limbs hurt. But mostly it was intense and ever-present. He had had small bouts of sleep, yet even in the sleep he had felt the pain. As he closed his eyes, he tried to will himself to go back to sleep, to shut out the horrors of the world, to numb the pain, even if for just a little while.

As he closed his eyes, Kendrick's mind raced with images. He saw himself as a boy, with his best friend Atme, the two of them sparring in the Legion; he saw himself with a girl he had loved, he could no longer remember her name, on a rowboat when he was younger; he saw his first battle, his first victory, his own surprise at his skills; he saw himself sitting around the table with his father, King MacGil, Gwendolyn, Godfrey, Reece, and even Gareth, all of them young, all of them happy. He saw King's court shining, majestic, impregnable.

And then Kendrick saw his father, standing before him, surrounded by white light. His father reached out a hand. He looked young and healthy, a bold and brave warrior, as Kendrick had remembered him. He smiled down.

"My son," he said, proudly.

The words filled Kendrick's heart with warmth. Kendrick had always, more than anything, wanted to be thought of MacGil's son.

"You are my firstborn," he said. "My true son."

Kendrick reached out to touch his dad's hand, but his fingers were just out of reach.

"We'll be together again soon," MacGil said. "But your time is not now. You must fight. You are a warrior. Do not give up. *Never* give up. Fight. Fight for me!"

Kendrick felt a hand on his wrist, and at first he thought it was MacGil's.

But then he opened his eyes and looked down, and saw that indeed there was a hand on his wrist. He was surprised to see a young, beautiful woman standing there, perhaps in her early twenties, laying a gentle palm on his wrist. She was studying Kendrick's pulse, and closing her eyes as if listening. She then opened her eyes and looked up at him. She had the most beautiful eyes he had ever seen. Almond shaped, they were a light shade of hazel and they complemented her face. Her skin was light brown, the coloring of the Empire race.

136

An Empire woman, he realized. He wondered what she was doing. Had Andronicus sent her? Was she about to kill him? From her smile and her kind touch, he could not imagine that she was. But what was she doing here, standing beside him, holding his wrist? He wondered if he were still dreaming.

"You're alive," she said to him, sounding surprised. She had the sweetest voice he'd ever heard; he ached to hear that voice again. He wanted her to keep speaking, and to never stop.

"Who are you?" he tried to ask, but the words came jumbled, his voice cracked, his throat dry.

"Sandara," she replied.

She looked up at him with hope, as if happy to see him alive. She reached up, and in her hand she held a black, fur cloak. She managed to climb up on the cross and drape it over his shaking shoulders. It was the smoothest, most luxurious fur he'd ever felt, and he had never cherished a piece of clothing more. He felt immediately warmed around his shoulders and chest.

"Why are you helping me?" he asked.

"Healing the sick is my calling," she said.

"But you work for the Empire," he said.

She looked around warily.

"I do," she said. "But not at night. They don't see all that I do. I do not like to see anyone sick. Empire or not. Regardless of whether their skin is the same color as mine."

Kendrick looked down at her, his heart melting with gratitude and appreciation. She extracted a sack filled with liquid, raised it to his lips, and he drank greedily as he felt water filling his mouth. He drank and drank, like a man crossing a desert who hadn't seen water in ages. He realized how dehydrated he was.

Finally, she pulled it away.

"Not too much at once," she said, "your body must get used to it."

Then she pulled out another small sack, put it to his mouth, and he tasted sweet wine. It was stronger than any wine he'd had, and it went right to his head. He felt lighter, tingly, and his pain lessened.

"It is not the best remedy," she said, "but it will do for now, to take your pain away."

"I don't know how to thank you," he said, feeling renewed for the first time in days. With the pain lessened, he was finally able to think clearly. "I owe you a great debt."

She looked down to the ground, sad.

"I fear you will not live to repay that debt," she said. "I hear the Great Andronicus will have you all executed tomorrow."

Kendrick felt a pit in his stomach, yet he sensed that it was true.

"Then why bother helping me?" he asked.

"Everyone is worth helping," she answered. "Every moment of life is precious."

She looked up at him, her eyes wet with tears, and he was touched to see how much she cared for him, a stranger. He felt a connection to her stronger than he could express, and he wished more than anything that he was free from this cross, to embrace her. He was sad to think that, in but hours, he wouldn't be alive to see her face again.

"Your kindness means a great deal to me," he said. "From these rags you can't tell, but I was once an important person," he said. "It is a shame you do not know me for who I am."

She smiled up at him.

"I don't care who you are," she said. "You are an important person to me now."

Kendrick looked at her and wondered.

"Why did you choose *me* to help?" he asked. "You gave me your only fur cloak."

She reddened in the night. She looked down and did not reply.

"I do not know," she answered.

"What would Andronicus's men do to you if they caught you healing the enemy?"

Sandara turned and looked warily over her shoulder; luckily, the Empire soldiers were distracted, huddled around bonfires, not paying attention to her.

"Death," she answered.

Kendrick's heart swelled.

"If I ever get free from here, I will find you. I will repay you."

"There is nothing to repay," she said.

She turned to go. Kendrick could not stand to see her go; he had to think quick to keep her here, and he blurted out the first thing that popped into his mind.

"Are you married?" he asked.

She looked at him, then looked down, and even in the dim light, he could sense her blushing.

Kendrick hated to be so forward, so tactless. But he knew these might be his last moments on earth, and he had no time for proper etiquette. He *had* to know.

"I am not, my Lord," she finally answered. She looked up at him meaningfully. "But even if you were a free man, it would be forbidden for someone of my race to marry someone of yours. It would result in death."

"I care for rules and penalties," Kendrick said. "My lady, if I am ever free from here, I will find you. Do not go far. Stay in the Ring."

She lowered her head.

"I must go wherever the Great Andronicus commands me," she said.

She suddenly turned and hurried, back into the darkness.

Kendrick watched her go until she disappeared, then he closed his eyes, seeing her face, her eyes, the color of her skin, the curve of her lips.

Sandara. Sandara. Sandara.

He repeated her name over and over in his mind, like a mantra. It gave him a reason to survive.

He would survive, he decided. No matter what, he would survive.

CHAPTER TWENTY THREE

Just as Thor thought the journey through the Great Tunnel would never end, they all, exhausted, weary, exited into the flat gray somber light of day. They squinted at the light, raising their hands to their eyes, even against the thick rolling gray clouds. They had been so used to blackness that this felt like stepping out onto the sun.

Thor was thrilled to be free from that cave. They had been marching all day and all night, through an endless cacophony of noise, harassed ever since that monster by small animals which they fought off all the way until the exit. As they emerged out the other end, it felt as if they had emerged to freedom.

A cold gust of wind smacked them in the face, and Thor leaned back and breathed deep, feeling like a rat emerging from a hole. As his eyes adjusted to the light, he blinked several times, in awe at the sight before him.

The cave had let them out onto a meandering path, glowing white, which wound its way up a high mountain range. As far as the eye could see were mountain peaks, seeming to stretch to the end of the earth, many of them capped with red. In the distance Thor saw a great burst of lava shoot up into the air, saw a cloud of black ash rise up, and knew the trail led off in the distance, beyond the top of the mountain ranges.

"The Mountains of Fire," Indra said. "The famed path to the Land of the Dragons. They say it is a path carved of bones."

Thor looked down and felt the unusual texture of the path beneath his feet, gleaming white, and as he examined it, he saw that she was right: the road was indeed a collection of bones, molded together, winding its way as far as the eye could see.

"The bones of who?" O'Connor asked.

They all exchanged a nervous look, and Krohn whined beside them.

Slowly, they continued marching, heading along the trail, twisting and turning their way higher and higher up the mountain range. Thor looked up and saw the trail wound its way impossibly high, and he wondered how they would make it. They were already exhausted. But they had no choice. This was the way to the Land of the Dragons, and they must go wherever the trail took them.

"Over here!" O'Connor called out.

O'Connor ran over to something gleaming on the side of the road, and reached down and picked up a small gold coin.

"What is it?" Elden asked, coming up beside him.

"There's something here, too!" Reece called, running over and picking up an ornate golden dagger left on the side of the road.

"I wouldn't touch that if I were you," Indra warned.

They turned and looked at her.

"Dragons covet their treasure," she said, "and they guard it jealously. These are the spoils of those who have tried to come their way. Everyone has died. These are their bones, and this is their treasure. The dragon's trophy. It is their way of boasting: they are so secure, they can leave treasure strewn about anywhere. It is also a warning."

Thor turned and looked up at the mountain trail, and as far as he could see, it glistened with treasure, priceless jewels and coins and weapons and shields and armor strewn all about.

"We can take what we see here, and bring it home and be rich for the rest of our lives!" Elden remarked.

Indra shook her head.

"Returning is the hard part," Indra said.

"The treasure we want is the most valuable of all, and the one we need the most," she said. "The Destiny Sword. We must not get distracted. I will gladly exchange all of this for that."

"Still, we can take whatever we can carry," O'Connor said.

"I would be careful of that," Indra said. "You will incite the dragons."

Thor studied the treasure, debating what to do.

"Each of you take just a few items that you cherish most," Thor said. "We don't want to get bogged down. Let the rest lie where it is. Our lives and our mission are more important than wealth. And these are the objects of slain men anyway. Much of it is haunted."

They continued on their way and as they went, they picked up various pieces of treasure, examined them, and sometimes kept them, and sometimes discarded them. Thor felt like every time he found a piece he loved, just a few feet later he found another that was even more precious and he exchanged it for that. The one he valued the most was a precious sling, its handle carved of ivory, its pouch lined with gold, and a sack of gold throwing stones to accompany it. He tucked it away, securely in his waist. Thor also found a dagger he loved, with an ornate gold handle, carved with images, and in a language he could not understand. It gleamed, the blade so sharp it cut his finger just to touch it. He tucked that one away, too, and found a shining gold gauntlet, studded with rubies, and as he slipped it on one hand, he could feel its power. He decided to wear it.

The only other thing he grabbed was a necklace. As soon as he saw it, he thought of Gwendolyn. It had a rope made of gold and a shining gold heart, laden with diamonds and rubies. He stuffed it deep in his pocket, with his ring, and he vowed to live long enough to give it to her.

The others found priceless treasure, too. O'Connor found a golden bow and a quiver of golden-tipped arrows that he slung over his shoulder, dropping his current one. Reece found a shield made of platinum which shone brighter than the sun, and which he slung over his back. Elden found a new axe, with a leather handle, and a double edge blade made of platinum, so shiny one could see one's reflection in it. Indra found a gold ring, which she stuffed into her pocket. Only Conven did not partake, marching down the road, looking off into the horizon as if he no longer cared for the world.

Krohn whined, and Thor looked over to see him nudging a piece of jewelry with his nose. Thor knelt down and saw that it was a collar for an animal, perhaps a dog, laden with rubies and sapphires. Krohn whined again, and Thor realized that Krohn wanted to wear it.

Thor lifted it and Krohn lowered his head as if he wanted to wear it. Thor clasped it around his neck, and Krohn leaned over and licked him.

Thor looked down at Krohn and it was shocking to see the shining jewelry standing out amidst his all-white fur. It made Krohn seem more regal, more powerful. It suited him perfectly.

They all continued hiking, higher and higher up the winding mountain trail, the wind getting stronger, the elevation making it harder to breathe. Thor soon found himself wondering if they would ever reach the summit. The mountain peaks seemed to stretch to the end of the world.

"I don't see any dragons," O'Connor finally said to Indra.

"Don't worry," she answered, "you will soon enough."

There came a low, distant rumble, like a growling noise, and the ground shook beneath their feet. They all stopped and listened. Thor recognized the sound at once from his time at The Hundred. The roar of a dragon.

It made it all real, and Thor swallowed hard, realizing how crazy this quest was.

They continued marching, and just as Thor was beginning to feel he could not march one step further, his legs shaking, they finally reached the summit of the highest peak. They all stood there, gasping, and looked out at the vista. The sight of it took their breath away.

Spread out below them was a vast valley with volcanoes everywhere. The lava spewed forth, filling the air with sparkling red, casting off heat so strong that it warmed the freezing cold day even from here. Rivers of lava flowed everywhere, and the land and sky were black with soot and ashes.

In the farthest distance, on the horizon, were roaring flames and smoke. There came a great rumble, somewhere out of sight.

The lair of the dragons. Thor could sense its power from here.

The view before them felt like one of the great wonders of the world. He had the same feeling he'd had when he saw the Canyon for the first time. Magical, mysterious, alluring—and dangerous.

Another gust of wind came, this one strong enough to knock them off balance, and Thor and the others looked at each other. They also stood rooted in place, hesitant to take the next step.

Finally, Conven stepped forward, descending down the trail, which sloped its way gently through the vast landscape, meandering around fields of lava, towards the ever distant lair of dragons.

Thor and the others followed, and as they marched and marched, Thor felt an increasing sense of ominousness, as if they were all being watched.

There came a sudden noise, a great flapping of wings, and Thor looked up and saw high up a huge dragon, soaring, circling. Luckily, it did not seem to spot them, but the flapping of the wings was so loud, Thor could hear it even from here. The wings were so wide they blotted out the sky, and from here the immense, primordial beast looked magical. Invincible.

Thor could not believe how close they were, after all this time, to finally nearing the Dragon's lair, the final resting place of the Sword. Thor could feel the Sword's energy even from here. He was excited to feel it was definitely here, within reach. His heart quickened.

Thor also felt a tremendous energy vibrating within, and he knew he was in a very powerful place, both physically and spiritually. He had never experienced anything like this before, and he felt overwhelmed by the sensation. He knew there would lie a tremendous battle up ahead for them. And he knew that the battle would be more spiritual than physical.

All of the boys looked up in wonder as the dragon flew by.

"And how are we supposed to fight that?" O'Connor asked. "Do you think our weapons would do any good?"

"Not to mention its flames," Indra said. "They will eviscerate you within moments."

"We must have faith," Thor said. "We are on a quest bigger than ourselves."

They continued marching and as they did, suddenly, a small volcano beside them burst, shooting up lava into the air. Sparks and a stream of lava poured down all around them, barely missing them, as they ran out of the way.

The deeper they went, the more of these small volcanoes burst, and the lava became more intense, their having to dodge it every few feet. It was like running through a minefield, and they still had quite a good distance to go until they reached the end of the fields.

As they went, all of them increasingly on edge, suddenly they all stopped as they heard an awful snarling noise behind them. The noise sounded like a tiger's growl, yet with fire in its throat. It sent the hairs on Thor's back on edge.

Thor turned slowly, as did the others, and was horrified at the sight: a small volcano exploded, the lava shooting up into the air, and as the lava fell towards the ground, it took the form of a large creature, twice the size of a guerrilla, made entirely of molten fire. As the creature leaned back its head and roared, it swung its arms and sent flame and lava flying everywhere. A small clump seared Thor's arm as it shot past him, making him scream out in pain.

They all hit the ground as flames and small bits and pieces of lava went flying everywhere.

"My shield!" Reece yelled.

Reece ran forward before the others with his new platinum shield, and as he held it out in front of them, they all took cover behind it; the shield magically expanded, becoming large enough to cover all of them.

Chunks of lava bounced off it, sounding like hail, hissing, denting the shield, sending up the acrid smell of sulfur and smoke

The monster, enraged, roared again, and the ground hissed as it charged right for them.

Conven jumped out from behind the safety of the shield, raised a sword high, and charged the beast; as he approached recklessly, he slashed the sword right through the monster's midsection. But the monster stood there, unphased, and Conven looked down, horrified to watch the sword melt in his hands, bending and falling limp to the ground.

O'Connor stood and shot golden arrows at it with his new bow; but the arrows, as they neared the beast, melted, too, all falling as flame to the earth.

Elden jumped up and threw his axe, which went end over end, right through the creature, searing, turning black, and landing out on the other side, melted.

Thor placed a golden ball in his sling, reached back and hurled it—but the creature merely raised a palm and caught the golden ball in mid-air, and the gold melted into a puddle at its feet.

The beast pulled back its hand, and smashed Conven across the face. Conven stumbled and fell to the ground, screaming, clutching his face as the blow left a burn mark along the side of his jaw. The beast then raised a fist to bring it down on Conven's exposed neck, and Thor knew the beast would burn him alive.

Thor stepped forward, held out his palm and closed his eyes. He felt the burning nature of this beast. Instead of fighting it, he tried to become one with it. And then, he willed his hand to send forth ice.

Thor opened his eyes to see a stream of ice fly out, radiating, covering the beast right before it could strike Conven. The beast shrieked as, bit by bit, the ice spread over him, and froze him in place.

Then, finally, the beast shattered, and melted into a puddle of water at their feet.

The others turned to Thor with a look of gratitude and relief, and Thor, spent, collapsed to his knees, his arm burning from the pain of being burnt, and drained from his use of magic. He was slowly becoming more able to control it, he noticed. But he felt it was also taking a heavier toll on him. He was not yet able to control his stamina, and he felt as if it had all been taken from him.

Reece and O'Connor came over and picked him up, helping to carry him as they all continued on their trek.

They continued, hurrying through the meandering lava fields, following the road of bones, trying to stay as far from the lava streams as possible. The smell of sulfur grew stronger in the air, as did the dark clouds of ash, the perpetual thunder, the explosions of fire. At some point, Thor knew, those sounds were no longer just the volcanoes: now, as they neared, they were also the sound of the dragons' breath.

As the trail dipped up and down, weaved in and out of lava fields, finally, it took them to a ridge, to a place where the land fell off before them and Thor saw something that would stay with him for the rest of his days.

Before them stood a great sea of fire and lava, sparking, bubbling, impossible to cross. Beyond that, there sat a land of black sand and sulfur, a huge cave dug into an ancient cliff. And filling the sky, flapping their wings, screaming, roaring, were hundreds of dragons, turning the sky black. They all shot flames from their mouths, all filled with fury, with bloodlust. Dozens more were nestled within the cave, guarding its entrance.

"The Dragon's Lair," Indra said.

They had found it. And somewhere, inside that cave, lay the Sword of Destiny.

CHAPTER TWENTY FOUR

Godfrey marched quickly through the night, traversing the back streets of Silesia, Akorth and Fulton beside him. As he looked over at his compatriots, he had to do a double-take to realize that they were his friends: the Empire uniforms they wore were so convincing, especially with the face plates down, that they fooled even he, their life-long friend.

As they marched into the unknown, Godfrey was proud of himself, and also a bit shocked: he'd had no idea that his plan, which was improvising and evolving as it went along, would get half as far as it did. He and Akorth and Fulton, he thought, made the most unlikely of heroes, the only members of the Silesian army still standing, slipping through the night, just the three of them, dressed in these ridiculous uniforms, left to oppose Andronicus' million-man army. It was so absurd that if Godfrey were watching it from a distance, he would laugh.

But this was real, and he was in it, and life and death were at stake—and Godfrey was not laughing. Nor were his friends. They all marched stiffly, terrified as they passed through camps of Empire soldiers patrolling everywhere, huddled around bonfires, their backs against the wind, trying to get warm. The three of them walked with their chests out, trying to strut with purpose, trying to act as if they belonged and were on a mission of great import.

With each new step Godfrey's heart pounded for fear of being discovered. He was terrified that someone would notice the mismatched size of his uniform or his crooked stripes or the direction they were marching, or stop to wonder where the three of them might be going this time of night. He increased his pace, as did his friends, and he could sense that they were as nervous as he.

Akorth and Fulton also reeked of ale, and it made him nervous; he wondered if a typical Empire soldier would drink as much as these two, and if it might give them away. He was sure that the ale they'd drank was helping to calm their nerves, but Godfrey didn't have any ale inside him himself, and it made him jealous. Still, he was happy to have the company, and he knew he would need them if he had any chance of pulling off what he was about to attempt.

Godfrey weaved in and out of the streets, determined to save his brother Kendrick. He had spotted him and the others on the crosses earlier in the day, and it had broke his heart. Godfrey had always had a soft spot for Kendrick, one of the only knights who had not been condescending to him, who had not made him feel like he was less than them. After spotting him, Godfrey had formulated a plan, and had bided his time, waiting with Akorth and Fulton until night fell, until they could make their move. Finally, the time had come.

"This will never work, you know that?" Akorth said, burping up ale beside him, stumbling, a bit off balance.

"It is probably the dumbest thing I've ever done," Fulton said. "Although I do admit I feel almost like a hero. It feels pretty good, I have to say," he said, smiling, revealing missing teeth.

"*Almost* is the key word," said Akorth. "You're just a bumbling drunk idiot in an enemy uniform, just like me. That doesn't make you a hero. It just makes you brave. Which also means stupid. We should all be back in the tavern, huddled up to a fire and some warm ale. Instead, here we are here, freezing our arses off for nothing."

"Shut up, both you!" Godfrey hissed.

They slowed to a walk, as a group of Empire soldiers passed them. The soldiers looked them up and down warily, and Godfrey prayed that they didn't notice anything out of order—or see him trembling.

They rounded a corner, and before they did, Godfrey saw the soldiers turn back and look over their shoulders, hesitating. But then, finally they kept walking. Godfrey breathed a sigh of relief. It was a close call. Perhaps they had bigger fish to fry; perhaps they were unsure; or perhaps they were just too damn cold.

"Listen you two," Godfrey whispered harshly. "Stop your bickering. You're right: it's reckless. And I don't know what the hell I'm doing. But I know how to survive. And so do you. So stop talking and follow me and do as I tell you. If not, then turn back and go home now. You might live today. But do you really think you'll make it here a month?"

The two of them looked at each other, then fell silent and continued to walk by Godfrey's side.

They crossed through a square of rubble and it tore Godfrey up to see the destruction all around him, to see all of his people bound together, enslaved, to see all the corpses. He realized how lucky he was that he wasn't lying there with the others.

They entered the courtyard and Godfrey's anxiety increased. There were more soldiers here, spread out in small groups, huddle around fires. But there, at the far end, in the shadows, he spotted what he had come for: a row of crosses, on which were bound the most important soldiers—including Godfrey.

"Keep your heads low as we march, but not too low," Godfrey whispered to the others as they marched across the courtyard, past rows of soldiers. "Act natural, like you belong here. Follow my lead."

They nodded back nervously.

Godfrey doubled his pace, trying to keep himself not from marching too quickly, too conspicuously, as they headed right up to the row of crosses and to Kendrick.

Kendrick hung there, hunched over on his cross, moaning, eyes closed. He appeared more dead than alive.

Godfrey hissed at him.

"Kendrick!"

Godfrey hissed several times, wondering if he was dead, when finally, Kendrick lifted his chin and opened his eyes slightly. His eyes fluttered several times.

Kendrick stared back at him in confusion, and then Godfrey realized: given his uniform, Kendrick thought he was an Empire soldier.

Godfrey lifted his face plate, revealing himself.

Kendrick's eyes opened wide in surprise.

"We've come to cut you down," Godfrey said. "Do you understand?"

Kendrick nodded quickly, and Godfrey climbed the cross, pulled his dagger out, reached behind him and cut the ropes binding his ankles, then his wrists.

"Set to work on the others!" Godfrey called out to Akorth and Fulton, and they broke into action, following his lead and cutting down the other soldiers.

As Godfrey cut the final rope, Kendrick suddenly collapsed off the cross, landing on Godfrey, knocking him down with him. Brom, Srog and Atme collapsed onto Akorth and Fulton, all of them stumbling down to the ground.

Godfrey had not anticipated that, nor had he anticipated Kendrick to be so heavy. Kendrick lay on top of him, moaning, like a ragdoll, and Godfrey got up, dragged him to his feet, and draped an arm over his shoulder, his heart pounding with excitement and fear that they escape before they were all discovered.

"Are you okay?" Godfrey asked.

Kendrick nodded.

"Don't worry about me," Kendrick said. "Save the others."

Akorth and Fulton dragged up Brom, Srog and Atme, and as Godfrey prepared to cut down more men, suddenly, a voice rang out.

"Hey, you there!"

Godfrey turned and his heart dropped to see a group of Empire soldiers, on the far side of the courtyard, running for them.

"What is the meaning of this? Who ordered you to cut these prisoners down?" they called out.

"RUN!" Godfrey yelled.

Godfrey, Akorth and Fulton began running, dragging Kendrick, Brom, Srog and Atme.

"This way!" came a voice.

As Godfrey ran, he looked over and saw, kneeling beside the stone wall, a beautiful women with brown skin, of the Empire race. She gestured frantically for him to follow and to enter into a small secret passageway hidden in the stone. Godfrey hesitated, wondering if he should trust her—but then he heard the shouts of the soldiers behind him, and knew he had no choice.

Godfrey led the others towards the woman, all of them ducking into the secret passageway in the dark shadows of the stone wall. As they all darted inside, she quickly slammed the metal grate behind them.

They found themselves inside a small, dark room, hidden behind the wall, and Godfrey kneeled beside the woman and looked out and watched with bated breath as the group of soldiers ran past, charging across the courtyard, looking for them. They had not seen where they'd went. It had worked.

"Who are you?" Godfrey asked, more grateful than he'd ever been.

"Sandara," she replied. "And you are very lucky to be alive."

CHAPTER TWENTY FIVE

Thor woke as first light broke over the horizon, casting an eerie blood-red glow over the fields of ash, over the valley of exploding volcanoes all around them. It had been one of the most harrowing nights of his life. They had all decided to settle in, to wait out the night until the dawn, when the dragons left their lair.

All night, Thor's dreams had been punctuated by the exploding noises of the volcanoes, by bursts of fire, by the searing heat of lava streams all around them. More than once he had been awakened by dreams that he was sleeping on the edge of the sun, only to see a stream of lava coming at him, and having to roll out of the way.

It was harder to breathe here, too, the clouds thicker, ash everywhere; he was nearly gasping for air by the time they awakened, ash in his ears and eyes and nose, on his cheeks, all over his hands. He looked at the faces of his companions, and saw that they were stained by ash, too. He could tell that none of the others had slept well; they all seemed sleepless and on-edge.

There arose another distant roar, the ground shaking, and the harrowing noises of the dragons began again. The first light broke to a chorus of screams, a huge cacophony splitting the air. As they all turned and looked over the ridge, watched the horizon, one dragon after the next lifted into the air, leaping out of the cave, off the edge of the cliff, their long claws dangling as they flapped their wings, flying higher and higher, screeching and arching back their necks. The creatures were hundreds of feet long, some black, green, purple and some scarlet, covered in ancient scales. They flew close to each other, then far apart, constantly weaving in and out in an intricate pattern.

One after the other leapt off the cliff, taking off in unison, like an army. In the distance, one dove down and breathed, filling the sky with flames, and Thor at first wondered what he was diving for.

Then Thor saw it. He was shocked to see, on the horizon, a contingent of Andronicus' army, led by Romulus. There, on the far side of the sea of lava, marched hundreds of men, shields held high, heading towards the dragon's layer. The dragons had spotted them.

Horrific screams arose as the dragons dove for them and breathed streams of fire, burning right through their shields. The shields melted and the soldiers, screaming, went up in flames; they panicked and ran towards each other, setting others aflame. It was chaos.

The rest of Romulus' army continued to march forward, and the rear rows stepped forward and hurled spears up at the low-flying dragons. But the spears merely bounced off the thick scales.

More dragons plunged, grabbing soldiers with their claws, and flying up with them, high into the air, playing with them, letting them drop, screaming, then diving down and catching them. They did it again and again, until finally, when they tired of the game, they flew the soldiers over the volcanoes and dropped them in. The men shrieked as they sailed through the air and were engulfed in flames.

Romulus' men were getting slaughtered. Finally, they turned and fled. But the dragons would not let them go. They chased after them, raining down fire on them, eviscerating nearly all of them.

"Now is our chance," Thor said, turning to the others. "The dragons have all fled the lair. They are preoccupied. We must quickly get the Sword, before they return."

"But how?" Reece asked. "We can't cross that sea of lava."

Thor knew they were right. They couldn't cross that sea. Even if they had a boat, it would melt in moments.

Thor closed his eyes, needing to draw on his power now, more than he'd ever had. He allowed himself to feel the power of this place. To become one with it.

As he did, he felt a very distinct energy. The energy of a dragon. It made him open his eyes wide in shock, as a current ran through him, from his fingertips to his toes. He felt a tingling, a throbbing in the very tips of his fingers, and as he opened his eyes, he saw a lone dragon lingering in the cave. It was smaller than the others, dark purple, with huge red, glowing eyes.

It turned and looked right at Thor. Thor sensed its name: Mycoples. It was a she. He felt her speaking right to him.

With a screech, Mycoples suddenly lifted into the air, flying right for them.

"A dragon is left behind!" Indra screamed. "It comes our way! We are finished!"

"No, we are not," Thor answered calmly. "Do not attempt to injure it."

152

The others listened, Reece lowering his spear and O'Connor his bow.

Thor felt the tremendous energy of the dragon rolling through him, and he felt a new power, radiating through his body. He raised his hands high to the sky, and turned his palms upward. He felt Mycoples coming towards them, and felt himself summoning her. He felt her *wanting* to come, as if she had been waiting for him. He felt a stronger connection to this beast than he had to do anything in his life.

Mycoples screeched as she neared. All of Thor's friends braced themselves in fear as she dove, but Thor did not. He knew she would not breathe fire, knew she would not attack. He knew her better than he knew himself.

Mycoples lowered herself slowly down to the ground, her great wings flapping, landing right before Thor. The ground shook as she did.

Mycoples turned and looked at Thor, her long tongue spitting, then retracting. Her soulful, glowing red eyes met his, and he felt as if he were meeting someone from another lifetime.

Mycoples turned and looked away, proudly. She sat there, as if waiting.

"Follow me," Thor said to the others.

Thor jumped up onto Mycoples' back without a fear, as if it were the most natural thing in the world. The others all looked at each other, dumbfounded. They stood there, too frozen in shock to move.

Then, one at a time, they all followed, jumping onto Mycoples back behind him, Indra taking Krohn.

As they all got on, Thor leaned forward and stroked the dragon's neck. Her scales were thick, smooth, and the feel of it electrified him. He leaned forward and whispered in her ear.

"Old friend," he said, "bring us to your home."

Mycoples jerked, and leapt up into the air.

She shot straight up, and Thor grabbed on with all his might, as did the others; they screamed and held on for their lives. Mycoples finally leveled out, flapping her huge wings as she flew them over the sea of lava. They were completely at her mercy; if she decided to drop them, they would all be dead in an instant. Yet Thor had never trusted anyone or anything more in his life.

From up here, as they looked down, Thor had the most incredible view of the Land of the Dragons, spread out below them. It was desolate and harrowing and breathtakingly beautiful. It was indeed a land of fire and power, all lit up by the blood red sun of the first light.

As they neared the lair, Thor stroked her neck, and Mycoples dove down low, right to the mouth of the cave, setting them down at the entrance. They all dismounted.

"Wait for us," Thor whispered to Mycoples before he left. She purred, blinking slowly and flapping her wings once, as if she understood.

Thor turned with the others, and they all raced inside the cave. There wasn't much time before the other dragons returned, and every second counted.

Thor was astounded. The cave was packed with mounds of treasure, towers of gold coins, jewelry, treasure chests, weapons— every manner of gold and treasure they could find. It was like an endless treasure tunnel, light gleaming off of everything, and as they ran through Thor had to check himself and resist the impulse to stop and examine, to reach out and grab some.

They ran and ran, Thor feeling the energy of the Destiny Sword ahead, pulling them in.

Finally, breathing hard, they turned a bend, and there, at the end of the cave, sitting right in the center, on a special pedestal, it sat.

The Destiny Sword.

They all stopped in their tracks, breathing hard, all staring, eyes opened wide in wonder. They were all too flabbergasted to say a word.

"Now what?" O'Connor asked.

"If no one can wield it," Elden asked, "how can we bring it back? The thieves took a dozen men just to carry it."

"Legend has it that only a MacGil, the true MacGil, can wield it," Thor said. "There is a MacGil among us."

They all turned and looked at Reece.

But Reece stood there and shook his head.

"I am not firstborn," he said. "I cannot be King. I cannot be the Chosen One. I'm just another MacGil."

"Still, you are a MacGil," Thor urged. "You must try."

The distant rumblings of the dragons arose, shaking the cave. They were beginning to return.

"Hurry," O'Connor said. "We haven't much time."

Reece stepped forward quickly, hurried over to the Sword, raised two hands, and with all his might, he tried to hoist it.

He grunted and groaned from the exertion—but nothing happened. It did not budge.

"We have nothing to lose," Indra said. "Why don't we all try?"

Thor looked back over his shoulder, watching the mouth of the cave, as the others all rushed forward, led by Elden.

One at a time, Elden, then O'Connor, then Conven tried to hoist it. Even Indra tried.

But it would not budge.

They all tried together.

Still, it would not budge.

"Come, help us!" Elden screamed.

Thor rushed forward, and as he neared the Sword, the strangest thing happened: the others all suddenly backed away, as if its energy repelled them. They cleared a wide circle for Thor.

Thor stepped forward, laid one hand on it loosely, and he felt an energy rush through him unlike any he'd ever experienced. It was like he was grasping the sun. Like he knew what it meant to be alive for the first time.

An intense energy shot through his arm and shoulder and his entire being, as Thor leaned back and suddenly hoisted the sword, easily, high overhead.

The others all looked at him with wonder and awe. An intense golden light shone off him, brighter even than the treasure, illuminating the cave, enveloping them all. As one, all of his friends dropped to their knees and knelt before him.

Thor could not understand what was happening. It was all too surreal.

Here he was, holding the Sword of Destiny, the sword that only a MacGil, only the Chosen One, could wield.

Who was he?

CHAPTER TWENTY SIX

Erec stood there, at the base of the gulch, standing alone before the Duke's army, peering into the narrow tunnel of blackness, waiting. He stood there, hands on his hips, displaying a sense of calm for all the eyes on him; yet deep down, he was anxious. His sixth sense told him Andronicus' men were close. He could not sit on his horse and wait. He had to be on his feet, on the ground, standing out front, before all the others. That was who he was.

Erec had gone over in his head his men's positions countless times, had rehearsed their strategy, had tried to think of every scenario, of everything that could go wrong. He felt confident, prepared. All of the Duke's men had been in position, waiting for hours, all trusting him.

But so much time had passed. Could he be wrong? Fleeting thoughts of doubt raced through his mind. What if Andronicus' army did not march this way? What if they were more cautious than he'd thought and circumvented the gulch? What if they were attacking Savaria, unprotected, right now? What if he had, for the first time in his military life, miscalculated? All of these people's lives depended on him. And so did Alistair's.

Erec told himself he had to stop doubting, and trust his instincts. He had made his choice and he needed to see it through. Although he had never met Andronicus, or his commanders, he felt as if he already knew them. He could always think how other commanders thought, had always had a talent of putting himself in their shoes. And he knew the topography of the Ring better than anyone—especially than any invader.

Which was ironic, considering that Erec was originally an outsider himself. He had been raised in the Southern Isles, and had arrived in MacGil's training as a boy. Perhaps because he had felt an outsider from the start, he had made it his duty to not take the Ring for granted, as those who had been raised here, but to memorize every nook and cranny, every contour, every mountain, valley and gulch. Especially from a military perspective. He knew how men advanced, he knew where they rested, and he knew where they retreated. He had studied all the histories, all the great battles. He knew how battles were won and how they were lost.

And everything he ever knew told him that this gulch was where Andronicus' men would advance.

As more time passed, the sun growing higher in the sky, the Duke's men grew impatient, and began to lose discipline; Erec could begin to hear squirming, coughing, sneezing, and the shuffling of horses. He knew time was growing short.

That was when it began. It started as the slightest tremor, one he could barely feel in the soles of his feet. He knew that they were coming.

Erec turned and mounted his horse, beside the Duke and Brandt, up in front of all the men. Their eyes were all on him.

"They're coming," Erec said to the Duke, looking straight into the gulch.

"I don't hear anything," the Duke replied.

"Nor I," said Brent. "Are you certain?"

Erec nodded, looking straight ahead.

"BRACE YOURSELVES!" Erec yelled out to the men. "INTO POSITIONS!"

The men scrambled, getting into their final positions, as Erec stood there, holding his ground proudly, right down the center of the gulch, several dozen warriors surrounding him. Their group would be just enough to goad the enemy, to give them assurance to come forward, into the gulch. If it was a good commander, he would charge forward, going for the easy kill. If it was a great commanders, he would hesitate, sense the danger, and retreat.

In Erec's experience, there were not many great commanders. Might and a trail of victories usually emboldened commanders, left them reckless, and led them to miscalculate. Even the greatest commanders fell prey to hubris, to the trap of momentum. Once victory is in your blood, Erec knew, it is hard to imagine defeat.

That was what Erec was counting on: at this point, Andronicus' men would be unable to imagine anything but victory.

Erec felt a distinct tremble, the ground shaking, the pebbles all around them shifting, tiny rocks beginning to slide down the face of the cliff. Erec saw panic in the eyes of the Duke's men as in the distance, at the far end of the gulch, Andronicus' army came into view.

At first, they were afforded a glimpse of but a few hundred men. But as they came closer, thousands more came into view. The army was as vast as a sea, and as Erec had anticipated, they all headed right for the gulch. Of course they would. With an army that size, who would ever stop them? Why bother scaling cliffs with all those men? The climbing alone would lose them days. An army that size had nothing to fear, and the gulch was the most direct route.

Erec stood firm, even though some part of him wanted to turn and run, as hundreds of Andronicus' soldiers walked their horses proudly into the gulch. They spotted him now, and they did not waiver.

A soldier rode out in front of them, stopped, raised a fist, and motioned for the others to stop behind him. From the looks of him he was their commander, a huge warrior with horns protruding from his head and a grimace which told Erec he had seen one too many battles.

The soldiers behind him came to an immediate halt, as their commander, perhaps fifty yards away from Erec, grimaced back. He suddenly looked, suspiciously, all around him, examining the gulch's contours, looking straight up at the walls, peering up to the top. Erec only prayed that his soldiers were well hidden up there, as he had commanded, and that none of them were peeking over. They were all, he knew, awaiting his command.

The commander looked in every direction, as if sensing something was awry. He was a better commander than Erec had expected, and he paused a moment too long.

Erec's heart pounded, wondering if he would turn his men back around. If he did, the strategy was lost.

Finally, the commander locked his sights back on Erec. He lowered his hand, and broke into a gallop, charging right for him. Inwardly, Erec smiled. As he had predicted, this commander had given into hubris.

Behind him, the Empire soldiers let out a great cry, charging right for him, narrowing the gap.

"HOLD POSITIONS!" Erec commanded the men, all of their horses prancing nervously.

The Empire came closer, perhaps thirty yards out.

"HOLD!" Erec yelled again.

When they reached a mere twenty yards away, Erec yelled:

"HORNS!"

Horns sounded all up and down the mountainside, and as one, all of his men appeared at the top of the cliff and began pushing boulders over the edge of the gulch. Dozens came rolling down the cliff, crushing and killing hosts of the Empire.

But something happened which Erec had not expected: the gulch narrowed too much towards the bottom, and the huge boulders got stuck, a good ten feet off the ground. It spared some of the Empire men an instant death and it also left enough space for the Empire soldiers to continue charging through, ducking beneath. It had slowed Andronicus's men, but it had not stopped them.

Now they had a battle on their hands.

Erec reached back and hurled his spear, and on cue, his men released their spears; they went flying all around him, impaling the barrage of soldiers, knocking several off their horses. But more and more Empire soldiers poured though, a never-ending stream, and Erec drew his sword and charged, the Duke, Brandt and several others at his side.

The gap closing, Erec drew his sword and charged right into the thick of soldiers. Erec was stronger and faster than just about any warrior, and the first one to charge was their commander. He swung down at Erec brazenly, with a high sword held loosely and high overhead; Erec deftly raised his shield, blocked the blow, and thrust his sword into the man's stomach in the same motion.

Without hesitating, Erec chopped off their commander's head, and it rolled to the ground below them.

Still, the Empire men kept coming.

Beside him, Brandt raised his lance and took out two Empire soldiers, while the Duke wielded his chained flail, knocking two men off their horses. The Duke's remaining men joined in, the finest men in the front lines, all rushing in to help.

But still more Empire men appeared, bursting through the gulch. Erec knew they could not hold them back for long. They needed to get those boulders all the way down, and block the entry.

"ARROWS!" Erec yelled.

On cue, arrows hailed down on the men, coming from the top of the gulch, and taking down the next round of Empire soldiers.

And the next.

And the next.

Corpses piled up, and it became harder for the Empire to get men through—yet still, the Empire kept coming.

Erec heard a sudden snarling noise, and watched as a pack of wild wolves was let go by the Empire. The pack burst through the gulch, over the group of corpses, and leapt into the air.

"WOLVES!" Erec yelled to the others.

The wolves lodged their fangs into their horses' legs, throwing them off balance and making them prance and buckle and throw the Duke's men to the ground. Beside Erec his friend Brandt hit the ground, then rolled out of the way quickly, as the Duke's horse keeled over and narrowly missed crushing him. All around them, soldiers fell, and they immediately had their hands full with snarling wolves.

All except for Erec. He rode his trusted companion Warkfin, a true battle horse, and Warkfin did not fall prey to the wolves as the other horses did. Instead, Warkfin leaned back as the wolves approached, calm and fearless, and spun around and kicked the wolves one a time, crushing their ribs. When the wolves went down, Warkfin stampeded them, killing them.

Yet still more wolves and men poured in through the narrow gap between the stuck boulder and the ground, and Erec knew that something had to be done. They had to get that boulder all the way down, to block the path of the Empire. It was too narrow and congested to get a horse in there; it had to be done on foot. Erec knew there was only one way to make that happen.

Not one to leave a risky mission to others, Erec leapt off of Warkfin and prepared to throw himself, alone, into the gulch and attempt the impossible. The second his feet touched the ground he was pounced on by a snarling wolf, who leapt for his throat; but Erec's instincts were well-honed and he sidestepped, drew his sword, and killed the beast in mid-air.

Erec then reached over and drew the one weapon he needed from Warkfin's harness: his war hammer. Hoisting it with two hands, he charged into the thick of battle, into the gulch. But not before swinging the hammer and crushing a wolf that was about to pounce on his friend Brandt's exposed back.

Erec charged head on, into the streaming Empire soldiers, heading for the boulder. Vastly outnumbered, Erec swung wildly. He took out soldiers left and right, though he paid the price, receiving countless minor blows and wounds. The narrowness of the gulch worked to his favor, preventing him from being completely surrounded by too many men at once.

Still, it was hard going. Erec fought with all he had, but too many men streamed in, and he was getting pushed back. The boulder was far away, and the tide of battle was turning. Erec found himself losing strength and knew that, in moments, he would be completely consumed.

*

Alistair paced the halls of the Duke's castle, her gut twisting, telling her something was wrong. She could hardly stand staying here knowing that Erec was out there, fighting for all of them. Cowering behind the safety of a castle wall was not who she was. She had remained behind only because she had promised Erec, only because he had been so intent on it. But she could stand it no longer.

She sensed that he was in great danger. That he needed her. She had to do something. After all, Alistair was no mere woman, no mere wife. She was daughter to a King, and wife to a noble warrior. Pride and loyalty ran in her veins, and nothing would change who she was.

Decided, Alistair crossed the room and stormed from her chamber, out into the castle hall.

"My lady!" came the voice of a surprised attendant. "Where are you going? You are supposed to stay behind the safety of these doors. I have been instructed to watch over you!" the soldier said, nervous, marching quickly alongside her down the hall, trying to keep up.

She ignored him, continuing to strut with purpose.

"The Duke would have my head if he found out I let you leave!" the soldier pleaded. "I must protect you from an invasion!"

But Alistair marched faster, throwing open the door at the end of yet another corridor. Finally, she turned to him.

"I do not need your protection," she said firmly. "Or anyone else's."

Then she turned and hurried down another corridor, taking the long stone spiral staircase down, two steps at a time, until finally she rushed out into the courtyard, the soldier hurrying after her.

Alistair ran to her horse, mounted and gave it a good kick. It took off at a gallop, racing across the courtyard of Savaria, through the arched open gate, to the shocked stares of the remaining guards. They looked as if they did not know how to react, as if they debated shutting the gates, but were uncertain.

Alistair did not give them time to decide: she burst out the gates, and into the open countryside. She rode alone, across the empty landscape, galloping for somewhere on the horizon, somewhere Erec was.

She would stop at nothing until she found him—and did whatever she could to save his life.

CHAPTER TWENTY SEVEN

Kendrick sat huddled against a wall, hidden inside the passage beneath Silesia, Godfrey, Akorth, Fulton, Brom, Atme, Srog and Sandara with him. The eight of them had been holed up there all night, hiding out from the slew of Empire forces looking for them. All night Kendrick listened to the hurried footsteps of soldiers scrambling, eager to find them. But they were too well hidden, thanks to Sandara.

They had all spent the night recuperating, Kendrick sleeping for the first time, stretching out his weary limbs, as did the others. Sandara had given them each water and wine, and had applied various salves to help heal their wounds. Although sore and stiff, Kendrick was beginning to feel back to his old self. It was surreal to be here, to feel alive again. He had been sure he would never come down from that cross alive again.

Kendrick looked over at his brother Godfrey with a whole new respect. He lay slumped against the wall, Akorth and Fulton beside him, three people in the world who Kendrick would never have imagined would aid in his rescue. Kendrick knew that Godfrey did not have the martial skills of a warrior—but he had to admire him for what he did have: craftiness, and supreme survival skills. After all, of all of them, Godfrey was the only one who had managed to survive, and to free them. He also had a lot of heart. Disguised as an enemy soldier, Godfrey could have ran away; instead, he risked death to come back for all of them. It raised Godfrey in Kendrick's eyes; he thought of him now as much as a warrior as any of his compatriots in the Silver. And he owed him his life.

"I have to thank you," Kendrick said, leaning over to Godfrey.

Godfrey looked up, surprised.

"You are my brother," Godfrey said. "There's nothing to thank me for. Besides, we didn't do much."

"You are wrong," Kendrick said. "You did a tremendous thing. You displayed bravery and valor. Most men in your position would have turned and ran. But you came back for us."

Godfrey shrugged.

"I shirked my duties my entire life," he said. "It was the least I could do."

"The hardest part of all of it was not having another drink," Akorth chimed in, smiling.

"This hero stuff is hard," Fulton chimed in. "If it came with a few pints of ale, it might be more tolerable."

Kendrick couldn't help smiling back.

"Don't worry," Brom said, leaning over. "If we make it out of here alive, I'll see to it you get an entire tavern named just for you."

"You are a wishful thinker," Akorth said. "We are completely surrounded. There are thousands of troops out there. We have nowhere to go. How will we survive this?"

"We're not," Fulton answered, shaking his head. "We're going to waste away in this tunnel, like a bunch of rats, and die here."

"Either that," Akorth said, "or surrender."

Kendrick shifted, agitated, having grappled with the same thoughts himself all night.

Kendrick looked over at Sandara, who sat against the wall, looking calmly down. She was even more beautiful in the dim light of this cave, beneath the flickering of the torch, than when he had seen her up on the cross. His heart beat faster looking at her.

"You helped us just as much," he said to her. "You risked your life for the enemy."

"You are not my enemy," she said. "I serve Andronicus out of obligation, not desire."

"Still, you risked death," Kendrick said. "For all of us."

Sandara lowered her eyes.

"I did what anyone else would have done," she said.

Kendrick felt his heart pulling for her, felt a stronger attraction to her than he had to anyone in his life. He wondered if she felt something for him, too.

"If we ever get out of here," he said to her. "I will find a way to repay you."

She slowly shook her head.

"No, my Lord," she said. "You already have. You allowed me to take action, to finally run from Andronicus' army. I should have done so long ago. I may die, with the rest of you. But at least now I will die as a free woman, and not as a slave."

"What is all this talk of death?" Atme boomed out. "I don't know about the rest of you, but I don't plan on dying on this day."

"Nor do I," Kendrick chimed in.

"Nor I," said Srog and Brom.

"I'm fine with not dying," Fulton said, raising a hand in agreement. "After all, I haven't had my full of ale. I'm not ready to go to heaven yet."

"*Heaven?*" Akorth laughed. "Aren't you presumptuous?"

Fulton reddened.

"Well if I'm going to hell, you're coming on my coattails," he answered.

"I'm paving my own way to hell," Akorth replied.

"Why don't we all pave our way together?" Kendrick asked.

They all turned to him, hearing the seriousness in his voice, falling silent.

"What do you mean?" Godfrey asked.

"I mean, I, for one, do not plan on lying here to die like a dog. Nor am I prepared to end my life in surrender, so that Andronicus can torture us."

"Nor I!" Atme shot back.

Kendrick, feeling emboldened, sat up straighter, feeling a new power rise within him.

"Then I say we fight!" Kendrick said.

"Fight?" Akorth asked, puzzled.

"We may all die," Kendrick said. "But we will die together. On our feet. Now is our moment, before we waste away. We will go out there and surprise them, and kill as many Empire as we can. And come what may, we will go out in one final charge of valor!"

The others cheered, jumping to their feet, each drawing their weapons.

Sandara stood and nodded solemnly to Kendrick. She walked to him, lay her hands on his forehead, leaned in and kissed it.

"May the gods be in your favor," she said, "in this lifetime and the next."

She crossed the room, undid the bolts, and opened the secret chamber door for them.

Kendrick led the others as they charged from the chamber. They emerged from the black hole into the bright light of morning, exiting in the Silesian courtyard, Kendrick squinting against the sun. There was a large group of unsuspecting Empire soldiers before them, and they all charged them with a great battle cry, and before the soldiers could figure out what was happening, they had slaughtered all of them. There were quickly a dozen dead.

Hundreds of Silesian captives, stood nearby and watched, bound to each other. Kendrick had an idea.

"FREE OUR BROTHERS!" Kendrick yelled.

The group of men ran to them and sliced their ropes, freeing one after the other.

The men broke free with a shout and ran and grabbed weapons off of the downed soldiers, and off of the corpses lying on the battlefield. The group grew larger by the second, each person freeing someone else. Soon there numbers swelled to over a hundred men.

The main camp of Empire soldiers, on the far side of the courtyard, were only beginning to realize what was happening, and they began to turn at the sound of the shouts. They clearly had not been expecting this. They stood there, shocked.

"CHARGE!" Kendrick shouted.

Hundreds of Silesians, led by Kendrick, let out a great shout, racing across the courtyard with weapons held high and vengeance in their eyes. Srog, Brom, Atme, Godfrey, Akorth and Fulton ran beside them, across the courtyard, towards the distant group of Empire soldiers, who now turned and charged for them.

Kendrick knew they had no chance of winning. But he no longer cared. This was what it was all about. Honor. Glory. Valor. He had fire in his veins, and he was prepared to fight the battle of his life.

CHAPTER TWENTY EIGHT

Thor, wielding the Destiny Sword in one hand, held onto the back of the dragon's neck with the other, as they soared through the air, racing away from the dragons' lair. Riding with him on the back of Mycoples were Reece, O'Connor, Elden, Conven and Indra, holding Krohn, all of them laden with the new weapons they had found. And Thor carrying the greatest weapon of all.

Thor was controlling Mycoples, leaning down and whispering in her ear, and she was listening. Thor felt as if he had known her his whole life, and he also felt within him an uncanny ability to control her. He felt in some ways as if he and the animal were one.

As they flew, a million thoughts raced through Thor's mind. So much had happened so quickly, he could hardly process it all. Here he was, flying on the back of a dragon, which he could hardly understand. It felt surreal. How did he have the power to summon it? To control it? Was it because Thor had some special power? Or because he had some special connection to this beast? Or was it both?

Most importantly: who was he? How was he able to wield the Destiny Sword? He had grabbed it out of desperation, not expecting, of course, to be able to hoist it. But ever since he had, he could not let go of it. The energy of it gushed through him like a river. Legend held that only a MacGil could wield it. Did that mean that he, Thor, was a MacGil? How was that possible? Was the legend wrong?

That also meant that he was the Chosen One. But chosen for what, exactly? How could he, a simple shepherd from the outskirts of the Ring, possibly be the Chosen One? He, a mere boy? He wondered if a mistake had been made.

As Thor reflected on how far they had come, on all that they had done to cross the Empire, he felt a sense of victory beyond description that they had made it this far, had actually found the Sword, had retrieved it, and were returning with it. He could hardly comprehend it. At the very moment when all had seemed darkest, somehow, they had prevailed.

The only way out is through.

Thor looked down as they flew, the landscape beautiful from here. Below were rivers of lava, volcanoes spewing forth fire and ash in the air. When they were down there it had been threatening; now, from up above, it was picturesque, like a huge painting unfolding beneath them. They flew through clouds that came and went. The farther they got, the more the clouds of ash and sulfur gave way to open sky and clear wisps of cloud.

They flew so fast, it nearly took Thor's breath away. They headed east, towards home, and Thor only hoped that they could return to the Ring in time to save his people. For the first time in a long time, he allowed himself to think of Gwen. To *really* think of her. To really imagine him being with her again. He had been afraid to dwell on it before, as he'd thought his chances of return were impossible. But now, for the first time, it felt as if it could really happen. And he allowed himself to believe once again.

Suddenly there came a distant roar from somewhere behind them, and Thor's heart dropped as he turned to see an army of dragons, soaring in the air, chasing after them. There were dozens of them, black and red and green, breathing fire, screeching. They were in a rage. Thor did not know if it was because they had taken the Destiny Sword, or because they had stolen their treasure, or because Mycoples had betrayed them. Whatever it was, they seemed set on vengeance.

"Faster!" Thor screamed, into Mycoples' ear. Her wings flapped harder and he felt himself lunge forward.

The terrain changed below them as they flew faster and faster, the landscape becoming a blur. They left the land of the dragons, flew over the mountain peaks, past the trail of bones, over the great tunnel. The salt fields appeared below, shining white; soon these passed, and they were crossing over rolling green hills. Then swamps, mountains, ridges, lakes....

On and on they went, and Thor felt as if he were watching their entire journey, his entire life, pass by beneath them.

They finally reached the jungle where they had first arrived at the Empire, a huge mass of green below, clinging to the edge of the Tartuvian sea. Thor looked down to see its waves crashing onto the shore. The air was warmer here.

"Our ship is gone!" O'Connor yelled behind him, and Thor looked down at the empty shores and realized he was right.

"We won't be needing that now!" Thor yelled back.

There came another roar and Thor turned to see the dragons were getting closer. They were breathing fire at them, and while it could not reach them, Thor felt an increasing sense of urgency.

"Faster!" Thor whispered to Mycoples.

The dragon flapped even harder, lunging forward again. Thor could feel her breathing hard, exerting all the energy she had, and he hoped he was not driving her too hard. Below them passed the Tartuvian, a vast expanse of yellow and blue. It rushed by, Thor able to spot the small whitecaps of its waves, the air turning moist; as they went, they flew over a fleet of Empire ships, dotting the ocean with their huge sails. Thor saw the men, tiny from here, like ants, and watched as they all stopped their rowing and looked up in wonder at the dragon flying overhead. No doubt, these soldiers were on their way to wreak havoc on the Ring.

"DOWN!" Thor commanded.

Mycoples dove down, right for the group of ships, and as they approached, Thor whispered: "FIRE!"

Mycoples breathed onto the sails, a steady stream of fire coming from her mouth, and as she did, one ship after the other lit up as the canvas sails caught. The huge wooden ships erupted into balls of flame, and Thor could see all the men below jumping ship, splashing into the water.

Mycoples ascended and continued flying east, towards the Ring.

Thor looked back and saw that the maneuver had cost them some of their precious lead: the dragons behind them were even closer. The plumes of black smoke from the sails had obscured their trail a bit, but Thor knew that wouldn't last.

"FASTER!" Thor commanded.

They lunged forward, the moisture in the air whipping them as they flew in and out of the clouds. They went so fast that Thor could hardly breathe.

Finally, on the horizon, Thor spotted the shores of the Ring. He saw the strip of beach, and saw, beyond that, the forest, and then the gaping expanse of the deep Canyon. His heart soared to have his homeland back in sight.

There came a sudden roar, and Thor felt the heat behind them and turned to see the dragons even closer, breathing fire, the flames getting so close that they nearly touched Mycoples' tail. He saw the huge, grotesque faces of the other dragons, too close. He could smell their sulfur smell from here.

Mycoples, despite her best efforts, just didn't have the energy to go faster. Thor knew that in just a few seconds, if they didn't go faster, they would all be dead.

"Please, Mycoples," Thor whispered, "for me. Just a little bit faster. Just one last burst of speed."

Thor felt Mycoples lurch forward, one last time, with all she had, racing them across the final stretch of Tartuvian, across the sand, the forest, and then, across the huge gaping Canyon.

Thor looked down at the Canyon from this perspective, and it took his breath away. It appeared as a huge gaping chasm in the earth, reaching to the bottom of the world, wider than he could ever imagine, as if it separated two worlds. Its swirling mist shimmered in all different colors, and Thor could feel its magical energy as they flew over it.

As the Canyon flew by beneath them and they finally reached its edge, crossing the threshold into the Ring, Thor felt the Destiny Sword vibrate in his hand. He held it high, and as he did, he sensed an invisible wall suddenly seal up behind them.

The Shield, he realized. The Sword had been returned, and the Shield was restored.

Thor looked back and behind them, the army of dragons, so close, breathed another stream of fire. Thor braced himself, realizing they were about to be engulfed in the flames.

But as they crossed into the Ring and the shield went up, the flames hit the invisible wall, just feet behind them, and stopped in mid-air. The dragons, too, suddenly came to a grinding halt, shrieking as they smashed into the invisible shield at the edge of the Canyon. They stopped in mid-air, screaming in pain, bouncing off it.

Enraged, they circled and circled, breathing flames at the Shield. But the flames simply rolled off of it, and the dragons could not get closer. They roared in frustration, but they could not get in.

Thor and the others cheered. For the first time since this whole saga had begun, since he and the others had set out on their quest, he felt safe. They were home.

Thor reached over and smiled as he stroked Mycoples' neck.

"You've done good, my friend," he said.

Mycoples purred in return, craning back her neck and lifting her wings. Thor knew she understood.

It all began to process in Thor's swirling mind. They were home. They were safe. The shield was restored.

Now, it was time to find Gwendolyn.

*

It had felt like an eternity since Thor had been back in the Ring. Having no news since his departure, he wondered what had happened in his absence. With the Shield down all this time, he feared for what may have come. Was Gwendolyn still in King's Court, he wondered? Was King's Court safe from attack? Was Gareth still ruling, and was Gwendolyn safe from him?

Knowing how long the Shield had been down, and seeing all those fleets of Empire ships at sea, Thor assumed the worst. He feared that Andronicus had invaded. And if he had, he figured the first place he would attack would be King's Court. Thor only hoped that Gwendolyn was still safe inside.

Thor directed Mycoples across the familiar countryside of the Ring, heading towards King's Court. As they flew, he appreciated his landscape from a whole new perspective. He noticed many familiar landmarks, and he felt so happy to be home. He prayed he never had to leave its borders again.

As they passed over a hill, King's Court came into view. Thor had been anticipating seeing it with excitement. But when they saw it, his heart plummeted.

What was once the glorious King's Court, the most magical and impregnable place in the world, was now just a hull, an empty burnout shell of rubble, completely burned down to the ground. Its walls remained intact, though even these were charred and sections crumbling. Its gates were torn off and the statues and banners of the MacGils had all been toppled. In their stead, Thor's heart sank to see, was instead a huge statue of Andronicus. And the banner of the Empire.

As they neared, Thor realized that there were no MacGil soldiers or citizens to be found. Just Empire soldiers, everywhere. Clearly, King's Court had been sacked, and it was now an occupied city.

Thor was speechless. King's Court. The bastion of strength of the entire Ring. Destroyed. How did that bode for the rest of the Ring? Thor did not want to admit it, but clearly, that could only mean one thing: they had been defeated in his absence. And Gwendolyn and the others had, most likely, been captured. Or worse, killed.

Thor knew Andronicus' reputation for savagery, and he broke down inside at the thought of anything happening to Gwen. He shut his eyes and tried to force the idea out of his mind; but a part of him already had a sinking feeling. Had Gwen died in the attack on King's Court? Was she down there somewhere? And if not, if Andronicus had wreaked that much destruction on King's Court, what other part of the Ring could be safe?

Thor whispered to Mycoples and she dove down to take a closer look. Thor directed her to the camp of Empire soldiers, occupying the city. As they descended, hundreds of Andronicus' men occupying King's Gate all turned and looked up. As they spotted the dragon, their faces all froze in fear.

They turned and tried to run, but there was nowhere for them to go. Mycoples breathed fire, and within moments, hundreds of them lay dead.

It was a small vindication for Thor. At least he had killed these men who had dared to occupy this sacred city. But what mattered most was that he find Gwendolyn alive, and unhurt.

They swooped down low and circled the city again and again. But nowhere were there any signs of humanity. It seemed as if everyone who had once been here was dead or gone. Thor wanted to touch down and look for her, but he knew it was pointless until they found some sign of life.

As they circled and again and again, Thor felt increasingly desperate. He did not know where Gwen could be. He started to wonder if maybe Gwen had fled King's Court at some point and if so, he wondered where she could have gone.

There came a sudden screech, high above, and Thor looked up to see his old friend Estopheles, screeching, circling above them. She flapped her wings and screeched desperately and seemed to be trying to give Thor a message.

Thor closed his eyes and listened, and he felt as if she were urging them to follow her somewhere. Estopheles turned and flew off, and Thor told Mycoples to follow.

They flew over the countryside, heading North, and Thor wondered where Estopheles was leading them.

"Where are we going?" Reece called out behind him. "King's Court is destroyed. My brothers and sister are back there. We must save them!"

"No," Thor said. "King's Court is no more. Estopheles is leading us elsewhere. I sense, to them. We must follow her."

They flew and flew, heading all the way North, along the edge of the Canyon. As the weather grew colder and they lost Estopheles in and out of the Canyon's mist, Thor was beginning to wonder if they were heading in the right direction—when finally, they reached it.

There, perched at the edge of the Canyon, sat a huge, red city.

Silesia.

Thor had seen paintings of it as a child, but had never seen it in person. The sight of it took his breath away. It was magical, blanketed in the swirling mist of the Canyon, with its two cities, one on the Canyon's edge and one built into the Canyon itself. It looked as if it sat on the edge of the world.

Even more startling, it was occupied by Andronicus's army. There must have been a million soldiers down below, covering the ground like locusts, camped out as far as the eye could see, and filling the entire city. It was unlike anything Thor had ever seen.

This city, unlike King's Court, had not been completely destroyed; nor was it empty of humanity, as King's Court was. Instead, down below, Thor saw hundreds of MacGil and Silesians, alive, bound to each other, slaves to Andronicus.

He also, as he looked carefully, saw something which gave him hope: there was a small group of soldiers, attacking a huge group of Empire. They were vastly outnumbered, clashing with a vast army of Empire soldiers pouring in through the gates. They were fighting bravely and holding their own for now—but within minutes he could see they would be outnumbered and overpowered.

As they flew closer, Thor looked down and saw Kendrick leading the pack. His heart quickened.

"DOWN!" Thor yelled.

Mycoples dove down, so close she nearly grazed Kendrick's head with her talons. Then she craned back her neck, opened her mouth, and breathed fire on the Empire soldiers, again and again and again.

Hundreds of Empire soldiers caught fire, shrieking, collapsing to their deaths.

Mycoples kept flying, lifting over the city gates, then diving down and breathing fire on the thousands of Empire soldiers camped outside it. Thor cut huge swaths through the crowd, destroying entire regimens within seconds.

The Empire soldiers who were not killed turned in a panic and fled, running for the hills. The entire army began to run, like a pack of migrating gazelles, farther and farther from Silesia. Many trampled each other to death in the chaos.

Thor circled back, and Mycoples flew back over Silesia and dove down and landed in the center of the courtyard.

They landed to the bewildered faces of Kendrick and the others, all of them in a panic at seeing a dragon. Then their panic turned to relief upon realizing that the Dragon was not going to harm them. And then, finally, it morphed to excitement and gratitude, as they all saw that it was Thor and the others, having returned from the Empire, dismounting from its back.

Thor dismounted from the dragon, and he wheeled the Destiny Sword. He raised it high, overhead, a light shining from it. As he did, the faces of all those around him froze in shock and awe.

There were still hundreds of Empire soldiers left inside the courtyard, and Mycoples purred and Thor sensed she wanted to attack.

"No," Thor said to her. "I've got these."

Thor burst forward on foot, raising the Destiny Sword high, and ran out by himself to meet the hundreds of Empire soldiers remaining.

As he charged, wielding the Sword, he felt different than he'd ever had in his life. It was like the Sword was a part of him. It was like it was lifting him up in battle, making each foot step lighter and faster. He didn't feel as if he was wielding the sword: he felt as if the sword were wielding him.

Thor met the enemy and swung the Sword, and as he did, a magical light shone forth from it. The Sword seemed to stretch out from his hand and he killed a dozen men in a single stroke. He raised the Sword again and again, charging right into the thick of the army, and swung relentlessly.

Within minutes, he had killed all of the men. Hundreds of them, all corpses, lying dead at his feet. And he wasn't even tired: on the contrary, the Sword filled him with energy.

Thor turned and walked back to his people, standing dumbfounded in the courtyard, watching the scene in shock.

They stood there, mouths agape, as he approached them, walking alone, holding the Sword at his side. Kendrick, Brom, Atme, Srog,

Godfrey and the others, dozens of members of the Silver, all famed warriors—they all looked to him with awe.

Thor stood there proudly, and he held the Sword high above his head in victory.

As one, all of the men raised their swords in a great cheer:

"THORGRIN!" they yelled out.

CHAPTER TWENTY NINE

Erec charged into the thick of the soldiers in the gulch, packed shoulder to shoulder, swinging his war hammer and turning it sideways to block blows, fighting ten men at once, using every ounce of his skills, every training he had ever received. He was beyond exhausted, but he would not give up. He only needed to gain a few more feet, to cut his way through this crowd, to reach the lodged boulder. If he could just knock it down, he could seal up the gulch and spare all his men from the tide of Empire. Without that, they could never win.

Erec fought with all he had, wheeling and swinging, ducking, leaping, kicking, elbowing and even head-butting. He received a great many blow, punches and kicks and elbows, shields smashing against him, swords slashing and bouncing off his armor. He was losing stamina as he struggled forward, never losing sight of the boulder. He fought for every inch.

Just a few feet away, Erec was stuck. He was simply too exhausted to fight back the tide of men, and he felt himself about to lose ground.

Please, God. I am willing to die on this day. Just let me reach the boulder first. Just give me one last burst of strength.

Erec summoned all the years of training he'd had. He thought of King MacGil, and his heart burned with a desire for vengeance. Not just for himself. But for the MacGils. For the entire Ring.

Erec screamed a great battle cry, and summoned a final strength from somewhere deep inside him, some place he did not know. He roared and rushed forward, knocking back two men at once and pushing his way the final few feet all the way to the boulder.

As he reached it, Erec raised the two-handed hammer high, and brought it down right on the center of the rock.

There came a great cracking noise as the boulder began to split.

Erec did it again and again, and finally, the boulder split in two. He smashed it one last time, and the boulder came tumbling down in a great pile of debris and dust, filling the gulch and completely cutting it off. The tide of Empire soldiers stopped. Finally, the gulch was blocked.

From behind Erec there came a great cheer of victory from his men, who had witnessed the scene.

But Erec suddenly felt a horrific pain in his back. It was the feeling of steel puncturing his flesh.

Erec collapsed to his knees, in agony. He turned to see one remaining Empire soldier still on this side of the debris. He had hidden in the corners, and Erec had missed him.

There came a shout, and Brandt rushed forward and stabbed Erec's attacker in the heart, killing him and sparing Erec from further injury.

Still, Erec felt the hot blood pouring out, and already felt the life force ebbing out of him.

"Erec!" Brandt cried out in concern.

Brandt reached down and grabbed Erec and picked him up, draping an arm over his shoulder as several of the Duke's soldiers rushed forward to help. They all dragged Erec out of the gulch, Erec feeling the pain with each step.

Erec lay there, blood trickling from his mouth, breathing hard, as they laid him down. It hurt to move. He felt his body growing colder, and he knew he wouldn't have much longer.

A horse came charging up, and as Erec looked up he could have sworn he saw Alistair, dismounting and running over. He wondered if her were seeing things. Alistair? How could she possibly be here?

She knelt down beside Erec, and held him in her arms. Erec could feel her love for him as she sobbed, the tears dripping down onto his face.

She held his face in her palms, leaned down and kissed his forehead.

"My Lord," she said, sadly.

As Erec felt the world grow lighter, whiter, the last thing he saw was Alistair, looking down at him with kind, compassionate eyes. He saw her lift her palms, and saw an intense blue light radiate from them. It was the most intense light he had ever seen, and he watched as she closed her eyes and laid her palms on his wound.

As she did, he felt his entire body filling with light and warmth. He felt his wounds healing within him, felt himself being brought back from the dead.

All the soldiers looked over at Alistair as the intense light grew brighter and brighter, encapsulating them both in a magic orb of light.

Erec, feeling stronger by the second, looked up into Alistair's mystical eyes and got lost in them. As he felt himself drifting into a healing sleep, he had enough energy for one final thought was:

Who is she?

CHAPTER THIRTY

Gwendolyn opened her eyes slowly, her head throbbing from the welt on her temple where she had been hit by the thieves. She looked around, and realized she was sitting on the forest floor, bound to a tree with coarse ropes. She wiggled, but they would not give. Sitting across from her, perhaps ten feet away, was Steffen, bound to a tree as well.

She heard muted laughter coming from somewhere, and she turned and looked over to see the group of a dozen thieves huddled over a small bonfire in the forest, roasting some sort of small animal, perhaps a rabbit. They shoveled food into their mouths and chewed with their mouths open, chasing it with sacks of wine, and laughing. They laughed too loud, elbowing each other, and were clearly all vulgar individuals.

"My lady," Steffen whispered urgently. "Are you okay?"

She nodded slowly back, getting her bearings.

"I'm sorry I let you down," he said, looking down to the floor in shame.

"You fought bravely," she said. "We were outnumbered."

"I have a plan," he said. "Play along with it."

Suddenly, the thieves turned their way.

"What have we here?" one of them called out. "The Queen and the midget are awake! Good morning, sleeping beauty!"

A chorus of crude laughter erupted, and the group jumped to its feet and began strutting their way. Gwen could see the daggers sitting openly in their belts, while some held daggers to their teeth, picking out bits of food and spitting them on the forest floor.

One of them walked up to her and kicked Gwen hard in the calf, while another kicked Steffen in his ribs.

"You too can talk all you want," one of them said, using the crude accent of the Southern Ring. "But you're not going anywhere. You see, will we finish this meal, and when we are done with our wine, we are going to take pleasure in torturing each of you. But first we are going to have a long night of pleasure with you, my lady," one of them said, stepping back and taking off his hat in an exaggerated bow, to the laughter of them all.

"Me first," said one.

"No you don't," said another. "You had the last one first. This one is mine."

The two of them shoved each other, then cursing, wrestling each other to the floor; finally, one punched the other, knocking him out, and stood. He was a huge, crude brute, with a big belly and a bald head, and he licked his lips as he looked over at Gwendolyn.

"I'm going to enjoy you," he said to her.

"You can have your way with us," Steffen suddenly called out. "But that would be the biggest mistake of your lives."

They all turned to him, then broke out in laughter.

"And why is that, little man?" one of them asked. "Are you going to do something about it?"

"It is not what I'm going to do," Steffen said. "It is what you are going to lose."

The thieves looked at each other with stupid, crude faces, lips hanging open, confused.

"Lose?" one asked.

"You see," Steffen said, "Gwendolyn here is not just a princess. She's a Queen. Of the entire Western Kingdom of the Ring. She has enough riches at her disposal to make all of you kings and queens yourselves, for the rest of your lives."

The thieves all looked at each other, then turned and looked at Gwendolyn with a new respect. They seemed unsure.

"And how is she going to produce this gold?" one asked. "She going to shake it from the trees?"

They all started laughing.

Steffen cleared his throat, undeterred.

"We are on our way to the Tower of Refuge," Steffen said. "I am sure you know of it. It is not far from here. The Queen's attendants will be waiting to greet us. They have chests of gold there. More than enough to buy her ransom and more. That is, *if* she is untouched. If we arrive there hurt in any way, or if we never arrive at all, I assure you, there will be nothing for you. You choose. Bring us to the Tower and become rich men—or harm us and remain in this forest as thieves and paupers for the rest of your days."

The thieves all looked to each other with a new expression. At first it was one of uncertainty; but then it morphed to greed.

"He's lying," one said.

"What if he's not?" another answered. "With if the little dwarf is right?"

"I can use that kind of gold," said one.

"So can I," said another.

"Forget the gold," yelled the big man. "I don't need more gold. What I want is to have my way with her. She's the prettiest piece I've seen in a long time. Maybe ever."

He began walking towards Gwendolyn, removing his belt—when another one of the thieves, unshaven with long hair, suddenly pulled a dagger and snuck up behind him and held it to his throat.

"Don't touch the girl," he warned, as the bald man stood still for fear of the blade. "We're getting that gold."

The big man, deferring to this one's authority, swallowed hard, and took a step back.

The leader with the long hair turned and pointed the tip of his dagger to Steffen.

"For your sake, your words best be true. If not, I will cut off your jewels myself, and feed you both to the bears."

*

Gwendolyn and Steffen were marched side-by-side, wrists bound with rope, led by the group of a dozen thieves, shoved as they stumbled forward, approaching the Tower of Refuge. They all emerged from the woods and entered the clearing surrounding the tower. The tower was immaculate, ancient and mysterious, built of a shining black stone. It was narrow, perhaps only a hundred feet in diameter, and it soared hundreds of feet high into the sky, a magical structure in the middle of nowhere.

Gwen felt the energy radiating off of it. This was clearly a sacred place.

The tower was built with but a single door, an arched, black door with no markings and no handle.

The thieves all prodded them into the clearing and closer to the door, until finally the leader stopped them, about twenty yards away.

"We're not going any closer," he said to Steffen, "until your people come out now—with the gold. You got one minute. Otherwise, we kill her. And you."

Steffen swallowed hard, then looked to Gwendolyn. She nodded back, understanding.

"I will summon my attendants," she said to the thieves.

Gwen recalled what Argon had told her, about how to summon the Keepers of the Tower. She leaned back and called out.

"Keepers of the Tower!" she called. "I have come to enter your walls!"

Gwendolyn waited in the silence, hoping, praying, that Argon was right. If not, she would be dead.

As time passed, Gwen's heart pounded in her chest. She was afraid that this might all be for nothing, that she might have her throat cut at any moment.

Suddenly, to her immense relief, the door opened.

Out walked seven knights, donning shining, black plate armor, from head to toe, their faces obscured by face plates with long, pointed noses. The seven of them walked in silence, in perfect formation, side-by-side. They donned gauntlets covered in sapphires, the only variation on their all black armor, and they each stopped together and faced them, standing at attention.

The thieves looked at each other, puzzled.

"What the hell is this?" asked one.

"Oh Keepers of the Flame!" Gwendolyn called out, remembering all that Argon had taught her. "I am here to devote myself inside these walls."

These were the sacred words that Argon had taught her to pronounce, the words that would gain one entry into the Tower of Refuge. Argon had told her about these men who stood guard: the Seven Knights. The Keepers of the Flame. They were seven magical nights, who, legend had it, had guarded the tower for centuries, prepared to keep out any and all enemies who dared to breach it. By Gwen's recital of these words, she immediately became an inhabitant of the Tower. And that made it the Seven Knights' sworn duty to protect her.

As Gwen finished pronouncing the words, as one, the knights silently strode forward, marching towards the thieves.

"Stay back!" one thief called out, his voice shaking.

The thieves were growing increasingly nervous, shifting, yanking on Gwen's and Steffen's ropes. One of them raised a dagger and held the blade close to Gwen's throat.

The Knights kept coming closer.

"Any closer, and the girl dies!" a thief yelled. But his voice shook with fear.

As the knights neared, they lifted their face visors.

The sight struck fear into the heart of the thieves. Even Gwendolyn was afraid.

Because behind the visors there was nothing. No faces. No bodies. Nothing.

The magical nights lunged forward, raising their swords like a flash of lightning, and attacked the thieves. Gwen blinked.

When she opened her eyes, all that was left around her were the corpses of the thieves, bloody, at her feet.

Gwen felt her hands freed, and she turned to realize that the knights had severed her ropes, and Steffen's too. The knights then stood back at attention, waiting beside her, as if for a command.

Gwen knew they were waiting for her. And she knew it was time to go.

She turned and looked at Steffen, and he stared back at her, still shocked.

"I guess this is where we say goodbye," she said, turning and examining the open door to the Tower with a sense of apprehension. It felt so final. As if she would never come out.

"I guess it is, my lady," he said sadly.

Steffen reached out and took one of her hands and kissed the back of it, bowing his head.

"And what will become of you?" she asked.

"Do not worry my lady," he said, turning back towards the thick forest. "My duty here is complete. You are delivered safely. I will survive. I always have. But know this: I wait for you. If you should ever leave this place, I wait to be in your service once again, for the rest of my days."

Gwen watched him go, disappearing into the forest. Then she turned and walked towards the open door of the tower. The Knights fell in behind her, accompanying her, and in moments, she was inside, the door slamming behind her. The finality of it echoed in every bone she had. She could not help but feel as if she had just been entombed forever.

CHAPTER THIRTY ONE

Thor marched quickly through the lower city of Silesia, accompanied by the MacGils—Kendrick, Reece, and Godfrey, the three brothers united again—and by Srog, Brom, Atme and several other soldiers. He held the Destiny Sword at his side, and the small group of men fell in beside him as they led him towards the hiding place of their mother, the former Queen.

Kendrick had filled Thor in on the events that had transpired since he'd left, and Thor ran them all through his mind. Andronicus' invasion; the destruction of King's Court; the Silesian siege. Gwen's becoming queen…. The only thing Kendrick hadn't yet told him was the one question he wanted answered most: what had happened to Gwendolyn?

When Thor asked Kendrick and Godfrey, they had each lowered their eyes and looked away. They would not tell him. When he'd asked why, they wouldn't say. And when he had asked where she was, all they said was that the last they had seen her, she had been in hiding in the lower city, and that she was rumored to have escaped. To where, they did not know. They had said that the former Queen knew, and Thor had insisted that they lead him to her at once.

The fact that they would not answer him left a weight in Thor's chest. By their expressions, he sensed something bad had happened to her, and he needed to know what it was. He felt overwhelmed with guilt for not having been here, at her side, through all of this. He just needed, desperately, to know that she was alive, that she was safe, and well. Only then would he rest at ease.

They marched through the lower castle, littered with the corpses of Empire soldiers who had been slaughtered by the freed Silesians after Thor had repelled the invaders. They hurried up the palace steps, and marched down corridors, Kendrick and Srog leading the way, until they reached the Queen's chamber. They all stopped before the door, now guarded by Silesian soldiers, and paused as the soldiers made way, then headed inside.

The Queen stood at the window, dressed in all black, looking mournful, more aged than Thor had ever seen her. She slowly turned and faced them, expressionless, stern.

As Thor examined her, he wondered. Here he stood, wielding the Destiny Sword. Did that mean that he, Thor, was a MacGil? Did that mean that the woman standing before him was his mother?

The thought of it sent a shudder through him. He knew how much she hated him. Was the reason why somehow connected to his lineage?

The Queen's eyes immediately fell to the sword in Thor's hands, and they widened in surprise.

"I need answers," Thor said to her, firm, in a rush. "I need to see Gwendolyn, right away. Where is she? Is she safe? What is all this mystery surrounding her?"

The Queen turned and looked at the others standing around Thor, then cleared her throat.

"All of you, leave us," she said.

The entourage filtered out of the room, except for Kendrick, Reece and Godfrey, who exchanged a confused look.

"What is it that you have to say to Thor that you cannot say in front of your own three sons?" Godfrey asked.

The Queen shook her head.

"It is not for your ears," she said firmly. "Leave us now."

The three of them slowly turned and walked out, closing the door behind them.

Thor and the Queen stood there, alone, facing each other. Thor's heart pounded even more as he stood opposite her, wondering what awful calamity might have befallen Gwen.

Thor could stand it no more: he rushed towards her, and cried: "Answer me! Where is she? Is she alive?"

The Queen nodded somberly.

"She is alive, yes."

Thor's heart flooded with relief. That was all he needed to here.

"Where is she?" he pressed.

"Far from here," she answered. "She has fled to the Tower of Refuge. In the farthest southern reaches of the Ring."

Thor looked back, puzzled.

"The Tower of Refuge?" he asked.

"It is a place for those recovering from calamity. For those who decide to take an oath and remove themselves from this world."

Thor stepped forward and grabbed the Queen's wrist in frustration.

"No more riddles! Tell me!" he yelled, his voice echoing off the walls.

The Queen lowered her eyes, and Thor could see that they were wet. She breathed deeply.

"Gwendolyn was attacked," she said flatly. "Raped. By Andronicus's men."

At her words, Thor loosened his grip, his mouth open wide in shock, his breath stopped in his chest. He stood there, and his entire body went cold. He could hardly breathe.

"She is not the Gwendolyn you once knew," she said. "She is embittered. Hardened of spirit and of soul. She lives. But her spirit does not."

Thor stood there, his mind reeling, dizzy from the news. He wanted to stab himself with his sword in his own heart, so overwhelmed with guilt for not being there to spare her.

"She pines for you," the queen said. "But she believes that because of what happened to her, you won't care for her anymore."

Thor reddened.

"That is ridiculous," he said. "Of course I do. I care for her just as much. Even more so. Why would that change my feelings for her? What kind of man do you think I am?"

"I told her," the Queen said. "But she would not believe it."

Thor shook his head.

"My love for her is as strong as it ever was. Even stronger."

"But you were not here to tell her that with your own words, were you?" the Queen asked. "So she has gone. To enter the Tower."

"Then I will go and find her!" Thor said, preparing to leave.

"She will not listen," the Queen said. "Those who enter the Tower never leave. I fear Gwendolyn is lost to you."

"*Nothing* is ever lost," Thor said. "You are a defeated woman. A widow. A pessimist. I am young and strong. My love for her will bring her back."

The Queen smiled wryly.

"And you are an optimist," she countered. "And naïve. You don't understand a woman's perspective."

"I don't need to," Thor separate "I know Gwendolyn. And I know who I am. And I know what we have. We can transcend all of this. This doesn't mean a thing."

Thor did not want to hear any more of this embittered woman's rants; he turned and prepared to leave the room—when suddenly something occurred to him, and he turned back to face the Queen.

"Why don't you want me to be with Gwendolyn?" he pressed.

At first she stared back at him blankly, but then she looked away.

Thor stepped forward, needing to know. He knew there was something she was hiding from him.

"The Sword," he pressed, feeling it throbbing in his palm. "Legend holds that only a MacGil can wield it."

She refused to look at him, and he sensed he was getting closer to the truth.

"Is that it? Is that why you don't want me near her? Am I a MacGil? Was MacGil my father? Is Gwendolyn my sister?"

The Queen looked directly at him, then finally, turned away.

Thor stepped forward, at the end of his rope.

"ANSWER ME!" he yelled, swirling with so many mixed emotions.

The queen slowly looked up, silent.

"Is King MacGil my father?" Thor repeated slowly, desperate to know.

She stared at him, her eyes hollow and cold.

"No," she finally said, flatly.

Thor froze, caught off guard. He had not expected that response. He was deeply relieved to hear that he was not related to Gwendolyn, which he had feared ever since he had been able to wield the Sword. He sensed that, finally, he was learning the truth.

"Then who is?" he pressed.

She looked away.

"He is my father, whoever he is. I have a right to know. Please. Tell me," he pleaded softly, exhausted.

She stared at him long and hard, and finally, she uttered one word that made Thor's knees weak, and would change his life forever:

"Andronicus."

A RITE OF SWORDS
(Book #7 in the Sorcerer's Ring)

"A breathtaking new epic fantasy series. Morgan Rice does it again! This magical sorcery saga reminds me of the best of J.K. Rowling, George R.R. Martin, Rick Riordan, Christopher Paolini and J.R.R. Tolkien. I couldn't put it down!"
--Allegra Skye, Bestselling author of SAVED

In A RITE OF SWORDS (Book #7 in the Sorcerer's Ring), Thor grapples with his legacy, battling to come to terms with who his father is, whether to reveal his secret, and what action he must take. Back home in the Ring, with Mycoples by his side and the Destiny Sword in hand, Thor is determined to wreak vengeance on Andronicus' army and liberate his homeland—and to finally propose to Gwendolyn. But he comes to learn that there are forces even greater than he that might just stand in his way.

Gwendolyn returns and strives to become the ruler she is destined to be, using her wisdom to unite the disparate forces and drive out Andronicus for good. Reunited with Thor and her brothers, she is grateful for a lull in the violence, and for the chance to celebrate their freedom. But things change quickly—too quickly—and before she knows it, her life is thrown upside down again. Her elder sister, Luanda, caught in a fierce rivalry with her, is determined to wrest power, while King MacGil's brother arrives with his own army to gain control of the throne. With spies and assassins on all sides, Gwendolyn, embattled, learns that being queen is not as safe as she thought.

Reece's love with Selese finally has a chance to flourish, yet at the same time, his old love appears, and he finds himself torn. But idle times are soon overcome by battle, and Reece, Elden, O'Connor, Conven, Kendrick, Erec and even Godfrey must face and overcome adversity together if they are to survive. Their battles take them to all corners of the Ring, as it becomes a race against time to oust Andronicus and save themselves from complete destruction. As powerful, unexpected forces battle for control of the Ring, Gwen realizes she must do whatever it takes to find Argon and bring him back.

In a final, shocking twist, Thor learns that while his powers are supreme, he also has a hidden weakness—one that may just bring his final downfall.

Will Thor and the others liberate the Ring and defeat Andronicus? Will Gwendolyn become the queen they all need her to be? What will become of the Destiny Sword, of Erec, Kendrick, Reece and Godfrey? And what is the secret that Alistair is hiding?

With its sophisticated world-building and characterization, A RITE OF SWORDS is an epic tale of friends and lovers, of rivals and suitors, of knights and dragons, of intrigues and political machinations, of coming of age, of broken hearts, of deception, ambition and betrayal. It is a tale of honor and courage, of fate and destiny, of sorcery. It is a fantasy that brings us into a world we will never forget, and which will appeal to all ages and genders.

About Morgan Rice

Morgan is author of the #1 Bestselling THE SORCERER'S RING, a new epic fantasy series, currently comprising eleven books and counting, which has been translated into five languages. The newest title, A REIGN OF STEEL (#11) is now available! Morgan Rice is also author of the #1 Bestselling series THE VAMPIRE JOURNALS, comprising ten books (and counting), which has been translated into six languages. Book #1 in the series, TURNED, is now available as a FREE download! Morgan is also author of the #1 Bestselling ARENA ONE and ARENA TWO, the first two books in THE SURVIVAL TRILOGY, a post-apocalyptic action thriller set in the future. Among Morgan's many influences are Suzanne Collins, Anne Rice and Stephenie Meyer, along with classics like Shakespeare and the Bible. Morgan lives in New York City. Please visit www.morganricebooks.com to get exclusive news, get a free book, contact Morgan, and find links to stay in touch with Morgan via Facebook, Twitter, Goodreads, the blog, and a whole bunch of other places. Morgan loves to hear from you, so don't be shy and check back often!

CPSIA information can be obtained at www.ICGtesting.com
Printed in the USA
BVOW08s1642230916

463094BV00001B/4/P